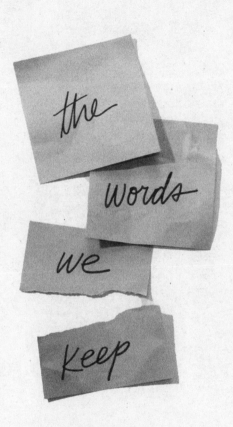

ALSO BY ERIN STEWART

Scars Like Wings

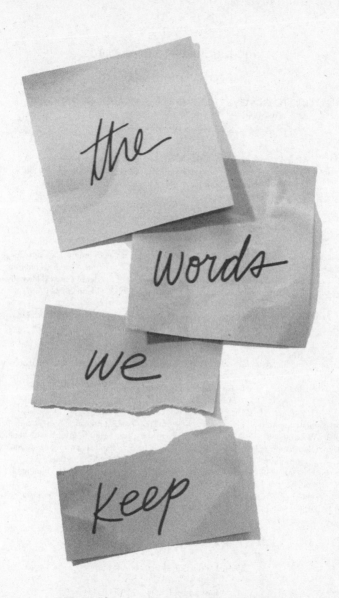

the

words

we

keep

ERIN STEWART

EMBER

To my mom,

who taught me to love words,

to use them well,

and to always believe in the power of my own

———————————

Text copyright © 2022 by Erin Stewart
Cover art and design by Casey Moses
Texture image used under license from Shutterstock.com

All rights reserved. Published in the United States by Ember, an imprint of Random House Children's Books, a division of Penguin Random House LLC, New York. Originally published in hardcover in the United States by Delacorte Press, an imprint of Random House Children's Books, a division of Penguin Random House LLC, New York, in 2022.

Ember and the E colophon are registered trademarks of Penguin Random House LLC.

GetUnderlined.com

Educators and librarians, for a variety of teaching tools, visit us at RHTeachersLibrarians.com

The Library of Congress has cataloged the hardcover edition of this work as follows:
Names: Stewart, Erin, author.
Title: The words we keep / Erin Stewart.
Description: First edition. | New York : Delacorte Press, [2022] | Audience: Ages 12 and up. | Summary: When sixteen-year-old Lily Larkin's older sister, Alice, begins to struggle with her mental health, Lily attempts to keep everything together and perfect, despite her own growing anxiety.
Identifiers: LCCN 2020052432 (print) | LCCN 2020052433 (ebook) | ISBN 978-1-9848-4886-4 (hardcover) | ISBN 978-1-9848-4887-1 (library binding) | ISBN 978-1-9848-4888-8 (ebook)
Subjects: CYAC: Mental illness—Fiction. | Sisters—Fiction. | Anxiety—Fiction.
Classification: LCC PZ7.1.S7457 Wor 2022 (print) | LCC PZ7.1.S7457 (ebook) | DDC [Fic]—dc23

ISBN 978-1-9848-4889-5 (paperback)

Printed in the United States of America
10 9 8 7 6 5 4 3 2 1
First Ember Edition 2023

Random House Children's Books supports the First Amendment and celebrates the right to read.

Penguin Random House LLC supports copyright. Copyright fuels creativity, encourages diverse voices, promotes free speech, and creates a vibrant culture. Thank you for buying an authorized edition of this book and for complying with copyright laws by not reproducing, scanning, or distributing any part in any form without permission. You are supporting writers and allowing Penguin Random House to publish books for every reader.

I find my sister's hand beneath the waves.

"I'm scared." My voice is small, carried away by the water—and so am I.

The ocean tugs me farther. We're too far.

But Alice reaches out to me.

"Take my hand," she says. "We're on an adventure."

And because I'm six and she's my much wiser and braver eight-year-old sister, I believe her. I let her convince me we're deep-sea explorers, returning from an expedition. I let her lead me, even though salt water fills my mouth, my ears, my everything.

We fight against the waves, hand in hand.

And then I'm on the sand. Dad's swearing. He's pounding on my back. He's yelling my name so loudly, it hurts my head.

Lily. Lily. Lily.

I'm choking, spitting out the ocean.

Dad falls to his knees, and he's hugging us, so tight I almost pop, and

1

we're huddled on the beach, and he's crying, and I think they're happy tears, but it's hard to tell.

"It's okay, Dad," I say, my voice stronger on land. "We were on an adventure! We were so brave!"

This only makes him cry harder, and Alice is crying, too, which makes no sense because she's the bravest one of all.

Ten years later, I'm by the shore again. Alone this time.

No deep-sea expedition. No adventure.

Just the crash of the waves and a stopwatch and the thud-thud-thud of my feet on the pavement. A text from Alice lights up my phone: Lily. Where are you?

I don't answer. I'm in the zone, pushing a little faster.

A little farther.

A little better.

Until my muscles are spent, and I turn toward home.

I find her on the bathroom floor. She reaches out to me, razor loosely in hand, words repeating on her lips:

I'm sorry

I'm sorry

I'm sorry

I stand, frozen, paralyzed by the sight of blood draining from her wrist, pooling on the tile.

Help me, she says.

In slow motion, I wipe her with a towel. Try to stop the blood. Find the source. But my shaking hands make it worse. Bright red on my skin. Smeared on the floor.

Help me.

But I don't know how. I barely know her, this lesser version of my brave big sister.

"Dad!" My voice echoes in the room, shrill and panicked and unfamiliar.

He finds us there, her head in my lap, her blood on my hands, waiting for someone who can fix this.

Dad scoops her up. Carries her, legs limp, blood dripping like a fairy-tale crumb trail down the stairs. He puts her in the car. Drives her away.

I clean my sister's blood off the tile. Off the carpet. Off me.

In the sink, the red spirals away, but not the echo of her whispered help me. *It fills my head, and I want to drown it out with screams. But I can't. I need to be strong. For Alice. For Dad.*

So because I can do nothing else, I make her bed

over

and over

and over.

Sixteen times.

Until it's perfect.

And when the sheets are straight, corners military tight and pillows fluffed, I rip it apart.

Just so I can put it back together.

chapter
1

Two months after the Night of the Bathroom Floor, it comes to my attention that I'm losing my shit at an alarming rate.

I use the term *losing* metaphorically, of course, because I've decided going insane is a process, and not a singular event, despite our eloquent idioms.

Snapped.

Meltdown.

Off the deep end.

But there is no lightning bolt of insanity. It's more like a drizzling leak you don't even notice until you're gasping for air, suddenly and irrevocably aware that you've drowned in your own thoughts.

I wonder sometimes if that's how it felt for Alice. I haven't had the chance to ask since Dad drove her away in the middle of the night and shipped her off to Fairview Treatment Center. Sure, I could send one of the ten billion emails I've started and deleted, or I could go with Dad and my little sister, Margot, to the weekly family visitation days, but that's a big fat no.

It's not like I don't *want* to see her, but I definitely don't want to see her like *that*, with all the other "troubled teens" at a place, according to the website, that promises to fix my big sister with horseback riding and trust exercises on the main lawn.

So until next month when Alice comes home from psych-ward sleepaway camp, I won't know if we're on the same slow train to loco-ville. All I know is that I, Lily Larkin, at the ripe old age of sixteen, am losing my freaking mind.

"Just relax." Sam slings her violin case onto the desk next to mine, doling out the same advice she's given me since we were freshmen. "That little vein on your forehead is getting angry."

"Relaxation will *not* help me ace this," I reply without looking up from my notecards, where I've written each line of my poem for today's presentation.

Sam plucks the cards from my hand. "As your best friend, it is my sworn duty to save you from yourself."

I swipe at them, but she karate chops my arm and sticks the cards into the back pocket of her jeans.

"It's just one grade. So chill, Lil."

"It's never just *one* grade," I say, rubbing my temple to momentarily release the tension wrapping my head. Note to self: I have *got* to get more sleep. "Not all of us can have your raw musical talent."

Sam's mouth falls open as she holds up her fingers, three of them wrapped in Band-Aids.

"Hello? First-chair bragging rights come with a price, too, you know."

"So don't tell me it's just one grade or one solo or one anything.

It's a never-ending domino effect to success, and if one piece is off, only the slightest bit not perfect, the whole thing goes to hell."

Sam frowns. "Depressing."

"But true."

It doesn't help that we're in the honors track, which means our dominos have to fall at a much faster rate. No breaks. No breathers. Just piece after piece, falling perfectly into place. Oh, and if you don't "specialize" in something like violin or swim team by the end of elementary school, what are you even doing with your life?

"So maybe just take it down from hyperdrive," Sam says. "Do you see anyone else freaking out?"

On cue, Kali plops down next to me, buried in her own notecards. Once upon a childhood, Kali was my go-to bestie, until it became clear in middle school that we were much better suited as frenemies. We're both word nerds and we're always pitted against each other in writing contests and class rankings, so now we're still friends but more the keep-your-competition-close variety.

"You ready?" Kali asks without looking up.

As if I didn't stay up until two a.m. writing these poems—and rewriting them. Every time I thought I was done, there was a smudge or weird spacing or a million other reasons to start again, over and over, until they were perfect.

"Oh, she's ready," Sam says. "She *always* brings her A-game."

Sam gives my arm a squeeze as a group of students and a bearded teacher I don't recognize file in, taking seats in the back row. The teacher waves them forward until they all move, groaning, to the front.

While Sam scrutinizes the intruders, I pull my cards out of her pocket. She throws her hands up in the air and gives me her most

7

disappointed look while I scan one last time through the words I'm going to have to say in a few minutes in front of everyone. My stomach's already tight at the thought. Although, if I'm being honest, my gut is always semi-clenched.

Mrs. Gifford claps to get our attention, her eyes and her frizzy red hair even more wild than usual. She introduces the new kids as the art class, and the bearded man as Mr. Friedman, the art teacher. No wonder I didn't recognize him. I've never actually been *in* the art room because (1) I have approximately zero artistic ability, and (2) my honors classes and the track team keep my schedule packed, leaving no room for artsy extracurriculars.

Gifford tells us the art kids are here "for something very exciting" and gives us time to practice our poems, although I strongly suspect it's because she's still nursing her daily Diet Coke. She doesn't even notice when Damon, late as always, slides into a seat behind me.

"Did you see him?" he says, leaning forward like we were mid-conversation.

"Who?" Kali asks, a singsongy lilt in her voice because *OMG! It's Damon!* who she's been in love with since fifth grade. She's never forgiven me for the regrettable month freshman year when I dated him, mostly because I believed that beneath his assholery, there was a boy worth liking. Spoiler: I was wrong.

Underneath, he's still a colossal tool.

"The psycho," he says in a creepy, horror-movie kind of way. He takes a long sip of an energy drink (the official last-period pick-me-up of the junior class) and nods to a boy who came in with the art kids, wearing neon yellow sunglasses to hold back a shock of black hair that sways with the rhythm of his hand moving rapidly on a pad of paper.

8

"I'm surprised they even let him in," Kali says.

"Let *who* in?" I ask.

"Micah Mendez. Got expelled from his old school. I heard someone found him perched on Deadman's Cliff, trying to, you know . . ." Damon makes a throat-slitting motion with his thumb.

Kali leans forward, whispering. "I read on the Underground," she says, referring to the tell-all cesspool of an online gossip page where people post the Ridgeline High rumor du jour, "that he had a full-on meltdown at his last school. Like, a calling-the-cops freak-out."

"I heard," Damon says, shout-whispering just loud enough that I'm sure the kid with the sunglasses hears, "he's certifiable. Been locked up in a nuthouse for the last year."

My stomach clamps so tightly, I almost lurch out of my chair.

"They're called treatment centers, you douche," Sam says. She shoots me a knowing look, but I quickly glance away, afraid Damon will intercept our stealth communication. Sam is the only one who knows about Alice, and that's how it has to stay. I don't need my family's dirty laundry coursing through the Ridgeline Underground rumor mill.

For all anyone knows, my big sister is still off at college, living in her dorm, staying out too late on weekends. I never mention that she came home a few weeks into freshman year, got into bed, and never got up again. That is, until the Night of the Bathroom Floor.

Alice is doing great. Alice loves college. We'll tell her you asked about her!

I've repeated the lie so much that sometimes I almost forget it's not the truth.

Almost.

How many treatment centers can there be around here?

Damon scoots his chair so close to me, I can feel his breath.

"Whatever. Bottom line, kid's a psycho. You should put *that* in your Word of the Day, Lil," he says, referring to my social media handle, LogoLily, where I geek out by making up new words. "*P-S-Y—*"

"I know how to spell, thank you very much." I take another look at the boy in the corner.

What are the chances it'd be the same center?

His hand stops moving and he looks up. I snap my own eyes away.

"And he doesn't appear particularly psychotic." I'm not exactly sure what a true psycho would, in fact, look like. But I do not think this kid is it.

Damon laughs. "That's the thing. You never know what's going on in someone's head." He points to each of us. "Any one of us could be a secret psycho."

His finger lands on me.

"Yeah, right," Kali says. "Lily's perfect."

Damon leans toward her, whispering dramatically, "Exactly. It's the perfect ones you have to be careful about. So tightly wound. All the pent-up crazy just builds and builds until—" He slams his palm on his desk. "SNAP!"

He leans back, laughing when I jump, my nerves congregated in my gut, twisting together into a bigger-than-usual knot.

"You are *such* a dumbass," I say, acting like I don't care about Damon's teasing or that this kid in the corner may know my family's secret. Except now he's staring at me. Like *right* at me. I meet the new kid's eyes, and he smiles *like he freaking knows me.* He half waves with a small piece of black charcoal chalk between his fingers. I turn away abruptly, forcing my eyes to focus on my poems.

"Uh-oh." Damon's eyes flash back and forth between me and the new kid like he smells fresh meat. "The psycho's digging our Lily."

"I'm not *your* Lily."

Even though we broke up *years* ago, Damon's never fully gotten the memo that I'm not his to torment. The knot in my stomach expands, undulating out in all directions. When I look again, the boy with the sunglasses is still laser-beam focused on me.

"Oh, this is too perfect," Damon continues. "You know what they say about freaks of a feather flocking to—"

"Seriously, Damon," Sam interrupts. "Must you incessantly compensate for your micro-penis by being the biggest dick on the planet?"

Damon leers at her. "Yeah, I bet you'd like to see what I'm working with."

"Keep it in your pants, Damon," I say, trying my level best to act like I'm not bothered by the boy in the corner. But the knot has completely taken over my abdomen now and is radiating waves of panic toward my chest. Even if it was the same center, he wouldn't say anything.

Would he?

"Do you *know* him?" Sam whispers to me.

I shake my head.

"Are you sure?" Sam straightens up, talking to me out of the corner of her mouth now. "Because he's coming over here. Right. Now."

chapter
2

Go away. Just go. Away.

I stare holes into my notecards. I pretend not to see him coming. Pretend I don't notice when he's standing right next to me.

"Lily, right?"

He puts out his hand for me to shake, his fingertips coated in black charcoal. I shake his hand, trying to ignore everyone staring, including Damon, mouth agape, obviously loving every second of this awkward encounter. I grip my pencil hard, trying to stall the dread that has moved from my abdomen to my throat.

Don't mention Alice.

Please don't—

"I'm Micah. Your sister and I—"

"Worked together," I say, making something up quickly. My words come out tight. "At the dog groomer last summer, right?"

He narrows his eyes at me, clearly confused about why I'm lying. His brown eyes hold mine for a second, questioning me, and I try to send the best *please just play along* look I can muster. He looks at Sam and Kali and then back to me.

"Sure. Sure. The dog groomer," he says slowly, unconvincingly. "Can't get enough of those little mutts."

He stands there for an interminable few seconds, rocking back on his heels, drawing attention to the fact that he's wearing neon green socks with monkeys on them, pulled almost all the way up to his shorts. Whoever this kid is, he's definitely not concerned about standing out.

"Psycho!" Damon coughs into his hand.

The boy with the sunglasses stares at him. "What'd you say?"

"Hey, dude. Just calm down. I don't want any trouble." Damon puts his hands up as if he's been challenged to a duel. "I was just saying those are some supercool socks."

The boy in the socks mutters a word in Spanish that I *know* is one of the bad ones, and as he turns to leave, his fingertips brush against the energy drink on Damon's desk, just hard enough to knock it over. The yellow liquid flows out across the desk onto Damon.

"What the hell, dude?" he yells, jumping up as a wet circle forms on his crotch. But the new kid is already walking away, hands raised like it's out of his control.

"Sorry, *dude,*" he says with so much disdain, I can taste it. Damon rants about how the school shouldn't let in "people like that," while dabbing at the wet spot with the paper towel Kali hands him.

"What was that about?" she asks, looking at my white knuckles death-gripping my pencil like it could save my life.

I shrug, biting back the panic. "No idea," I lie. "You heard Damon. The kid's crazy."

I'm pretty sure I know *exactly* what that was about, but I'm not about to spill my guts right here, with Damon just waiting for some juicy morsel of gossip. He'd just *love* to know where my sister's been these last few months. The Germans have a word for it—*schadenfreude*—finding joy in the misery of others. And I'm not going to give all my über-competitive classmates the satisfaction.

I try to return to my poetry, but my mind is gone.

What if he knows about the Night of the Bathroom Floor?

What if he tells everyone about Alice?

The more I fight the what-ifs, the more they push back, edging me out until I feel the familiar sensation that I'm floating up and out of myself, watching my life through a spotless pane of glass.

I watch the scene like a movie reel: Gifford calling up the first row of students to read their poems. Sam gets up and reads hers, a rhyming, iambic-pentameter metaphor about violin strings stretched too thin.

By the time Gifford calls me up, I've left my body completely. I watch me stick my notecards and a pen into my 365-day planner, clutching everything to my chest like a security blanket as I walk zombie-like to the front of the room. I see everyone's eyes on me, who is not really me because I am floating high and free above this Lily-not-Lily, who stands there, silently.

I'm frozen, like that deer Dad hit on the highway last year. Like I'm about to get smashed to bits by a fifty-ton moving vehicle.

Could you look any stupider?

I can't remember a single word, so I open my planner to the note-cards. But my mind is stuck on the boy with the sunglasses.

What if he tells?

My skin itches—little buglike crawlies on every inch. I see my fingers scratch their way up my arm to my neck.

Kali leans forward in her chair, her face twisted in disgust.

"Ewww, stop. You're bleeding."

I see me wipe a smear of blood from my skin onto my pants.

"Lily?" Gifford's voice pulls me back into my body. A shot of adrenaline floods through me.

What if he tells?

The thought vibrates me from the inside, like I'm going to jump out of my own skin.

When did it get so hot in here?

Damon twirls his finger beside his ear and points to me. A boy next to him hides a laugh under his hand.

"Are you okay?" Sam mouths from her desk.

I nod and give Sam a thumbs-up.

Another lie.

WHAT IF HE TELLS?

The words on my notecard jumble together.

Get a grip, Lily.

A tingling starts at the tips of my fingers.

A block of concrete slams into my lungs.

Just calm down.

But I can't.

It's too late.

I'm not getting enough air.

I want to scream.

But I'm paralyzed.

Everyone is staring at you.

Can. Not. Breathe.

My head's not connected to my body anymore.

Am I even *in* my body?

I feel like I'm dying.

Am I dying?

You're definitely dying.

My heartbeat thuds in my head, whooshes in my ears.

A new, racing rhythm thumps through my body like a second heartbeat.

Pulsing.

Pounding.

Deafening.

Little pricks of light shoot in from the corners of my eyes.

Darkness kaleidoscopes in. I have to get out of here.

I force my legs to move, and before anyone can stop me, I run.

chapter
3

I dash to the bathroom across the hall and barf.

Twice.

Leaning against the stall wall, I flush away my vomit and slump to the cold floor. I hug my knees to my chest, making myself as small and tight as possible.

I'm okay

I'm okay

I'm okay.

Against my fingertips, my pulse races in my neck. One hundred forty.

I breathe in deeply, then release the air slowly, slowly.

Until slowly, slowly, my heartbeat fades from the back of my head.

The rhythmic pulsing gathers itself again in my chest.

Little by little, I reclaim my body.

But not my mind.

It's still spinning, churning out unwanted thoughts.

It's getting worse.

You're *getting worse.*

And then, the biggest thought, the one that screams the loudest each time my mind and body betray me:

What if you're going crazy?

Just like her.

What if . . . you're already gone?

chapter
4

The Evidence

1. My body has a mind of its own.
2. My mind has a mind of its own.
3. My big sister already snapped.
4. I have a constant sitting-at-the-top-of-a-roller-coaster feeling. Except I never drop.
5. Can. Not. Shut. Off. Brain.
6. Almost hyperventilated during a run.
7. Freaked out at school because a boy possibly (okay, almost definitely) knows Alice from rehab. Currently sitting on the bathroom floor like a weirdo.

I stare at the strikes against my mental health.

Writing the words in the back of my planner, seeing it in ink, makes it feel real. I've known something was wrong—something was off—since my first heart-pounding, mind-racing, breath-stealing freak-out a few weeks after Alice went to Fairview. I was alone on a late-night practice run through the neighborhood, running the same path I'd taken on the Night of the Bathroom Floor. While I ran, the memories flashed, fast and fresh: Alice's blood. *Help me,* she says. I don't know how.

My heart ended up in my throat, beating a million miles a minute, and my lungs pinched off my air until I couldn't run anymore. I've lost control a few times since, but I've managed not to have a repeat during school, in front of everyone—until now. (Thank you, Mr. Monkey Socks.)

I'd give anything to just stay on this floor all day. But someone's gotta keep those dominos falling in line. I hoist myself up, dipping my head down slightly to stop the ground from spinning. At the sink, I splash water onto my face and slap my cheeks a little in the mirror so I don't look quite so Queen of the Undead. This latest and greatest episode has left my body drained, like it's run a marathon. The kind I can never win.

With a coarse paper towel, I wipe the trickle of blood from where I scratched my neck in front of the class.

They all think you're nuts.

I pop in a piece of gum to hide the sour bile taste in my mouth and tug my ponytail tight, ignoring the pulsing in my skull, the weary in my bones.

They're right.

When I emerge, the boy in the monkey socks is leaning against the bank of lockers in an otherwise empty hallway. Fan-freaking-tastic.

"You okay?"

"Fine."

20

He jogs a few steps to catch up to me, and his eyes lock on mine from behind thick black half curls of hair that fall in front of his face.

"It's just, you looked like you were about to have a panic attack in there."

"I don't have panic attacks."

~~I have brain attacks. Body attacks.~~

I keep those words to myself. No need to go blabbing about my questionable sanity so my classmates can call *me* a psycho, too. And whatever is happening to me is not *just* a panic attack, because that would mean it's all in my head, and how can that be when my heart's racing and my skin's buzzing and my lungs are gasping for air?

"Well, whatever it was, I'm sorry if I said something wrong. You know, about dog grooming with your sister?" He puts air quotes around the words *dog grooming* like we're in cahoots. "It's just, Alice talked about you all the time at Fairview. You look just like her."

I stop short in the hall. We're only three doors away from the English room, and the last thing I need is to walk in together.

Freaks of a feather.

"Look, Micah—it's Micah, right?"

He nods.

"One, I am *nothing* like my sister. And two, you can't just go broadcasting stuff like that."

Micah tucks his curls behind his ear. One eyebrow curves upward when he smiles.

"Stuff like what?"

"Stuff like"—I lean in closer to him—"Fairview."

He leans in close, too. He smells like ashy charcoal and wood shavings rather than the standard I Just Bathed in Axe Body Spray eau-de-boy.

"Why are we whispering?"

A couple of junior girls from the track team walk by, and I straighten up, pulling away from him.

"Just trust me."

"Thanks for the tip." He flashes an easy, genuine grin just as Principal Porter rounds the corner, his mouth puckered in its usual I-hunt-children-for-sport demeanor.

"Mr. Mendez," Porter half shouts down the hallway. "At Ridge-line, we stay *in* class during class time."

"On my way, sir," Micah says, straightening up to give a small salute with his black-tipped fingers. Porter looks from him to me, probably trying to figure out what we're doing together.

"May I remind you that you're here on a *probationary* basis," he says. "Don't give me a reason to change my mind."

He stares at both of us like *Well, get going, dummies* until we turn and speed walk back to the classroom. Inside, everyone is sitting in pairs, like they're about to board an ark. Two by two, they turn to stare at us. At the front of the room, Gifford smiles.

"Wonderful!" she says. "Our final partnership has returned!"

A classroom's worth of eyes land on us.

Did she say *partnership*?

As in Lily and Micah, partnership? As in this-can't-be-happening partnership?

Gifford asks me if I'm all right. "It's normal to get some jitters reading your work in public," she whispers to me.

"No, it's not that. I—" I start, the class still staring.

~~I'm losing it.~~

22

"I think maybe I'm coming down with something."

Liar, liar, crazy pants on fire.

Gifford ushers us into two desks at the front of the room, assuring me I'll have a chance to make up my poetry reading.

"You've missed our spiel, you two, but Mr. Friedman will give you the SparkNotes version." She's talking so fast, her frizzy red hair vibrates.

"We're combining our classes to explore what happens when words and art collide," says the art teacher with the straggly beard. He interlaces his fingers and holds his joined hands up to the class. "The power of art. As one."

More specifically, Gifford adds, we need to come up with a project that's both written and visual, that shows the power of art in a community. We have seven weeks, and this project will be 20 percent of our grade. Half the project is what we say, and half is finding a creative way to share it with as many people as possible. They turn us loose to create! *Mine the depths of your artistic genius!* Their enthusiasm makes me want to curl up and sleep for a million years.

And I'm stuck with *this* kid?

The other partnerships are chattering away, introducing themselves, and Micah's just staring at me, that same I'm-getting-away-with-something grin on his face with his eyebrow cocked upward.

"What's so funny?" I ask.

"You don't like me, do you?"

"I don't *know* you."

"And yet, you hate me." He leans toward me, whispering, "Just so you know, Alice is the one who asked me to check in on you."

"Hold up. *Alice* is worried about *me*? First of all, that's hilarious, and second, as you can see, I'm doing just fine without her."

"Clearly." Micah studies my face in a way that makes me want to run away again. "How come I never saw you on visitation days?"

"Just haven't made it yet." Technically, it could be true. She's got another month at Fairview, so I *could* still go visit, but I highly doubt she's eager to see me, considering our last interaction included such highlights as me standing there helpless while she nearly bled out. I push the memory of razor blades out of my mind because I'm trying to pull off an I'm-*not*-crazy vibe here. Damon catches my eye across the room—his pants are dry but he's still death-staring Micah. "Look, I don't know how else to say this. I do *not* want to talk about my sister."

He holds up his hands, guilty.

"Okay, okay. Message received, Little Larkin."

"Don't call me that."

"So many rules." He smiles again. That eyebrow reaching for the sky. A scar runs through it, separating it right in the middle. "Why so many rules?"

"I don't know. Why do *you* have so many questions?" I stare him down, but he doesn't look away. "Look. I guess we're partners."

He leans back in his desk so that the front two legs come up. "Looks like it."

His hands are clasped behind his head, elbows pointed outward, and from this angle I can see a tattoo on the inside of his wrist. A semicolon. I've seen it before online, the symbol for someone who lived after attempting suicide. *Is Damon right? How many of the rumors are true? Public meltdowns? A death wish?* He follows my eyes to his wrist and then stares at me, daring me to ask.

"I just need to know you're going to take this seriously," I say instead.

He tips his desk back down, looking me straight in the eye.

"It's art. I never take it seriously."

"It's twenty percent of our grade."

"So?"

"So, I care about my future."

"And I don't?"

"I'm just—"

"You're just making some bold assumptions, is what you're doing."

I take a deep breath. "Let's start again. Since we're stuck together—"

"Oooh, bad start."

"Since we're partners—"

"Better."

"We should come up with a plan."

I take out my planner and open it to the calendar.

"We have seven weeks." I draw a red star on the project's May due date. "So let's break that down by week, and then give ourselves a week to finalize, and—"

"Are you for real?" He pulls my planner away. I try to snatch it back, but he's already thumbing through it. My heart starts beating toward panic again. *My list of crazy is in there.*

It takes all of two seconds for my heart rate to skyrocket.

Do not freak out again.

Do not freak out again.

"Please give it back," I say.

He puts his hand over his mouth and shakes his head.

"This is the most anal-retentive thing I've ever seen. And yet, I can't look away."

I grab the book, shove it into my backpack, and zip the pack tight.

"Look, you don't have to *get* me. I don't have to get why you're wearing monkey socks and sunglasses indoors. We don't even have to actually work together. Why don't you just worry about the art and I'll worry about the writing. We'll get together in a few weeks and find some way to put them together. Deal?"

He smiles again, his eyebrow shooting up. "Is that another rule?"

"Is that another question?"

He leans back again, arms folded, like he's trying to figure something out. Thankfully, mercifully, the bell rings and he tips his charcoal piece to his forehead. "See ya around, partner. Let me know if you need help."

"I don't need help."

~~And you'd be the last person I'd ask, anyway.~~

Damon and a group of guys flank both sides of the doorway so that Micah has to pass right through them. They make monkey noises as he does and knock his backpack off.

"Watch your back, Manic Micah," Damon says.

In one day, he's already got a reputation, a nickname, and an enemy in the biggest douche-nozzle at Ridgeline High.

If anyone needs help, it's that kid.

This place is going to eat him alive.

Ridgeline Underground

354 likes

Heads up: Micah Mendez is dangerous. He basically
attacked Damon today and I heard he went full psycho on
a kid at his last school. Like stomped him into the ground.
Anyway, don't let his dumbass socks fool you.

45 comments

I believe it. Kid's weird and trying WAY too hard.

I like his socks!

Bets on how long until he offs himself?

20 bucks says he can't even do that right

chapter
5

After class, my head's still woozy from my freak-out.

But duty calls.

I chug an energy drink until my heart's doing the cha-cha. Sam and the rest of the track team are already four minutes into our twenty-minute warm-up run by the time I drag my butt out to the field.

"Tardy. Twenty push-ups after warmup," Coach Johnson bellows as I run to catch up with Sam.

"Soooo," she says. "Are we going to talk about it or just blow past it?"

"Blow past what?"

"You. Sprinting out of class."

"Oh, that."

"Yeah, *that*."

"It's nothing."

Sam stops dead on the track, hand on her hip.

"No. You do not get to act like that. Not with me, basically the be-all and end-all of best-friend-dom, just like all the Sams before me."

28

"All the Sams before you?"

She shushes me with her hand in the air.

"Please save all your mockery until the end of my soliloquy." I gesture for her to continue. "As I was saying, take a look at the finest heroes of all time. Frodo. Captain America. Jon Snow. What do they have in common?"

"Capes? An unhealthy affinity for hair gel?"

"Incorrect," she says. We start running after Coach threatens more push-ups. "A Sam. Jon Snow has Sam Tarly, lovable nerd. Frodo has Sam, loyal hobbit of the Shire. Even Captain America had a trusted Sam sidekick. But every time you shut me out, you are robbing me of my birthright. My heritage by name."

"Must you always be so . . . extra?"

"Must *you* always be so secretive?"

Sam waits for an explanation, but I don't have one. The heat from the rubber track radiates onto my legs. My body drags, but I push through.

Breathe in, breathe out.

Just move forward—one foot in front of the other.

"Is it about Alice?" she whispers as a trio of girls runs alongside us.

I wait for them to pass before I whisper back, "That boy from the art class. The one with the socks? He was at Fairview with her. He almost said it in class, in front of everyone."

"So you ran?"

"Yeah."

And also there was the whole heart racing, lungs collapsing, head spinning thing.

"Even if he told, Lil, it's not like *you* went to Fairview."

Not yet.

29

We round the corner where Coach is writing each of our names on a whiteboard with a number. *Lily Larkin: 1.7 seconds.* That's how much I need to cut off my 400 meter if I want to have a shot at state in two months.

"What's the big deal if he's your partner for *one* project?"

The big deal? The big deal is that I exist in two *very* different worlds. The one where I win races and get straight As, and the one where my brain is breaking and my sister is in a rehab center because hers already broke. Two Lilys, and never the twain shall meet, at least not if I want to keep at least one Lily sane. And getting all chummy with Micah *definitely* qualifies as worlds colliding.

For a second, I almost tell Sam everything. Tell her how I've been losing control since Alice left. How I stay up until the sun comes up most nights, locked in an ever-tightening spiral of what-ifs. About the list in the back of my planner and how I slip out of myself sometimes, become a spectator in my own life.

Across the parking lot, Micah's pedaling away on a bright orange bike, ignoring Damon and the posse of jerks taunting him.

Certifiable.

That's what Damon called him.

That's what people think about kids who go to treatment centers or make lists about why they're going insane.

And that's exactly why I can't tell—anyone. Not even my best friend.

"I think I'm just stressed," I say.

Sam rolls her eyes and mock waves to me.

"Hello? It's junior year. It's supposed to be stressful. I've been up till one every night this month practicing for my solo." She holds up her bandaged fingers while we run.

"Right? It's just a lot, sometimes." An unexpected lump lodges in my throat. "Take the right classes. Get the right grades so you can take better classes. Cram your schedule full so by the time you actually get to college, you're ahead of your classmates, already winning a competition you didn't even know you entered."

Sam stops running and grabs me by the shoulders.

"Listen to me. It sucks a fat one. We know this. But we're going to get through it, get into college, party like hell senior year, and then bust out of this joint."

"If we're lucky," I say. "Did you know the acceptance rate at UC Berkeley was only seventeen percent last year?"

She throws her head back in exasperation.

"Lily Larkin. Do *not* make me take away your Google."

"No, seriously. What if I don't get in? Dad wants me to follow in his Golden Bear footsteps so badly, and everybody will think I'm a total failure and—"

"You'll end up living under the overpass and eating soggy Cheetos from the trash can to survive?" Sam bumps my shoulder with her fist. "You're going to be fine. We're *all* going to be fine. We're almost there. Just hold on a little longer."

We run the rest of the path out to the end of the school property, where the track intersects the Pacific Coast Highway sidewalk. The ocean stretches out in front of us. We're just about to turn right, follow the regular loop back up to the school, when Sam grabs my arm.

"I know what you need." She looks down at the beach and then back at me, eyebrows lifted in invitation.

"Uh-uh. Coach already thinks I'm slacking." He's not wrong. I've stopped doing my practice runs. I've tried taking a different path, but the memories of Alice always find me, and my body and brain go berserk and I turn back before I even break a sweat.

If I didn't need a win at state to polish off my college apps in the fall, I'd probably stop running altogether. But I've worked too hard to quit now, and the team's counting on me, and Dad's counting on me to get into Berkeley, and I'm not about to let everyone down.

"Coach will live," Sam says, smiling as she runs down the steep stairs scaling the cliff. She yells back at me, "What *you* need is a detour."

I glance at the school behind us, where Coach is berating some terrified freshman, and I follow her down the stairs, taking them two at a time until I land on the soft beach. And then we're off, sprinting toward the water's edge. We run along the space where sea meets shore, dodging the waves as they surge toward us. Our footsteps fall like secrets in the sand.

My lungs fill with salty air as I breathe deeply. My mind feels clearer out here, running free. No finish line.

The beach is ours except for the shape of a person way out on Deadman's Cliff, a glowing silhouette in the slanted sun. Sam's black hair shines, too. With the sun streaming across her face, the uneven sand beneath our feet, I let myself believe her.

You're going to be okay.

Wet sand clings to our shoes as we run back up the steps, leaving the freedom of the wide-open beach.

"Totally what I needed."

"Exactly. Because I'm Sam. Best friend extraordinaire." She puffs out her chest and puts her fists against her hips like a superhero. "And you can be my sidekick—Anxiety Girl!"

I laugh and point my fist toward the sky, acting stronger than I feel. "Jumping to the worst possible conclusion in a single bound!"

"Should we get matching capes?"

"Definitely."

Back at the track, Sam takes off with the long-distance runners while I pay my push-up penance. After, I take my spot on the starting blocks with the sprinters. 1.7 seconds. That's all I need.

"Pick up the pace, Larkin," Coach yells when I'm halfway around the 400-meter track. "Second place is first loser."

I dig my heels into the spongy rubber blacktop, my quads propelling my body forward. Sam's right. We're almost there. Hang on a little longer.

I train my eyes on the finish line.

Just keep running.

LogoLily's Word of the Day

curternus (n) The act of running toward a goal that keeps moving, ever so slightly, out of your grasp, as if you're a hamster on a wheel to nowhere, believing that if you can just go a little more, a little farther, you'll win.

From Latin *cursus* (running) + *aeternus* (eternal)

chapter
6

Pack the lunches.

Write a poem.

Extra credit for bio.

Laundry.

My mind ticks through my to-do list as I spread mayo on bread for tomorrow's lunches for Dad, Margot, and me.

Staci (yes, that's right, with an *i* and only an *i*; don't get me started) loiters around the kitchen nervously while I work.

"I can help, you know," she says.

If I didn't have a down-to-the-second system already in place, I'd probably let her pitch in. Alice and I had a fine-tuned method for running this place before Staci and Dad got married last year, and I'm still doing just fine as a one-man band. Nothing screws up the rhythm more than someone else getting in on the act, especially Dad's brand-spanking-new wife.

"Thanks. I got it."

"I'm just standing here."

She reaches out to put the apple slices into the baggies. I slide them over to me.

"Seriously, Staci, I don't need help." I slap the top of each sandwich into place. We've managed just fine without a mom for ten years, and we're not in the market for a replacement. She leans against the countertop with a heavy sigh.

"Everyone needs help sometimes, Lily."

She watches me put apples and lemon juice into baggies. The tense silence makes my heart speed up, which is the *last* thing I need after my epic freak-out today. Fortunately, Dad strides into the room, armed with an over-the-top smile and Scrabble.

"Hashtag family game night?"

He jiggles the box, sending the tiles clinking against each other.

"Do we need to have the hashtag talk again?" I say.

"What?" He holds up his hands innocently. "I *totally* used that right."

"If you're older than fifty, you did *not* use it right."

He chuckles and slings his arm around my shoulder, pulling me tight against him. Even though I'm gaining on his six-foot height, my head still fits perfectly in the space between his chest and shoulder. Always has. When I was little, pretending to be asleep so he'd carry me to bed, I believed this pocket of space was mine—a little piece of Dad carved out just for me.

"Well, hashtag my bad," he says.

Groan. "Dad. Seriously. It physically pains me."

His chest shakes as he laughs. "All right, all right, I get it. Your old man is not cool. But I might just be smart enough to kick your butt." He shakes the box again, trying to ply me with my favorite

36

game. Dad's a self-proclaimed logophile (aka "lover of words") just like me. "How about it?"

On the floor, my backpack bulges at the zipper. My stomach squeezes—it's gonna be another late night. Geometry chapter test, Spanish oral on camping trips (because learning how to say *Let's pitch the tent* in español is going to come in handy one day), and now this poetry project with a partner who doesn't give one flip. After today's episode, all I want to do is sleep, but if I'm going to outrun whatever is wrong with my brain, I can't stop.

I keep my freak-out and the list in the back of my planner to myself. Dad has enough to worry about.

"C'mon. Thirty minutes? We got pizzaaaaa." He draws out the word like he's a used-car salesman selling me a lemon, which is actually the perfect metaphor for Larkin family time lately.

Maybe it's because this family feels hauntingly incomplete without Alice. Or maybe it's because Dad and I have spent most of our "together time" these last two months desperately tiptoeing around The Things We Don't Say. We talk about school. About the weather. About oddly specific German words. But never about the night she left. Our family is already stretched thin at the edges, trying to pretend everything's okay. If we pick at that particular thread, we might unravel.

Sometimes I think the silence is the only thing holding this family together.

But Dad's shaking the Scrabble box so eagerly, I can't let him down. I look at my backpack again, mentally cramming thirty minutes into tonight's homework schedule.

"Carbs *and* wordplay? How could I say no?" I say, zipping up the lunch bags and ignoring the knot in my stomach.

"Pizza's here!" Staci shouts up the stairs to Margot.

I'm more than a little shocked that she's letting us eat what she calls "gluten-stuffed cholesterol pies." Ever since the Night of the Bathroom Floor, Staci-with-only-an-*i* and Dad have been on an all-natural kick. Something about chemicals and well-being and how *we could all do with a little less toxicity.* All I know is, our pantry went from Lucky Charms to various iterations of granola mixed with hemp hearts and flaxseed.

Staci carries in the pizza and starts dishing it up on the island for me. "Pepperoni or Hawaiian?"

"Hawaiian."

Dad groans from the pantry. He's a staunch supporter of the Coalition Against Fruit on Pizza.

"I really do have a lot of homework," I reply.

"No, no, by all means," he says. "Have your fruit in marinara sauce. Who am I to stand in the way of bad taste?"

Staci slides a triangular piece of paper-thin dark brown crust and a drizzle of what maybe, sorta resembles cheese onto my plate.

"What is *that*?" I say.

"Pizza."

"I respectfully disagree."

She holds up the label from the box. "It's all-natural! Non-GMO, gluten free, dairy free—"

"Joy free."

Dad laughs, but puts his arm around Staci's shoulders, tugging her head against him—into my spot.

I look away, trying to ignore the ache in my chest. It's not the usual palpitation-induced tightening, more like a dull ache right behind my ribs. An ephemeral thud of sadness.

Margot trounces down the stairs in a full-on, honest-to-goodness black robe, complete with a maroon-and-gold emblem on the chest, the latest in her Harry Potter obsession. She found Mom's old books in the basement after Alice left for Fairview, and almost immediately began sorting everyone into their Hogwarts house against their will.

"Any letters from Hogwarts today?" I say. I know I shouldn't tease her, but come on—she's a ten-year-old WEARING A CAPE.

She sticks her tongue out at me. "For the one-hundredth time, I do not think I am an *actual* wizard."

"Your attire begs to differ." I take a bite of undigestible pizza. "Just saying you're *really* blurring the lines between reality and fantasy here."

Dad bops Margot on the head with the Scrabble box. "Enough Potterverse. Let's play."

Staci arranges Dad's tiles on the coffee table. (They're always on the same team.) Margot and I share Dad's über-competitive DNA, so after a few rounds, I'm lost in the game and in my family, and today's drama fades away. My stomach feels almost normal as I sit here, focusing on seven little tiles as if they're the most pressing thing in my life. Like Alice is actually just off at college, and I didn't have an epic bathroom meltdown today, and that Micah kid didn't almost out my secrets, earning me a tell-all post on the Underground with the other hot gossip.

I even silence my phone when the alarm for my thirty minutes of free time goes off.

I'm ahead by ten points, waiting on Dad to play the winner-take-all word I know he's building, when he clears his throat and inches forward on his couch cushion so that his knees touch the Scrabble board perched on the coffee table.

"Girls. I want to talk to you about something." His voice is serious. Very un-Dad-like. My stomach instantly retightens. "Alice is coming home."

I pause with my newly picked tile in midair. "What? Like, here?"

"Well, this is her home," he says calmly, like his words don't explode around me, sucking the oxygen from the room.

"When?"

"Tomorrow."

"I thought she had more time," I say. The grip on my stomach has already started its march north toward my throat. She left in January. It's only March. "Wasn't it supposed to be three months?"

"Well," Dad breathes out slowly. "The counselors think she's ready."

Did anyone bother to ask if *we're* ready?

Dad continues. "And she seemed really good on our last visit, didn't she, Margs?"

Margot nods.

Staci pipes up, her face beaming with an overzealous smile. "What wonderful news. This place hasn't been the same without her."

"Is she going back to school?" I ask.

"Not yet." Dad flips a *Y* tile between his thumb and pointer finger. "She'll stay here for a while."

Well, that pokes a ginormous hole in our Alice-is-away-at-college ruse. And how can we *not* talk about it when she's right here?

"So, what do we tell people?" I ask. I think of how Damon talked about Micah today. If people know about Fairview, Alice won't be able to just waltz back into her old life.

Dad studies the Scrabble board like the answer is hiding in the triple-word score.

40

He sighs. "Let's just tell people that she's taking some time off for a work-study project. That's something college kids do, right?"

"So we should lie about it?" Margot asks.

"It's not a lie, honey. It's more like—"

"An omission," I offer.

Dad nods. He tousles Margot's crimped hair.

"Exactly," he says. "We do that sometimes to protect the people we love. But trust me, this is going to be a good thing, girls. Alice will be home, and things can go back to normal."

Ah, the lies that bind.

Margot smiles. Dad's words don't explode for her. She wasn't there when I found Alice. Crumpled on the bathroom floor. She didn't see Dad lift her or hear the tightness in his voice when he called 911. She's too young and too lost in her fantasy world to see what's happening here.

Our big sister left because something was wrong with her.

Something Dad couldn't fix.

And now she's coming home.

Dad lays out a word that immediately bumps him ahead of me on the scorecard, but I'm not really here anymore. I'm watching family time from outside my body. Through the glass, I see them, laughing and placing tiles. I see me, playing my part, smiling when I'm supposed to smile.

But inside my head, the worries have slithered in, uninvited.

This is how it always starts.

With a thought.

A whispered what-if.

What if Alice is different now?

What if everything's different?

As my mind spins, my heart races. I'm suddenly hyperaware of the air moving in and out of my lungs.

What if you forget to keep breathing?

Dread branches out through my body. My right hand starts to tingle. I shake it out, but the pins and needles won't go. Margot shoves me with her elbow.

"Earth to Lily," she says. "Your turn."

I blink back to life. The glass shatters. Dad is staring at me, and so is Staci. Well, she's staring at my left hand, which is scratching off the scab on my neck.

"Actually, I—I really do have a ton to do tonight." I empty my tiles back into the box lid.

Dad studies me now, his face still serious.

"You okay, kiddo?"

I hoist my heavy backpack up, the weight of it almost crushing me, and I slap on my everything's-just-great face. The last thing this family needs is one more member losing their grip on reality.

"I'm fine."

Not a lie.

Exactly.

Just an omission.

Because that's what you do for the people you love.

Alone on my bed, I try to calm my body.

Breathe in.

Breathe out.

Just breathe.

I do *not* need a doubleheader meltdown today.

Across the room, Alice's empty bed stares back at me. On the night she left, I meticulously tucked in the corners of her navy-blue comforter. Sixteen times. *If I can just fix this bed,* I thought, *maybe Dad will stop looking so scared.*

Alice's desk is just how she left it, though—a mess of papers and projects. Crochet needles from when she made what turned out to be a hideously deformed scarf. Recipes from her *Top Chef* phase. Hot-pink Post-it notes, where Alice would scribble her ideas. She was always trying something new, always living life 110 percent.

Pictures on her desk show off Alice's big smile (best in the senior class) and even bigger hair. She's standing between Margot and me at her high school graduation, her cap barely holding down her long, brown, curly hair that always occupied as much space in any room as she did—big and boisterous and everywhere.

Everything from her hair to her smile to the bright red shoes below her grad gown screams Alice, at least the Alice I knew before she left for college. When she showed up on the front porch a few weeks into the semester, stripped of her Alice-ness, Staci gave her pills from the organic health-food store, insisting that her iron and B vitamins were low. Dad said she was going through a phase. That she needed rest.

I saw the thin cuts on her arms that she tried to hide, but I kept it to myself. Figured it was another one of Alice's fleeting ideas, like when she went Goth for a month. I expected it to pass.

I didn't expect the Night of the Bathroom Floor.

Or the word Dad uses in hushed tones on the phone with the Fairview counselors: *bipolar.*

What if Fairview changed her?

Stole the pieces that made her, her?

I try to put Alice and her expedited homecoming out of my head while I bust through my homework in a few hours. (Thank you, energy drink nightcap.) The black, chalky fingerprint in the corner of my planner, courtesy of my new problematic project partner, keeps pulling my attention. Will everyone treat Alice like they do Micah— rumors and *I heards* swirling?

Before I turn out the light, I stand up and walk the distance between Alice's bed and mine, one foot carefully placed in front of the other.

Seven steps.

When I was little, after Mom died, that was all it took. Seven steps and one flying leap, and I was safe, tucked in next to Alice's side, where the monsters under the bed couldn't get me.

The best thing to do, she'd say, *is make friends with the monsters.*

And somehow they stopped being scary. Alice was like that. Brave and smart, with all the answers.

I run my fingertips across her perfectly made bed and wonder which version will be coming home tomorrow: the girl who tackled life head-on, or the broken girl from the bathroom floor.

Back in my own bed, sleep flits just out of my grasp like always. Memories—freeze-framed moments—fill my head, circling like snakes, biding their time, lunging every so often to take a nip: Me, frozen, staring at the blood. Dad carrying her down the stairs. Me, running from the classroom today. Sitting on the bathroom floor with my list. Micah ignoring the *cuckoo* calls.

I cover my head with my blanket. *Just stop.*

But my brain doesn't listen.

Never does.

Across the room, a beam of moonlight illuminates Alice's perfectly made bed through the dark.

Seven steps.

But where do you go if your sister is gone? And the monsters have moved from under the bed to inside your head?

1:27 a.m.
You never visited her.

1:40 a.m.
She probably hates you.

2:00 a.m.

> **To:** TheOneAndOnlyAlice@jmail.com
> **Subject:** SORRY . . .
>
> Alice,
> Dad says Fairview has a no-cell-phones rule. That blows.
> So I hope you're checking email. Just wanted to say I'm
> sorry I never made it over there. I've been super busy. I
> hope you're feeling better.
> Lily

2:03 a.m.

Conversation moved to Trash.   Undo   ✖

2:15 a.m.

> **To:** TheOneAndOnlyAlice@jmail.com
> **Subject:** WELCOME HOME!
>
> Dear Alice,
> Can't wait to see you tomorrow! So excited!!
> Love,
> Lil

2:20 a.m.

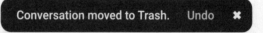

3:00 a.m.

She's definitely gonna hate you.

chapter
7

The light wakes me before my alarm.

It's too bright. Too early.

Margot snuck into my bed at some point like she's done every night since Alice left. I always wake up with a toe up my nose.

In the bathroom mirror, dark circles shadow my bloodshot eyes. I don't even know what time my brain finally shut down last night. I kneel on the cold floor over a pink-hued section of tile grout. So much for the hours Dad spent in here with a can of Clorox and a 100-percent-blood-removal mission. I guess even industrial-strength solvents can't get rid of everything.

On the lip of the bathtub, my razor catches my eye.

What if you don't stop her this time, either?

I grab the razor and search under the sink and in both our desks for anything with a blade or sharp edge or the slightest bit of skin-cutting ability. I throw all the scissors and toenail clippers and even a pencil sharpener with a tiny blade into an empty shoebox and shove it under my bed.

A rumble shakes my floor, and I stumble down the stairs to where Staci, still dressed in her workout clothes from early-morning yoga, is trying to drag Dad's desk across the wood floor in the office.

"It's too early for redecorating." My whole body aches. A vise squeezes my head.

"I'm not redecorating." Staci pushes her body weight into the back of the wooden desk, which doesn't budge. "I'm re-energizing."

She puts her hands on her hips and stares at the massive desk that usually has all of Dad's books stacked on it for the lit classes he teaches at the community college.

"The ancient art of feng shui," she continues as if I've asked. "Your sister needs good vibes when she comes home. We all do. And the first step is opening up the home's natural energy potential. And things like this"—she points to the desk—"need to be in command positions."

There's no way Staci's moving that sucker alone, so I help her reposition the behemoth into the far corner, which is apparently the perfect location because it's equidistant from both walls and facing the entry door, aka the primary energy portal. I don't have the heart to tell her she's rearranging deck chairs on the *Titanic*.

In the kitchen, Margot's slurping cereal while Dad throws things into a box on the island.

"You feng-shui-ing, too?" I ask.

"Just some overdue cleaning," he says, tossing an aspirin bottle into the box. It lands on a pile of other medicine.

"Think Alice will like my new look?" he says in a clear attempt to change the topic from the contents of the box.

Dad rubs his fingers down the beard he's let grow since Staci said facial hair is *distinguished*. He's posing like a supermodel, cracking

Margot up, who doesn't seem to notice or care that Dad's "cleaning" is actually to make sure Alice doesn't down a fistful of aspirin when she gets home.

When Margot runs to get her backpack, Dad stops posing to contemplate the set of knives on the counter like he's trying to solve one of his Sunday morning crosswords. He rubs the back of his neck while he stares at it.

"Dad?" I ask. "You good?"

"Fine, fine," he says absentmindedly before picking up the whole set and plunking it into the box.

Before English class starts, my mind is on Alice when it should be on coming up with a killer poem for this project. A vague ache wraps around my head, so I bunch up my hoodie on my desk and rest, only to jerk awake from a particularly vivid flash of Alice with deep red slices up her arms.

What if this is how it started for her?

Sleepless nights and incessant thoughts.

Heart-racing episodes on bathroom floors.

Sam stops by my desk. "I feel it is my responsibility—nay, my duty—to tell you that you look like shit."

"I'm aware, but thanks."

"Rough night?"

"You could say that."

~~Oh, and my brain is broken.~~

"Alice is coming home," I whisper. "What if—" I stop, unable to articulate the scenario in my head. The one where I don't find her in time. The one where the blade goes too deep.

49

Sam gives my hand a squeeze as the bell rings.

"Hey," she whispers, calm and sure like always. "It's going to work out."

To start today's Writers and Artists Unite! session, Friedman delivers an impassioned diatribe on the power of art to transform. "Expose the dark places to the light." He gestures wildly as he talks. "The parts that scare you most, that's where the artist is born, for fear comes from the mind. And art comes from the heart."

Micah's desk is butted up against mine, but we're working separately, unlike the other partners, who are deep into brainstorming, talking loudly and excitedly about their projects. Micah's drawing in a sketch pad, his black hair falling into his eyes. His sunglasses are bright pink to match his socks, which today feature watermelons. I swear this kid is asking for attention, and not the good kind. His hair dances with the rhythm of his hand, holding a pen instead of charcoal this time.

Whatever he's working on comes so effortlessly, I'm jealous. I stare at a blank page in my notebook. Normally, my poems kind of pour out, fully formed, as if they already existed in some ethereal space and I'm just the conduit—the hand that holds the pen. But my wellspring of creativity seems to be having a dry spell since Alice left. The only words I can conjure are the ones I make up on LogoLily.

Micah's staring at me.

"What?" I ask.

"Just feeling sorry for that pencil." He points to my mouth, where I've inadvertently chomped my pencil almost to bits. I dust the shavings off the desk.

"Guess I zoned out for a minute," I say, as if that explains the fact that I've just wood-chippered my Ticonderoga No. 2.

"Yeah, you were going full beaver over there." He nods to my blank page. "Writer's block?"

"No."

Liar.

He thumbs the corner of my notebook, flipping the empty pages.

"Clearly." He searches my face, just like he did yesterday. "Could this have anything to do with our mutual friend coming home?"

My heart stops.

"You know about that?" I whisper.

He nods. "Emailed me last night."

"Did she say anything else? Like, is she excited? Nervous?"

~~Fixed?~~

Micah leans back, a slight smirk on his face. "Those sound like excellent questions for Alice," he says, clearly enjoying that he knows something I don't.

I want to push for more, but Damon is watching us from across the room, ready to pounce on any opportunity to tease me for being buddy-buddy with *Manic* Micah. I lean back, stifling all the questions I want to ask about Alice as I return to my blank page, trying to ignore the pang of guilt—or maybe jealousy—that strikes me right in the breastbone.

This random boy knows more about your sister than you do.

Thankfully, Gifford summons me to her desk before I end up on the bathroom floor again.

She sticks a pencil into the red frizz that is her hair. She already has three in there. I picture her shaking her hair out at night, emptying an office supply closet onto the floor. What Gifford lacks in self-awareness she more than makes up for in enthusiasm. She's taken an interest in my writing since freshman year, when

I was one of only three students who showed up for her creative writing club.

"Lily, dear," she starts, "I'm not broadcasting this to everybody, but there's a lot more to this project than just a grade."

She tells me the details—how Ridgeline will sponsor one team for a summer art-and-writing workshop at UC Berkeley, all expenses paid. How attendees will meet all the department heads and get a leg up on the competition for fall admission.

She keeps talking, but my brain is stuck. All the worries about Alice give way to only one thought: *Berkeley*.

Gifford with her lipsticked teeth and pencil-holder hair has given me the answer I didn't even know I needed: I can't control which version of Alice comes home from rehab, but I *can* control this. I can win.

And once I'm at Berkeley, whatever is wrong with me—the list in the back of my planner—will be ancient history. As long as I keep moving, whatever got Alice can't get me, too. And Margot won't lose another sister to the monsters in her head, and Dad won't have to send another daughter off for cerebral repairs.

I can stop my family—and myself—from unraveling.

"You know I'm a fan of your poems, and I think you have a real shot here. But for this contest, we want something raw. Something real. Something that tells us who you are." She smiles wide, a pink lipstick smudge on her left incisor. "Can you dig deep?"

Yes.

A million times yes.

To get into Berkeley, I can do anything.

"Definitely," I say, holding my notebook to my chest.

I practically float back to my desk. Micah, however, is less than wowed.

"So?" He shrugs when I tell him, like I've just told him the hot lunch today is chicken nuggets and not that this one project could determine the entire trajectory of our lives.

"So, it's my dream school. We *have* to win."

He taps his pen on his sketchbook and cocks his scarred eyebrow upward. "Alice told me about this," he says.

"About what?"

He waves the point of his pen in a circle in my direction. "This. How you are."

"How exactly *am* I?"

"You know—gotta be the best. Get the best grades. Win *all* the races."

"Alice said that? I mean, she talked about me?"

What else did she tell him?

"Yeah, sometimes between smoking weed and getting body piercings in unspeakable places, we'd do normal kid things like talk and stuff." He leans forward like we're sharing a secret. "And she told me *all* about you."

The way he says it makes my heart speed up, but I feign annoyance rather than panic.

"Let's not pretend like you know me."

Micah smirks. "Oh, I think I've got you pegged, Little Larkin."

"Lily."

"Right," he says, directing his pen at me again. "You were the kid who had a coloring book, and every single page was perfect. You *always* drew inside the lines."

I open my mouth to protest, but he cuts me off.

"No, wait! Scratch that. It's even worse, isn't it? *You* were the kid who re-outlined the drawings before you colored them in. I'm right, aren't I? I'm totally right."

"A lot of kids did that."

"Riiiiiight." His eyes are dancing with his smile now, and I can't help noticing that he has little gold flecks in his brown iris.

"Okay," I say. "If we're pretending like we know each other, then *you* were totally the kid who scribbled with no regard for the lines, but your parents stuck it up on the fridge anyway and declared it a masterpiece."

He shakes his head. "First of all, my dad died when I was seven, so no plural parents here, and second of all, I am a staunch opponent of coloring books."

"I'm sorry. I didn't know—"

"Well, how would you? Few people share my particular rage about coloring books."

"No, I meant about your da—"

"I know what you meant," he says dismissively. "But seriously, we hand kids a picture of a duck or a cow and tell them *this* is the only way a duck or a cow can look. So they never venture outside the lines, and then we wonder why we're raising a generation of drones. Don't *even* try to convince me otherwise."

"Wouldn't dream of it." I'm smiling and I'm not even sure why, except that the possibility of a clear path to Berkeley has me almost giddy, and Micah's smiling at me in this no-bullshit way, and besides, how many high school boys get passionate about coloring books? It's almost . . . endearing. *Almost.*

"Hot takes on coloring books aside," I say, "the fact remains,

54

I *need* to win this. And I've got"—I look at my blank page—"nothing."

Micah studies me again, a look on his face like we're sharing a secret I'm not in on yet.

"I *could* help you, seeing as we are partners and all."

I lean back and fold my arms. I didn't think Micah was even paying attention to this project.

"*You* write poetry?"

"Not a word. But I may have some ideas on unblocking you. Rediscovering your artistic mojo."

I roll my eyes. Should have known he wasn't *actually* taking this seriously.

"Again. Not blocked. My mojo is just fine." The bell rings, and I pick up my notebook as I stand. The blank pages scream at me. "But, since we *are* partners and all, go ahead. Tell me these ideas."

He wags a finger at me, his smile shooting his eyebrow upward. "Nice try, but I was specifically told to work *on my own.* It was an official Lily Larkin rule, I believe." He closes up his sketchbook when I lean over to sneak a peek and holds it to his chest as he stands up. "Unless, of course, you've decided you *need* my help."

We stand in silence for a few awkward seconds, waiting each other out.

"You're gonna make me beg, aren't you?" I say.

"I'm very patient."

I wave Sam ahead when she stops to wait for me for practice. My mind wages a mini war with itself.

In this corner, lifetime champion and all-around fun-buster: Doubts!

You know what they say about him.

Certifiable.

And in this corner, newcomer but serious contender: Desperation!

You need this win.

Your family needs this win.

He might be your only chance.

"Fine. Will you please, all-knowing and wise art guru, help me rediscover my muse?"

"Yes." He picks up my hand, draws a small sketch of a Winnie-the-Pooh bear on my palm, and scribbles a note in the corner of my notebook—*@100-acre-wood.* "Come find me."

Then he disappears into the crowded hallway, his neon pink socks shining from a sea of khaki and denim.

"He is *so* weird," Kali says, flipping my hand over to see what Micah drew. "I'm just glad *I* didn't get stuck with him."

I ignore her and text Sam on my way to the locker room.

Me: you were right

Sam: I'm sure it's true, but why?

Me: everything's going to work out.

Sam: and this change of heart thanks to . . .

Me: the doors of UC freaking Berkeley swinging wide open

Sam: get out

Me: I will not

Sam: what do you have to do?

Me: WIN

* * *

I float through track practice. I even shave half a second off my 400 meter. Coach pats me on the back, tells me he knew I'd get my groove back. I take a cool-down lap next to Sam, whose telling me all about how her spotlight solo piece next month could land her the coveted first violin spot.

"I would be concertmaster, which is like the gold star for college apps," she says as we run. "And you're going to Berkeley. It's all happening, Lil!"

Sam's infectious positivity and the promise of this English contest keeps me smiling all the way around the track, all the way home.

Until I walk through my door.

A blue duffel bag sits in the front hallway.

Alice is home.

chapter 8

I find her in the kitchen, sitting on a bar stool, arched over a bowl of cereal. Her hair is short. Boy short.

It stops just below her ears, with the buzzed base coming to a small point like an arrow down the nape of her neck. Without her bigger-than-life hair, she's barely recognizable. It's still curly, but less wild. Tamed somehow. Her clothes are less, too. Less loud. Less colorful.

Less Alice.

She's reading the Lucky Charms box in front of her. How do I play this? Big, teary welcome-home hoopla? *Oh, how I missed you!* Casual, no big deal? *Hey, girl, haven't seen you since you lost your mind. How are things?*

I'm still debating when she turns abruptly and spots me standing there like the socially awkward idiot I am.

"Hey," she says.

"Hey."

Nailed it.

I get some milk from the fridge, where I see a one-page tip sheet called *After Treatment Care: A Family Guide* under a cheesy magnet that says, WE MAY NOT HAVE IT ALL TOGETHER, BUT TOGETHER, WE HAVE IT ALL. I pause long enough to see the top tip: *Everyone moves at their own pace. Give your child time to adjust.*

"Just some light reading Staci put up," Alice says. *"How to Feed and Care for Your Psychotic Daughter."*

I don't know if I'm supposed to laugh or what, but I smile because Alice kind of, sort of does. Not a *real* Alice smile. Her lips move but her eyes don't change. Definitely not the *best smile in the senior class.*

From her drab clothes to her short hair to her lackluster smile, she's just—less.

She watches me pull a bowl from the cabinet and pour myself some cereal. For a second, our eyes meet, and I'm back on that night, her eyes begging me to help her.

I look away. "When'd you get back?"

"'Bout an hour ago."

"Good to be home?"

She munches a mouthful while contemplating my question as if I've asked her the meaning of life.

"What's up with the furniture?" she asks.

"Staci."

She nods like this explains it.

"She got to the pantry, too." I point to the Lucky Charms. "Only allowed those in because they're your favorite. And don't even get me started on the handmade soap situation," I continue, because I'm not

59

sure what else to talk about. "I swear they are made of straight-up forest mulch. Yesterday, in the shower, I literally cut my thigh on a twig."

The second I say it, it's all I can hear—*cut, cut, cut.* The sharp sound of it fills the air, and to make it a billion times worse, I look at her arms. She's wearing long sleeves even though it's already warm for March in Southern Cali. When she sees me eyeing her wrists, she pulls her sleeves down farther.

You should have stopped her.

I shake off the thought. For all I know, her skin is healed, pink and soft and new. Perhaps people, like skin, regenerate.

She stares at the soggifying little shapes disintegrating in her milk.

"Since when do you eat Lucky Charms with a spoon?" I ask. She *always* picks out the marshmallows straight from the box, eating only the brightly colored pieces and leaving the dregs for the rest of us. It was always pretty obnoxious, actually, but kind of her signature move.

She studies the cereal like it's a riddle. "Since now, I guess."

The sound of her chewing fills the air.

"I like your hair," I say, even though I don't. I liked her old hair.

With one hand, she pulls at the short, springy ends. "I wanted something different."

"It's cute."

She half laughs, but her eyes still aren't in it. "You've always been a terrible liar."

"No, really," I protest. "It's—"

not you at all

"—fun."

60

"Well, Dad hates it," she says. "I could tell because he kept complimenting it."

She goes back to chewing, and my mind goes blank. I've never had trouble talking to her before. This is Alice, for crying out loud. My sister who I've slept with a million times. The girl who taught me how to curl my hair and use tampons (not at the same time, FYI). The girl who has shared my room and my secrets my whole life.

Seriously, Lily.

Say something.

Anything!

But it feels off. *We* feel off.

Even the silence feels wrong. Like we're both trying to sidestep a land mine between us.

You should have visited her.

Should have been there for her.

If I could just make her smile or laugh her big, deep Alice ha-ha that could fill any room, any space, maybe we could be us again. Normal. Isn't that what Dad promised?

But the space between us is filled only with heavy silence, weighed down by the words we keep.

~~I'm sorry.~~

~~I missed you.~~

~~Are you still. . . . you?~~

I'm picking the scab on my neck again, and when I force my hand away, I see the Winnie-the-Pooh sketch.

"I met a friend of yours from Fairview," I say in desperation. "We're partners on this project. Micah?"

She pauses midchew like she might actually talk to me.

"I don't want to talk about Fairview." She keeps eating, her eyes fixed on the back of the cereal box like it's the Holy Grail of cardboard, a secret message hiding somewhere between the riboflavin and high-fructose corn syrup. Finally, when the silence has grown so big I can taste it, I blurt out something just to fill the void.

"I'm sorry I didn't come visit. I've been really bus—"

She pushes back on her stool abruptly, screeching the legs against the floor. She rinses her dish in the sink and turns to me, arms folded. "Let's not do this."

"Do what?"

"This." She gestures to the space between us. "Whatever this is."

"I just wanted you to know," I say. "It's not like I didn't *want* to come."

"Well, I'm home now," she says. "You're off the hook."

You blew it.

You totally blew it.

I make one last-ditch effort to salvage this conversation—salvage the us we used to be—as she walks away. "I'm glad you're back."

The words feel small.

So do I.

She stops and turns to me, a forced smile on her lips beneath dull eyes.

"Seriously, Lily. Lying is just not your thing."

LogoLily's Word of the Day

essombra (n) When someone you once knew disappears.
Not dead, still breathing, and yet . . . gone.

From Latin *esse* (to exist) + Spanish *sombra* (shadow)

chapter

9

Alice isn't any more Alice when I come into our room after packing tomorrow's lunches. At dinner, she said about two words, despite Dad's best efforts to get her laughing and Margot's litany of questions about Fairview. Luckily, Staci and Dad filled the silence with chitchat while we chomped on some tofu concoction, trying *way* too hard to pretend tonight was just like any other night.

"Sorry I left such a mess," she says, standing in the middle of the room, looking at the piles of half-finished projects.

"It's fine." I scoot back on my bed to lean against the wall, pulling out my planner. She picks up the graduation picture of her and her best smile, shakes her head, and puts it in a drawer.

"Did you make my bed?"

Sixteen times.

"I wanted to help."

She nods, studying the room like it's been a lifetime instead of two months. "What's with Margot's cape?"

"She's been reading Mom's books. She's waaaay into it."

Alice pulls pajamas from her drawer. "Harmless cosplay, or full-on psychosis?"

"Unclear."

"What about Dad? He looks old. Well, older."

"He's—"

~~exhausted~~

"—fine. We're all fine." I add this last part even though she didn't actually ask about me.

She nods and heads to the bathroom, but stops at the threshold, staring at the tile floor.

"You okay?" I ask.

She looks at me like she's surfacing from an alternate dimension, and I want to tell her she can share her monsters with me, and I'll tell her about mine and how I'm scared, every single second, that she's going to hurt herself again. How I might shatter if she does.

"Fine," she says before stepping in and closing the door. The shower beats out a steady rhythm, and I double-check to make sure the box of blades is still under my bed.

I'm busting through tonight's Spanish review when Dad appears in my doorway, his reading glasses perched on the tip of his nose, his eyes tired.

"You still up, Lily pad?"

"Yep."

He sits on the bed next to me and hands me half a chocolate chip cookie.

"Life's too short for tofu," he says, smiling. "Besides, you only YOLO once."

I take the cookie even though I'm not hungry.

"Dad, seriously. The slang is not your friend."

He laughs lightly and looks toward the bathroom, where the shower's still going.

"How long has she been in there?" he asks, checking his watch.

"Not too long." I almost tell him about the box of razors under my bed, anything to make him look less worried about what Alice could be doing behind closed doors.

His eyes rove over her side of the room, where her blue duffel bag sits on the floor, still packed, like it's standing at the ready.

"How does she seem to you?" he asks.

~~Muted.~~

~~Broken.~~

"Different."

He nods, his eyes never leaving Alice's bag.

"Dad." I clear my throat. "With bipolar disorder, is it, like, treated? Like it's gone? Or, I mean, what if—could she—"

He pats me on the thigh as I stumble over the memory of the Night of the Bathroom Floor.

"All that matters is she's going to be better now." He holds my hand, squeezing it three times, his unspoken signal for *I love you.* "You leave the worrying to me, all right? That's *my* job, and I take it very seriously."

Just above his temple, a patch of white hair matches the shoots of gray in his beard. His brow is furrowed, forming a strong crease right in the middle of his eyebrows. Alice is right, he looks older. For all his dad jokes, all his unrelenting efforts to make everything okay, he's worried.

"I'm in the running for a poetry contest," I blurt out. Dad looks up and smiles, momentarily erasing the crease in his forehead.

"Oh yeah?"

"Yeah. Winner gets a scholarship to a Berkeley summer program, and Gifford says I'd basically be guaranteed a spot freshman year."

Okay, so I embellish a little, but it's worth it because Dad fist-pumps into the air, his wrinkles morphing from worry to smile lines, and I breathe a little easier.

"A Golden Bear just like your old man!"

Before I can stop him, he breaks out into a rousing, but whispered, rendition of the school's fight song, and even though I don't need all this fanfare, I'm glad I've made him happy—for a moment. And I know, more than ever, that a win is exactly what this family needs.

When he's finished his ode to his alma mater, he pats me on the back.

"That's amazing, honey. Really. Just amazing. Berkeley on the horizon, and you're still gunning for the state finals, right?"

It's the first time he's asked about my running since Alice left. Before, he always wanted to hear about my times and would put all my meets on his calendar. He still tries to get there when he can, but I guess he's got bigger things on his mind now than me running in circles.

I nod. "Got a real chance this year."

If you can get your times down.

He scans my bed, all my textbooks and notebooks and flash cards, like he's seeing them—and me—for the first time in ages. "You're not pushing yourself too hard, though, are you?"

I shake my head, but for an instant, I wish I were young again, that he'd tuck me into the spot just below his shoulder, next to his heart. And he'd tell me it's okay, and I'd believe him because he's my dad and dads don't lie.

Maybe I *can* tell him. About the bad thoughts and the panic that keeps surging through me and how I'm sitting at the top of a roller coaster, waiting for this massive drop that never comes. How I'm 99 percent sure I'm as messed up as Alice.

Yes, I'm going to tell him. Even though his eyes are tired and one more disappointment could kill him, or at least maim him. But we're all the walking dead around here anyway. What's one more flesh wound?

I breathe deeply. The words form on the tip of my tongue.

~~Ask me again.~~

~~Ask me how I'm doing.~~

~~Just ask.~~

~~I'll tell.~~

But he doesn't ask. Instead, he says he's proud of me and stands up, eyes lingering on the bathroom door for a second as the water turns off.

He kisses the top of my head. "What did I ever do to deserve such a perfect daughter?"

My chest deflates. I swallow my words.

I hide them deep behind my ribs, tucked neatly by my heart, with all the other words I keep.

Alice returns, hair still damp, and gets into bed without a word.

I disappear, too, into the pages of my notebook, still trying to think of a poem because even though Micah says he'll help me, I have serious doubts about this whole muse-discovery plan. On my hand, the Winnie-the-Pooh sketch he put there stares at me, and I can't help wondering about Manic Micah. How many of the Underground rumors are true? And why did he offer to help me?

And what, exactly, was I thinking? That a boy with monkeys on his socks and a super-sketchy past can help me with this poem?

Help me write something good enough to save this family?

Something that tells us who you are, Gifford said. *Something real.*

Real is a stranger with short hair and scars on her arms sleeping across the room from me. Real is me sitting on the bathroom floor, staring down a list of crazy.

Reality is too real.

My brain can't focus with the lump formerly known as Alice across the room. She's perfectly quiet, but I know she's there. Seven quick steps, one flying leap, and an eternity away.

In the dark, the monsters come calling.

You should be able to write this poem without Micah's help.

You should be able to talk to your sister.

You should

should

should

should

The shoulds pile up like so many cars on the highway that screech and skid into each other, unable to stop. With Alice across the room, sucking up all the oxygen, they're louder than ever. I end up in the bathroom, staring at a row of medicines in the cabinet with long names and harsh consonants. Each one is labeled with Alice's name. Each one shouts its orders: TAKE EXACTLY AS DIRECTED. TAKE WITH FOOD. TAKE TWICE A DAY.

EAT ME!

DRINK ME!

TRUST ME!

Tell your doctor right away if you have new or worsening depression or suicidal thoughts. May cause dizziness and drowsiness and an irrational impulse to chop off all your hair. Don't operate heavy machinery. Or be anything like the person you've been for the last eighteen years.

I don't know what I'm looking for exactly. Maybe a clue? Some crystal ball. *What can you tell me, little white label? What's Alice's future? What's mine?*

But seeing her medicines makes my skin too tight. Makes my breath catch in my lungs.

I slam the cabinet shut. My face looks like Dad's in the mirror. Same wide jaw and green eyes. Same purply circles under them. My long brown hair is straighter than Alice's, but still has a hint of Mom's frizz.

I stare until my face goes fuzzy. Like when you say a word too many times. My face loses its definition.

Loses its meaning.

My eyes focus on a few stray eyebrow hairs. My hand fumbles in the drawer for my tweezers.

The hairs pinch as they leave my skin.

One. Two. Three. One more.

The hair breaks, leaving a small stub. I dig the tweezers in until blood beads on my skin. But I keep going.

Deeper.

Deeper.

It stings.

But I control the hurt.

A little deeper.

And . . . got it.

In the mirror, my cheeks are flushed.

I wipe the pinpoints of blood from my eyelids.

Not a single hair running wild.

Perfect.

Q   I think I'm going c   ✖

Q   I think I'm going crazy
Q   I think I'm going crazy song
Q   I think I'm going crazy reddit
Q   I think I'm going crazy meme
Q   I think I'm going crazy country song
Q   I think I'm going cross-eyed

LogoLily's Word of the Day

locuration (n) The process of slowly losing your mind,
like a frog in a boiling pot of water who doesn't notice the
heat until it's too late, so you're left watching yourself boil
because it all happens so slowly, so imperceptibly little by
little, unwanted thought by unwanted thought, until BAM!

You're cooked.

From Spanish *locura* (crazy)

chapter
10

"Time to spill the tea."

Sam's tuning her violin on my bed, both of us still in our track uniforms from an after-school meet. I won my heat, but my time was up. Definitely not good enough for state.

"What is the dealie with your English partner?"

"Micah?" I write down an equation for my math homework.

"Oh, don't *even* try to play dumb with me." She points her bow at me before pulling it across the strings, as her fingers dance impossibly fast on the strings. The music is low and haunting and incredible.

"You're going to kill your solo."

"I better." She sighs as she lays her violin in the velvet case and snaps it shut. "Or my parents will literally kill *me*." She rests her chin in her hands like she's waiting for juicy gossip. "Nice try on changing the subject, by the way, but back to the boy. I saw you two deep in conversation the other day."

I shake my head, pretending like I'm focused super hard on this quadratic equation.

"It's not like that. Like, at all."

"Then what *is* it like? What's *he* like?"

I search for the words to describe Micah. His weird mix of know-it-all bravado and indifference, plus the flash of passion when he talked about coloring books, and another flash of humanity when he offered to help me. We haven't had another collaboration, so he hasn't elaborated on how exactly he's going to help me find my muse, and I haven't had time to go searching for the enigmatic 100-acre-wood to ask. I see him in the halls, though, mostly alone, a new pair of whimsical socks every day, and a smile on his face.

"I haven't given it much thought," I say, still piecing it all together. "But it's like I can't quite figure him out. The rumors about him don't seem to jibe with the guy who draws cartoons on people's hands, and he offered to help me on this project, which he doesn't have to do, and I can't tell if he's, like, a total a-hole, or just completely different from—"

Sam's grinning wildly at me.

"What?" I ask.

"That's a lot of thinking about someone you're not thinking about." Sam shuts my math book. "And, a-hole or not, you have to admit the boy is adorbs. Those weird socks? That black hair? The little scar in his eyebrow? Come to momma."

I shrug. "If you say so."

"Don't tell me you're not into his whole vibe. It's so . . . unique."

"Not my type." Not that I have a type. Between track and my honors classes and taking care of things around here, there is zero room in my life for breathless romances. "Besides, I barely know him."

Sam pulls out her laptop matter-of-factly and lies on her belly next to me, her legs kicking up behind her. "Shall we do some recon, then?"

First she scrolls through the Ridgeline Underground. Micah Mendez comes up with two hits: one post about Micah being a violent psycho, and the second, a photo of him standing on a cliff over the ocean, his arms wide, the wind blowing his black curls. The post simply reads: *A Boy on the Verge?*

"Is that Deadman's Cliff?" I ask.

That's been the nickname for the steep jut-out by Crater's Cove since I was about seven and the local news station kept playing the footage of a local man's dead body. Mom had died the year before, so I was a little death-obsessed, and I kept watching the body covered in a white sheet like a bloated whale on the sand, washed ashore like so much seaweed. The news anchor kept saying *apparent suicide.*

"So, Damon's right," Sam says. "Boy's got a death wish. Ooh, do you think it's true about the fight at his old school, too? Maybe that's where he got that scar. I bet it is. Should've known by the socks: boy's wild." Sam's eyes are blazing as she rattles off her theories. "Let's keep looking, shall we?"

Nothing shows up when she types his name into her social media. I open my notebook to the page where he's written *@100-acre-wood.*

"He gave me this."

Sam smiles wide.

"Of course he did." She taps it into her screen. "Got him!"

She pulls up a wall of photos. Little squares of charcoal drawings, interspersed with quotes and vibrantly colored sketches of the Winnie-the-Pooh gang.

"That's . . . unexpected," Sam says.

I point to the first drawing on the page. "Is that Damon?"

Sam makes the image bigger, and it's definitely Damon, except Micah has drawn him as a caveman, knuckles dragging on one side, and the other hand holding an energy drink.

"Well, the kid's got balls," Sam says. "Or he's *looking* for a beat-down."

The charcoal drawings on the page are haunting—dark streaks creating even darker images. A girl in a bathtub with long, flowing hair covering her naked body peers out with black eyes. His page is a strange juxtaposition of the brightness of the Winnie cartoons and the darkness of his charcoal—the same perplexing mix as the artist himself.

"Whoa, that's intense." She points to a boy drowning in water, one hand reaching up to the sky. "You sure you know what you're getting into here?"

"I'm not *getting into* anything. He's my partner. If my entire future didn't hinge on this project, and by relation him, we wouldn't even be having this conversation."

She winks at me. "Whatever you need to tell yourself, Lil."

"Besides," I add. "Even if I *was* into him, which I am not, boys are not a good idea right now. Between Alice and this poem and needing to shave off that last freaking 1.7 seconds—"

~~and losing my mind~~

"—I can't handle one more thing."

Sam flips over on the bed.

"What you *need* is to de-stress." She raises her eyebrows suggestively. "Some sexy artist action should do the trick."

"I hate to inform you, but boys are not the answer to everything."

"Except you totally want him to dip his paintbrush—"

I throw a pillow at her head to stop whatever obscenity was going to end that sentence. She dodges and rolls off the bed, and is aiming the pillow back at me when Alice walks in.

"Hey, Alice. How are you?" Sam's voice is suddenly tight. She hasn't seen Alice since Fairview, although I've told Sam how Alice is a ghost, moving around us like an echo. As if to prove my point, Alice is wearing a gray sweatshirt and sweatpants, a drab shadow of the bright dresses and vintage finds she used to wear.

Alice says she's fine and sits on her bed, staring at us until Sam says she'd better get going.

"We'll finish this later." She drops the pillow on the way out with a wink.

"No, we will not."

After Sam's gone, Alice cocoons into her comforter even though it's only eight p.m.

"You told Sam about Fairview, didn't you?" she says, a floating face in a sea of blankets. "About me."

I swallow the lump in my throat.

"Yeah." I whisper like it's the dead of night even though the evening light is still slanting into the room. "But just her, I promise. No one else."

"I could tell."

"How?"

She looks at me across the space between us. "I can always tell." She nods to my computer screen, where Micah's page is still up. "He's not your type, by the way."

I shut the laptop, feeling like she just busted me outside his window with night-vision goggles.

"Oh, I know. We're just partners on this project."

"He told me."

"You guys still talk?"

"Yep."

I want to ask her more. About him, about Fairview. About why she's different now from the big sister I grew up with, and if maybe it's the same thing that's wrong with me. Maybe we could help each other. But Alice clearly doesn't want to talk, because before I can get my words out, she flips over, turning her back toward me.

In the silence, my mind hops from worry to what-if and back again for an hour, and eventually lands on the Boy on the Verge. The scar in his eyebrow, the semicolon tattoo on his wrist. He's unstable, violent, psychotic—I've heard all the rumors. Still, I revisit his page, scrolling through the juxtaposition of the bright cartoons and dark drawings. What would it be like to put yourself out there like that? To be, unapologetically, yourself? *Here I am, world. Like it or not.*

That's the kind of poem I need for this contest. I may not be able to figure out Micah Mendez, but I do need this win. I type out a message and sit for at least ten minutes, my thumb hovering over the little arrow button.

9:00 PM

LogoLily: So, about my artistic mojo . . .

I close my eyes and hit send.

100-acre-wood: Ah, you have come to the master, ready to be enlightened?

LogoLily: I'm sorry, I seem to have interrupted you in the middle of an ego trip.

78

100-acre-wood: No, wait! I'm done. I'm done. Let's find your muse.

LogoLily: . . .

100-acre-wood: Saturday? Crater's Cove. 4 pm

LogoLily: My muse is hiding at the beach?

100-acre-wood: That's the thing about muses. They're almost never where you expect them to be.

LogoLily: I'll be there.

100-acre-wood: Sleep well.

~~Never do.~~

The last bit of light from the window has faded, so when I turn off my phone, my eyes adjust to the darkness.

This could easily be the stupidest thing I've ever done.

chapter
11

Saturday late afternoon. Beach parking lot.

I'm here despite the cacophony of monsters in my head shouting that putting my future into the hands of a boy I hardly know with a questionable past is probably not my hottest idea. Plus, I'm not sure I'm up for whatever Micah has in store, because I got almost zero sleep and am dragging serious butt.

Staci convinced Dad to let Alice go out with friends last night to "get back to normal." But Alice going out meant Dad was up pacing, and I was checking my watch, checking the blades under my bed, checking, checking, checking to make sure life wasn't spiraling out of control again. Alice made it by her ten p.m. curfew, but I was too rattled to sleep.

In the slanted sunlight, I close my eyes, bury my toes in the cool sand, and lean back on the rock wall bordering the parking lot. The warm sun and the salty sting of the air transport me back to a summer day more than ten years ago.

Alice and I are burying Mom in the sand. She's covered up to her chin, her laugh trilling on the breeze. Dad's videoing like always. Margot is in Mom's belly, and a sickness is in Mom's heart, but we don't know it yet.

We don't know anything. Except this moment. Our parents and each other and the sun and the sand sifting through our fingers.

When I open my eyes, they're gone, Mom's laughter scattered by the ca-caaas of seagulls dodging overhead. Micah waves from the beach parking lot, holding two rakes with long, metal tines.

Rakes? RAKES?

Yeah, this was a mistake.

Abort! Abort!

"You came," Micah says.

"You sound surprised."

"A little." He squints into the sun that hangs just above the horizon line. Then he marches down the beach without another word. My bare feet sink into the warm sand as I trail behind him. He's sans socks today but still has on his neon sunglasses, a T-shirt that says NORMAL PEOPLE SCARE ME, and a pair of bright orange swim trunks. When he reaches a clearing just below a craggy rock formation, he jabs the rakes into the sand.

"So, here's the deal," he says. "We start with art."

"What does art have to do with me writing poetry?"

"Nothing." He smiles easily. "And everything."

I shake my head. "Art is definitely not my thing."

He points the handle of a rake toward me. "As I recall, *you* reached out to *me* for help."

"Yes, but—"

"Well, do you want it or not?" He raises a finger into the air like he's just remembered something. He pulls a paper from his backpack and hands it to me. "And to take this project to Lily Larkin level of anal-retentive, I even made a list. Try not to get too excited."

Micah's Mentoring Rules

1. No questioning the process.
2. No quitting until the project is done.
3. No falling in love with me.

Heat rushes to my cheeks. "Falling in love with you?"

"I saw that in a movie once, and I've always wanted to say it. I'm also waiting for a chance to use 'You killed my father; prepare to die,' but that didn't really seem to fit here."

I hold out Micah's list of rules to him. "I'm sorry. I think this was a mistake. I actually really need to focus on the poem."

"All in due time."

"This isn't a joke. It's my life. It's serious."

"That *does* sound serious." He doesn't take the paper, just offers me a rake. "For this to work, you're going to have to trust me."

"I don't even know you."

"True. And we *are* up against a lifetime of coloring-in-the-lines indoctrination. But wasn't there ever a time, maybe just once, in a moment of sheer, reckless abandon, that you wanted to draw what *you* wanted to draw?"

He waits for me to open up—divulge my secret wild side. But the truth is, I *like* drawing inside the lines. I'm good at it. It's who I am. I wouldn't even be on this beach with this boy if my family didn't absolutely need this win.

But we do.

"Or maybe," he continues. "Is it that if you don't try, you can't fail?"

"Fine." I pluck the rake from his hand. "Teach me how to art."

The cove stretches out before us in a lazy *C*, hugging the waves as they peak and break and spill over the beach. Micah sweeps his arms wide toward the ocean.

"Lily, today the world is our canvas." He drags the tines of his rake through the sand, leaving wet, dark lines behind it. "And the sand, our medium."

He keeps pulling the rake, making a twirly design in the sand, and then he stands back and gestures like *Ta-da!*

"You know the tide's just going to wash that away, right?" I say.

"I'm aware of how the ocean works."

"Then what's the point?"

He smiles like my question amuses him. "See, that's your problem."

"My problem?"

"You're so worried about *the point* of it all."

My mind tries to come up with a rebuttal. But he's right. I used to write poetry for fun. I loved making the words sing on paper the way they did in my head. Now writing's a chore. Even running, the one place where I felt free, is a weight. An item on my growing to-do list.

I sigh. "What do I draw?"

"Whatever you want. Doesn't have to be perfect." Micah's already lost in his work, sweeping his rake effortlessly through the sand, trailing dark lines behind him in unpredictable patterns. "In fact, better if it's not. Perfect is boring."

I start pulling my rake through the sand, moving it this way a few feet, then turning and going the other way. I pause and look back at what I've done.

What even is that?

You're embarrassing yourself.

If he can do it, why can't you?

Are you totally worthless, Lily?

Are you listening?

Lily?

Well, are you?

"So, tell me about your poetry. Still blocked?" Micah says as our lines bring us together. "Sorry, sorry. Still in denial about being blocked?"

"Rude," I shout to him as we get farther away again. "And it's not writer's block."

"Then what is it?"

~~Life block.~~

~~Alice block.~~

~~Brain block.~~

"I don't know. It's like everyone is *expecting* something. Gifford thinks I have important things to say, and my dad just *knows* I'm going to win, but I can't even write anything, so maybe I was wrong. Maybe I'm not a poet after all." I've gone off course while talking and walked straight through my own lines, leaving big ol' footprints in the design. "Well, crap. I've already messed it up."

Micah just laughs. "Know what Bob Ross would say?"

I try to cover up my mistake by kicking more sand on top.

"Bob Ross, as in TV painter guy with the white-boy Afro from the eighties? Always talking about happy little trees?"

"The very same. Kind of a personal hero of mine."

I shield my eyes from the harsh angles of the sun to look at him. "That's . . . surprising."

"Why? Bob Ross was an icon. Always upbeat. Giving art to the masses. Spreading joy like syphilis."

"First of all, ew. Second, I do *not* get you." I stand back, studying him, trying yet again to figure out the enigma that is Micah Mendez. "On one side you're into Winnie-the-Pooh and brightly colored socks, and apparently Bob Ross, and then on the other you're . . ."

I pause, thinking about all the things I've heard about him. Suicide. Fistfights. Certifiable.

"Handsome? Witty? Pick a word, any word."

"Well, we can eliminate *humble*."

He flicks a rakeful of sand in my direction with a teasing smile that inexplicably makes my stomach flutter. I silently curse Sam for all her sexy artist talk.

"I know what they say about me, you know." Micah leans on his rake, eyes on the sand. "A Boy on the Verge. Manic Micah."

My gut tightens. "You know about that?"

Does he know I called him crazy on the day we met?

He must totally hate you.

"Yep. And it's hilarious because I'd give my left nut for some mania, but alas, my malady of non-choice is depression."

"That's just the thing," I say. "You don't *seem* depressed."

Micah laughs. "I'll pass your glowing Yelp review along to my therapist." He's standing next to me now, shoulder to shoulder, and I don't know why he's so close until he looks down, and he's added his footprints to mine, and now it looks like they were part of the design all along. "Anyway, as I was saying, Bob Ross would say there are no mistakes, just happy accidents."

With the setting sun on his face and his black curls dipping in front of his eyebrow with the scar, I can't help thinking Sam's right: he *is* kind of adorable.

I turn away before I find myself wanting to know more about this boy and his scar.

No time for boys.

"Why are you helping me?"

Micah squints in the sun, looking at me like he's choosing his words carefully. "You had this look. This *help, I'm drowning* look in your eyes. I mean, your eyes are beautiful—" He clears his throat and his face flushes red, and I'm sure mine does, too, so I look down at the sand. "But also sad, all at once. And I just wanted to help."

He smiles awkwardly, and the sun is warm and the sand is cool, and I let his answer be enough. I keep drawing my lines, and before long, I'm off on my own path, making circles and curves and lines. Just like running, it has a rhythm to it. Pull and turn and pull again. And like with writing—at least the way writing used to be—the less I think about it, the easier it comes. And soon I'm lost in it, thinking about nothing but the feel of the sand giving way, the sound of the waves.

Across the beach, Micah practically dances as he draws, his body twisting and turning, his rake an extension of his body. I try not to notice the way his arm muscles flex as he grips his rake.

"Time's up!" Micah declares from across the beach, which is lined with our creation, but from this angle, it looks like nothing more than a bunch of messed-up sand.

"Now what?" I yell to him.

"Now," he says, chucking his rake into the sand, "we swim!"

And then he's running toward the ocean, ripping off his shirt as he goes. He high-knees it over the waves and dives in, headfirst. I follow behind, toeing the foamy white, eyeing the huge DANGEROUS RIPTIDES signs that dot the coast each spring.

"What are you waiting for?" Micah whips water from his hair, rocking slightly with each wave.

"I just don't, exactly, love the ocean."

You mean hate/fear/avoid at all costs?

Sitting with my legs pulled to my chest, I watch from the safety of the shore as the waves tower above him, and he dives beneath the foam. Each time he disappears, I hold my breath until his black hair pops out again.

With my heart in my throat, a memory stirs—one I've tucked deep.

I'm six and Mom's gone and Margot's here instead, and we're back at Newport Beach on Dad's everything-is-still-the-same, I'll-prove-it trip. He dips Margot in the waves while Alice and I swim out.

Let's see how far we can go, she says. *Follow me.*

But we're too far.

And I'm trying to swim back to the shore. It keeps floating away.

Dad and Margot are little dots.

Dad's waving his arms.

But I'm tired.

I don't want to swim anymore. Don't want to fight.

I flip onto my back. Floating is easy.

The water holds me. Folds me into itself.

The ocean tugs me away.

I'm sorry.

Then Alice's head is next to me. She's grabbing me, pulling me back.

It's okay. Let me go.

It's too hard to stay.

But she tells me we're on an adventure. Gets me to follow her to the shore, where Dad holds me so tight, I think he'll never stop.

"Where do you go?"

Micah's voice brings me back. He's sitting next to me, dripping wet, his hair slicked against his head except for one defiant curl falling into his eyes.

"What?"

"When your eyes are open and your body's here, but you're somewhere else."

The water laps against my feet. How do I explain where my mind goes? How I float out of myself?

"The ancient Scottish have a word: *sjushamillabakka,*" I say. "Where the sea meets the shore. Not quite water, not quite land. An in-between border realm."

Then I tell him about the time I almost drowned. About how Alice got me to swim out too far.

"You know the scariest part?" I say, and I'm not sure why I keep talking, except part of me feels like this boy with the semicolon tattoo might understand. Maybe he's the *only* one who could. "How natural it felt to let the water take me. Like part of me almost wanted it to." I look at the sand rather than meet his eyes as I tell him this piece of the story I've never told anyone else. "Sometimes that feeling comes back to me, of the in-between—the *sjushamillabakka.*" I scrape my finger through the sand. "Not really dead. Not really alive. Just floating somewhere in the middle."

I half expect him to tell me I'm off my rocker, because let's admit it, I am, but instead he smiles, a gust of air whipping his black curls in front of his eyes. And Micah, the artist with the scar on his eyebrow, looks at me, his words half carried away by the wind. "And you say you're not a poet." He searches my face. What does he see in it? In me? "You're different."

Little jolts of electricity prick my skin. Can he see the monsters in my head? For a split second, I think he can.

"I'm pretty normal."

He shoves me lightly and I'm keenly aware of how close his body is to mine, half-naked and wet and glistening in the sun. "Relax. It's a compliment."

"How is *that* a compliment?"

"Because normal is overrated. I'm a pretty good reader of people, and you are not like everyone else."

"I see we're back to you pretending to know all about me."

"Actually, just the opposite. I'm enjoying the fact that I may have had you, Lily Larkin, track star, super student, all wrong." He leans back on his elbows, beads of water sparkling on his chest. "You know, it's not the worst thing in the world to have someone know who you are."

Then, suddenly, he looks at the water flowing past us onto the beach and grabs my hand as he jumps up, pulling me with him.

"We're about to miss it!"

"Miss what?"

He winks. "The whole point."

Micah picks up the rakes and his shirt as we run up the beach, up the side of a rocky overhang, all the way to the edge, where we stop short of flying into the air. The beach spreads below us, shades of light and dark, wet and dry, creating a swirling, sprawling design. It's complete chaos, all the lines and curves and circles intersecting at random, but somehow it makes sense.

He learns forward on the rock, his eyes wide like a little kid's. "This is it!"

A wave flows up the beach, licking our artwork, then another, until the water overtakes it, dragging the sand down the beach and our creation with it.

As the sea devours our art, one wave at a time, we're silent, like we're watching something sacred. Our design disintegrates slowly, stubbornly. Wave by wave, piece by piece, the sea swallows it.

"It's unbelievable," I whisper.

He meets my eyes. "Yeah," he says. "It is."

He turns back to the beach, where our art is almost gone. The sand sinks as the tide reaches higher, like some sort of cosmic balancing act. One thing waning, one growing stronger.

Micah inhales sharply when the water washes over the last piece of it, pulling the sand out to sea.

Our design is undone.

It's sad.

And beautiful.

All at once.

chapter
12

I replay every moment in my mind on the drive home. The way Micah looked at me—*saw* me. The way my body buzzed standing next to him, overlooking our art. The way it's still buzzing now. And perhaps the most incredible part, how for a brief moment, the monsters shut up.

But the thoughts of Micah and the beach cut off abruptly when I see Dad on the porch, pacing, one hand gripping his phone, the other raking through his hair.

"It's Alice," he says. The buzzing in my veins gives way to ice. "I told her to be home by eight. But she's not answering her phone."

Dad's trying not to panic for my benefit but is failing miserably. My monsters return with a vengeance.

What if she needs help?

What if she's hurt?

What if she's hurting herself?

Staci's face is lined with worry as she puts her hand on Dad's shoulder, tells him to come inside. "She's out with friends. I'm sure she's fine."

Dad shakes his head as his call goes to voicemail. "She could be anywhere. Doing *anything*."

His voice falters on the *anything*, and I have to go upstairs to escape the look on his face, the worry he usually hides.

In my room, I text Alice a short plea: Please call. Dad's scared.

~~So am I.~~

I check the box under my bed. All blades present and accounted for.

"What are you doing?" Margot's voice makes me jump guiltily.

"Just cleaning up." I shove the box back to its hiding spot. Margot has traded her wizard getup for her pajamas that make her look way younger than ten because they're about six inches too short and feature some sort of unicorn monstrosity. Her eyes are pink and brimming with worry.

"Do you think she's okay?"

I nod, trying to be reassuring, but Dad's *anything* rings in my head.

"You should be getting to bed," I say.

She shakes her head. "Not until Alice is back."

I don't have the heart to tell her *our* Alice doesn't seem to be coming back—now or ever. She jumps into my bed and curls into my side next to the history textbook I should be studying.

"Where do you think she is?"

"Honestly, Margs, I don't know."

She snuggles closer. "What's wrong with her?"

"I don't really know that, either. But seriously. Sleep. Now."

Margot sighs. I'm clearly failing her on the big-sister front.

"But it's not, like, contagious, right? Like, we won't get it?"

While she talks, she bites the fingernail on her ring finger.

"It's not the flu," I say, swatting her hand away from her mouth. "It's in her head."

"So it's not real?"

"No, it's real. But it's like her brain is . . ." I pause, searching for the right word. *Sick?* Not quite right. *Broken? Diseased?* Still feels wrong. It's not like Alice has worms eating through her frontal lobe. I think through all the definitions and WebMD entries I've read about bipolar disorder since her official diagnosis. Basically, she swings wildly between manic highs and depressed lows. Looking back, I guess the ups and downs have always been there, but that was just Alice. She could be moody, unpredictable, but what teenager isn't? And she'd always swing back again—until she didn't. "I think— I think it's more like her brain isn't working the way it used to."

Margot nods thoughtfully, her body toasty warm next to me, snuggled up tight just like Alice and I used to do. Within three minutes, she's out, her chest heaving up and down rhythmically.

I text Alice again—no answer—and even turn to the 100-acre-wood.

> **LogoLily:** Any idea where Alice went tonight?

> **100-acre-wood:** No. Why? What's wrong?

> **LogoLily:** Nothing.

~~But also, maybe everything.~~

There's so much else I want to say to Micah—about the beach, about how my mind felt free for the first time in months—but the moment has passed. Like always, Alice has eclipsed anything and everyone else. She's always been the center of whatever room she enters, like a supernova, all light and sparkle and energy. But here's the thing about explosions—bombs or supernovas or really anything that erupts in a startling display of grandeur and light: when they're done, and the fire has all burned out and the show is over, they always leave a hole.

So we're all here, standing on the edge of the Alice-shaped chasm, all our gravity still pointing to her. And even though I feel like I might vomit at the thought of something bad happening to her, I kind of hate her for it.

Almost midnight, and still no Alice. Margot's zonked out beside me, and the words of my history book blur, and Dad's footsteps fall up and down the front hallway in a steady, nervous rhythm. I absent-mindedly pick at the tiny scabs by my eyebrows, crusty reminders of my too-deep excavation the other night.

Stop it.

Why do you keep doing that?

People are going to start noticing a bunch of scabs on your face.

But my mind starts spinning and my fingers start picking because somehow it helps calm me, keeps me from having a full-on meltdown again. So I slide my hand to my waist instead and find a small bump. A hair follicle maybe. Or a scab. A piece of not-quite-perfect skin.

I pick it off.

I find a fresh one and pick that, too. Then another.

And for a moment, my brain resets. My body unclenches. Before long, blood coats my fingertips.

What are you doing?

I need to clear my head.

What I need is a run. A run like before my brain started short-circuiting, when the beat of my feet and my heart were my safe space. *My* space.

I slip my hand out from under Margot's head and tie on my running shoes. Downstairs, Dad's sitting at his desk, rubbing the back of his neck, his face wan, his shoulders slumped low. He looks so different from the superhero Dad of my childhood—strong and capable with all the right answers and a kiss that could make all the owies go away.

But now he has the same expression as on the Night of the Bathroom Floor—helpless.

I don't want to bother him, so I tell Staci I'm just doing my regular route around the neighborhood. She looks almost as lost as Dad when she glances up from the phone she's staring at like she can will Alice to call. She nods absentmindedly, and I slip out.

My feet hit the pavement in a familiar rhythm. One foot in front of the other. Thud-thud-thud. Just me and the breath pushing in and out of my lungs. A nighttime rain has wet the streets, and I inhale the sweet scent of the jasmine bushes as I breathe deeply, trying to calm my body, my mind. I've run this neighborhood so many times, I know all the twists and turns by heart.

Before I can stop it, my mind shoots back.

It's January, and the night is cool, and I've been trying to hit regional qualifying times.

After, her blood on my hands.

Help me, she says.

I'm helpless.

Worthless.

I make her bed. Sixteen times.

Back in the present, the memories flash, fast and furious and fresh. My heart gallops ahead of me. My lungs reach for air. The all-too-familiar wave shivers down my arms to my fingertips, grips my throat.

I turn back the way I came, hoping to get home before a full-on episode strikes. That's the last thing Dad needs tonight. I reach my house, still on edge, and dip my head down to stop the wooziness.

Seriously. What's wrong with you?

Runner's block.

Writer's block.

Just . . . blocked.

I stealth in the front door. A voice fills the house.

Alice.

My body deflates with relief—she's here.

And she's yelling. Words tumbling out, angry and pointed. "I'm eighteen. You're treating me like a child!" She keeps going, saying she's done with therapy. How it's not working. How none of this is working.

Staci and Dad try to talk her down, try to convince her that it *is* working, that it's just going to take time. They don't even sound like they're convincing themselves.

I tiptoe up the stairs and close my door to block out the sharp sounds. Margot has switched from my bed to Alice's. An hour later, when the voices have settled and Alice finally comes in, she looks from our little sister to me.

"What's this?"

"She's been doing it since you left," I say. "Gets scared in her own room."

Margot wakes slightly when Alice shifts her over.

"You're home," Margot says, reaching up to pull Alice down by the neck. "I was so worried."

"I'm home," Alice whispers, and re-tucks Margot. She doesn't even change into pajamas before sliding into bed. She turns to me in the dark, her short, un-Alice curly hair backlit by the streetlights through the window. Even though I can barely see her, I can tell she's looking at me—like, *really* looking at me—which is two parts unsettling and one part nostalgic.

"I didn't mean to scare everyone." Alice's voice is small and tight. "It's just, sometimes, I can't breathe here, you know?"

I do.

~~I do know.~~

I almost say it, too.

But someone has to hold this family together.

LogoLily's Word of the Day

nullaspire (n) The feeling of not getting enough air. Your chest is moving. Lungs inflating. But you're still left gasping for breath, wondering if you've ever truly inhaled.

From Latin *nulla* (none) + *spirare* (to breathe)

chapter
13

That night, I dream I'm in the ocean.

    Alice walks toward me.

    Made of light and water, air and love.

    But she can't reach me.

    She disintegrates into the waves.

    I scream for her but suck in only ocean.

    Salty and cold. It fills me.

    A wave tosses me

    upside down,

    right side up—

    tumbling me like a rag doll.

    I want to swim up.

    Out.

    But I can't tell up.

    Or down.

    Or out.

    So I just keep spinning

turning

tumbling.

The waves whisper to me.

Come.

Join us.

It's easy.

Just let go.

I believe them.

Let them take me.

I become the sea.

I gasp awake, my lungs hungry.

The edges of my dream remain.

Water.

Waves.

Alice.

"You were screaming," she says in the darkness.

I suck my voice back in.

Inhale it like seawater.

Deep.

Deep.

My lungs fill

with ocean

and words

and screams.

*   *   *

I wake again, more fully and drenched in sweat.

Alice hovers at the side of my bed—a ghost in the night.

"You were doing it again," she says.

"Sorry."

"Are you okay?"

"Yeah. I'm—"

terrified

"—fine."

She retreats to her side of the universe, and I stare at the ceiling, my finger pressed against the vein in my neck—165. My fingers are sticky and my side hurts. In the bathroom mirror, I lift my shirt and turn sideways to get a better angle on the side of my abdomen, right above where my jeans normally hit. There, where no one else can see, is a patch of bright red, angry splotches where I've ripped open my skin in my sleep.

Disgusting.

I wipe the blood off my stomach, rinse it from my hands.

Back in my bed, I open my planner to the last page, to the evidence of my questionable sanity. I add a new line.

8. Am clawing myself to shreds.

I can't keep doing this.

Across the room, Margot's huddled up tight next to Alice, holding on for dear life.

We can't keep doing this.

Even if Micah does help me find my muse (which is still a *huge* if), it's going to take a lot more than UC Berkeley to save this family.

I flip to a blank page of my planner and make a new list.

The Plan

> 1. Win this poetry contest.
> 2. Get the REAL Alice back.
> 3. Fix my own crazy.

Simple.

Easy.

Totally doable.

Except I have no idea how.

Q How to help someone with b

Q How to help someone with bipolar

Q How to help someone with borderline
personality disorder

Q How to help someone with body dysmorphia

Q How to help someone with bulimia

Q How to help someone with body image
issues

Q How to help someone with back pain

Q Why do I pick

Q Why do I pick my skin

Q Why do I pick my lips

Q Why do I pick my scabs

Q Why do I pick my nose

Q Why do I pick my scalp

Q Why do I pick my nails

Q Why do I pick fights with my boyfriend

Q Brain won't stop

Q Brain won't stop thinking

Q Brain won't stop racing

Q Brain won't stop thinking at night

chapter
14

The Google gods diagnose me with about a million disorders, and as much as I hate to admit it, there may be something to Micah's panic-attack theory. My late-night internet deep dive tells me it's like the survival mechanism we learned about in biology. Your body pumps blood and oxygen to your arms and legs, getting ready to either battle or run. Your pulse spikes. Your lungs inflate. It's simple science, fight or flight.

But what if there's nowhere to run?

And the only person to fight is yourself?

By school on Monday, I have exactly no muse and no ideas how to help Alice or myself.

I also have zero idea how to act around Micah. We haven't talked since the beach. If I could, I'd Google *how to be normal around a boy after sharing an oddly intense moment atop a cliff while he was half-naked and you had just spilled intimate details about your messed-up mind.*

Alas, no search engine in the world is equipped for my next-level neurosis.

And my brain is doing what it does best—taking something shiny and new and turning it ugly.

You've already told him too much.

He probably does this all the time—takes girls to the beach, makes them feel endlessly interesting and unique.

And you fell for it.

And you shared.

So. Much.

Idiot.

Idiot.

Idiot.

It doesn't help that every time I look up, Sam shoots me suggestive eyebrow signals from across the room. So now I'm sitting across from Micah during today's collaboration session, staring at my empty notebook, trying not to think about the way he looked at me as we watched our art slip away.

"Earth to Lily." His voice brings me back to reality. "Where are you today?"

~~With you~~
~~on a beach~~
~~in the in-between.~~

"I'm here."

"Could've fooled me." He's tapping his pencil on his sketch pad. "You freaked me out Saturday night. Alice made it home?"

"Yeah. If, in fact, the girl they sent back from Fairview is Alice."

"What does that mean?"

"It means—I don't know. It means she's not herself."

"Yeah, well, Fairview's supposed to change you," he says. "Changed me."

105

Of course. Micah's been at Fairview. He probably knows all about getting back to normal after treatment. Probably knows more about bringing the *real* Alice back than I could ever find online.

"So," I say, trying to act casual. "Were there a lot of people with bipolar disorder there?"

"Some."

"And do they, like, treat it, or is it something that takes time?"

He's eyeing me suspiciously now. "If you want to know about Alice, you should ask Alice."

"Yeah but, just, how long does the medicine take to work? And what about therapy? She doesn't want to go anymore."

"Oh! I know! Talk. To. Alice."

"Fine. Just tell me this—will the medicine fix her?"

Micah frowns. "Fix her? I'm sorry, has Alice broken?"

"You know what I mean."

"Actually, I don't."

He's waiting for an explanation with an expression on his face that says I'm a total jerk. All my thoughts of beaches and boys and soul-searching looks scatter to the wind.

He hates you.

Kali flops down in a seat next to me, and for once I'm grateful for her interruption.

"Can you believe about the summer scholarship?" she says.

"Gifford told you?"

Kali smiles, but it's not really a smile, more like a wolf baring her teeth. Very unsettling.

"What? You thought you were the only one in the running?" Before I can stop her, Kali reaches across me and grabs my notebook. "Let's see what you've got."

She flips open the emptiness. Page after page of jack squat. Zilch. Nada. She turns from the nothingness of my notebook to the nothingness of me, and I want to crumble into dust.

"No way," she says, her smile becoming even more predatory. "Don't tell me straight-A Lily Larkin is having writer's block?"

Damon has sauntered over now. My heartbeat picks up speed.

Do NOT freak out.

I look around for Gifford, but she and Friedman have left the room, so I try to recall the pages of suggestions from my late-night Google search on how to stop a panic attack in its tracks.

Join a club!

Get a fidget spinner!

Just stop thinking.

Mind over matter.

Deep breaths.

I inhale as deeply as I can, but my chest seems to be stuck, and I'm scratching at a scab on my stomach even though I told myself I wasn't doing that anymore, but it's not working, and just as I start slipping out of my body, Micah stands up, grabs the notebook, and tosses it back to me.

"Like she's going to let you see our idea. You'd probably just steal it because, believe me, it's A-mazing. Right, Lily?"

Micah's staring at me, offering me an out.

"Definitely." I sit up straighter. "Amazing."

Kali flashes her smile-not-smile again and flounces off, her ponytail whipping unnecessarily hard behind her. But Damon doesn't leave, just grabs Micah's sketchbook from his desk.

"As long as we're sharing ideas—"

He covers his mouth in faux shock before turning the drawing toward his buddies. On the page, Micah has drawn a boy, his mouth wide, screaming. And inside that mouth, the same boy, screaming again. And so on and so on, screaming boy spiraling back into eternity.

"Dude. That's messed up," Damon says. "They teach you this at the loony bin?"

In one movement, Micah's in Damon's face, his hands balled into tight fists, his eyes full of darkness and rage, so different from the boy on the beach. Is this the Micah everyone whispers about, the one who got kicked out of his old school for fighting? And Damon's telling him to "Settle down, man," and Micah's looking around, like he's waking from a trance, seeing everyone staring at him, and just as quickly as it started, he sits back down, trains his eyes on his desk, opening and closing his fists slowly.

Damon holds the pad out to Micah, who doesn't even move one millimeter. Damon laughs and chucks the pad into the metal trash can by the door, but Micah just stares at his desk, eyes forward, jaw gritted tight as Damon pops open an energy drink near Micah's ear.

"Payback's a bitch," Damon says before dumping the liquid in after the sketch pad.

I wait for Micah to say something. To defend himself like he defended me a second ago. When it's clear he's not going to, I jump up and shove Damon out of the way.

"Do you have to be such a tool *all* the time?"

He smirks and drains the rest of the drink into his mouth before chucking the empty can into the trash. I pull out the sketch pad and let it drip dry for a second before handing it to Micah. He wipes it with the sleeve of his hoodie, but the screaming boy is all but obliterated.

"Why didn't you do anything?" I whisper once the onlookers have dispersed. *Show's over, folks.*

"Nothing to do," he says, ripping out the wet pages. "You heard Principal Porter. *Probationary* means 'play nice, keep my head down.' Damon would love nothing more than for me to go all Manic Micah and get kicked out of here. Prove the rumors right."

He stops trying to salvage the drenched notepad and throws it back into the trash. He closes his eyes a moment, and when he opens them, the darkness is almost gone.

"So," he says. "Are all the guys at Ridgeline such Neanderthals, or was I just lucky enough to piss off the biggest douchebag in the place?"

"Just lucky, I guess."

"And *you* dated this king of the d-bags?"

"Who told you that?"

"I have my sources."

I want to ask more about these dubious sources, since I've seen Micah talk to exactly no one since he got here, but I'm hung up on the fact that he *knows* about my dating history. He's asked about me.

"First of all, that was freshman year, so it hardly even counts, and second of all, I have officially filed that under things I regret doing in high school." My cheeks warm up when Micah raises his eyebrows. "I mean, I didn't *do* him, do him. I've actually never done—"

I take a deep breath. "Wow, I'm saying a lot of things here, and I'm just going to—" I make a sound like I'm rewinding the last few seconds. "And we'll just pretend like that never happened, yes?"

Micah shakes his head, grinning wide. "No way. That may have been my favorite moment of our partnership so far. Flustered looks good on you, Lily."

I look down at my desk, biting my lip as my cheeks burn once more, which is all sorts of stupid.

"Well." I clear my throat. "I'd like to personally apologize on behalf of Damon and all the Ridgeline d-bags. And also, to say thank you. For saving my butt with Kali back there. I kind of froze."

"Yeah, I picked up on that."

"But she's right, you know. We still don't have anything solid."

One quasi-transcendent day at the beach isn't going to beat Kali or help keep my family and future from falling apart.

"Hey, we can't give up now. Not until round two of Discovering Your Muse with the Micah Method."

"Oh, it's a method now?"

"That sounds like questioning."

"Oh, wow, it's a method now!"

"Better. Friday after school? My house."

"Shall I bring my own rake?"

The bell rings and Micah gathers up his stuff, but before he goes, he gives me that I've-got-a-secret grin again with his eyebrow reaching upward. "Oh, did I forget to tell you? *You're* in charge this time."

Ridgeline Underground

56 likes

Whoa. Guys. Check out Manic Micah's page @100-acre wood. Some weird shit on there.

15 comments

WTF

What's with the cartoons?

Go back to Fairview, freak.

LogoLily: You up?

100-acre-wood: Always.

LogoLily: What did you mean, *I'm* in charge?

100-acre-wood: I mean it's your turn to capture the muse. Show me what inspires you. Teach me something about poetry. Anything.

LogoLily: Micah. I can't even write a poem. How am I supposed to teach you?

100-acre-wood: I don't know. Think outside the lines.

LogoLily: ゛

100-acre-wood: You did *not* just use an emoji.

LogoLily: What? It's the language of our generation.

100-acre-wood: I refuse. Little cartoons to express emotion?

LogoLily: This from the boy with a profile pic of WINNIE-THE-POOH!

100-acre-wood: officially insulted emoji

LogoLily: hold on

LogoLily: looking for an anti-establishment-damn-the-man-burn-all-the-coloring-books emoji

100-acre-wood: we're done here emoji

100-acre-wood: (but also, excited to be inspired emoji)

chapter

15

At school, Micah's been claimed.

He no longer walks the halls alone. He's been interviewed and accepted by a clan—the Artists. The girls wear shorts and black pantyhose and an obscene amount of black eyeliner. The guys have wannabe dreads and share Micah's air of indifference about the names that Damon and his ilk shout at them in the parking lot. A few of them even wear socks like Micah's.

When I pass him at school, we smile, but we orbit in different circles. At night, though, when my house is dark and I'm willing myself to sleep, we meet in the 100-acre-wood.

In the ethereal space of the internet, we talk every night. He asks about LogoLily's Word of the Day. I tell him that I make up words to make sense of the world.

Tuesday, 11:15 pm

LogoLily: It's like we have these 26 letters. That's it.
26. But you can arrange them a million different ways

to mean a million different things. They become yours.

LogoLily: Does that make me a total weirdo?

100-acre-wood: Yes.

100-acre-wood: But the world could use more weirdos.

He talks about the drawings he's working on, and how his dad was an artist before he passed away. He talks about how drawing helps him feel like his dad's not really gone. He tells me he has to— *has* to—draw to keep everything from festering on the inside. Art saves him, keeps him in the here and now.

Wednesday, 10:23 pm

LogoLily: So art is like your medicine?

100-acre-wood: No, Zoloft is my medicine. Art is my high.

LogoLily: How do you just put it out there like that for everyone to see?

100-acre-wood: Have to. Have to get it out. Get it into the light. Feels less dark that way.

LogoLily: Aren't you scared what people will think?

100-acre-wood: It's not brave if you're not scared.

In the quiet of my room, with nothing but the sound of Alice breathing from seven feet and a lifetime away, I tell him things, too. That I'm trying to qualify for state in the 400 meter. How my mom died when I was six because her heart only had enough strength left to bring baby Margot into the world before it gave out. How it's UC Berkeley or bust.

Thursday, 1:15 am

100-acre-wood: Why Berkeley?

LogoLily: It's the best. And it's always been the plan.

100-acre-wood: Should have known there was a plan involved.

LogoLily: So if we win, you'd turn it down?

100-acre-wood: I would.

LogoLily: No way.

LogoLily: Is that what the 100-acre-wood is all about? Boys who never want to grow up?

100-acre-wood: Could *not* be more wrong. And also, that's Neverland. College just doesn't fit into my plan.

LogoLily: Which is?

100-acre-wood: Don't make too many plans.

Some things, though, I don't tell him. Like about the episodes that send my brain into overdrive and my fingertips searching for skin to pick. Or about the night I found Alice. Or how I have to bring her (and me) back to save this family.

I know Micah has secrets, too. Like what happened at his old school. The way Damon shoves him in the hallway or the posts about him on the Underground. The semicolon tattoo on his wrist.

I don't ask about the words he keeps, and I don't tell him mine.

Some things are just better left unsaid.

Each night, I find myself waiting for that little *Ding!* And despite my best efforts, I find myself wondering about him. It's stupid, really, how much I think about him. About which rumors are true. About how this boy with his bright socks and big ideas doesn't seem at all like a Boy on the Verge. About how his art is dark but his smile is light.

Like I told Sam, my brain has no room for boys. It's just nice to have someone to talk to in the darkness. It's also a nice distraction from the Alice of it all.

Since the Night of the Missed Curfew, she's stopped going to her weekly therapy and started sneaking out in the middle of the night. I pretend to be asleep while she stealths out of the house. I lie in the dark, my mind spinning, fingers picking, until she comes back. Most of the time I don't even know I've started scratching at my skin. All I know is, it helps me focus on the pain instead of the panic of where she's gone, what she's doing.

This is what Micah doesn't understand. Alice does not want to talk with me about *anything*.

Mostly, we all try to stay out of her way. I bury myself in homework while also trying to come up with whatever it is I'm supposed to do for my next muse-discovery meeting with Micah. Margot's lost in Harry Potter, and Dad's still trying to convince everyone that things are back to normal, except he's taken on extra evening classes just to escape. And Staci? She's appointed herself the captain of the Alice Pep Squad, constantly trying to yank Alice out of her post-Fairview funk.

Alice, come do yoga!

Go for a walk!

Find a hobby!

Figure out what the hell you want to do with your life before you drive us all crazy, too!

So far, she's helped Alice sign up for online classes and convinced her to join her daily yoga sessions, which is more progress than I've made on my help-Alice-be-Alice-again plan. Every online search I do ends up with the same answer: *Give your loved one time. Be there. Give them space.*

So I give her space. So much space I can barely see her anymore.

And the only progress I've made on my own brain is that I've clipped my fingernails so short that I can't scratch holes into my stomach.

In the evenings, we sit down to vegan/organic spreads created by Staci because *pleasant family mealtimes* is one of the top Fairview tips.

So, we sit, doing our darnedest to obey the rules, around a dining table with inedible food, *trying* so hard I fear one of us might burst into flames. I watch from outside my body, like we're on a sitcom. Tonight's episode: "Family Pretends Everything Is Fine!"

```
Camera pans out, revealing a perfectly normal
family, eating some sort of Elmer's-glue-
looking tofu.


                    DAD
  How was school today?


Lily, who is not really Lily because real Lily
is doing backflips on the ceiling, inspects
jiggly substance on her fork. Puts it back onto
her plate.


                    DAD
        (Tapping hand like it's a faulty
        microphone.)
  Hello? Is this thing on?


                  MARGOT
  My team got into the final round of Math
  Olympiad!


                    DAD
  That's great, honey. You gonna win?
```

                    MARGOT

    Definitely! I made a whole set of flash
    cards!

                     DAD

    That's my girl.

Margot beams.

More scratching of forks. The Sister Formerly
Known as Alice pushes food around on her plate,
making eye contact with no one. Lily-not-Lily
wonders if everyone else is doing backflips on
the ceiling, too. Under the table, she picks at
her skin. Turns out short fingernails are no
match for monsters.

                    STACI

    This is so nice, having everyone around
    the table.

Dad lays hand on top of Staci's.

                     DAD

    I feel like we're finally putting this
    whole thing behind us.

        THE SISTER FORMERLY KNOWN AS ALICE
    And by "this thing," you mean me?

                    DAD
    No. Oh, honey, no. That came out wrong. I
    just meant—

        THE SISTER FORMERLY KNOWN AS ALICE
    Yeah, thanks. I know exactly what you
    meant.

Shoves her chair back abruptly and stands,
plate in hand.

        THE SISTER FORMERLY KNOWN AS ALICE
    Can I be excused?

Dad nods. Alice exits. The entire room
exhales. Dad pushes back from the table
slightly, runs his hands through his
hair, and stares at his barely touched
tofu.

                   STACI
            (Squeezing Dad's hand.)
    It's an adjustment period. For all
    of us.

                    DAD
            (Putting on his everything's-
            fine face.)
    Lil. How's that poetry contest coming?

                              LILY

    Perfect.

Under the table, Lily bleeds where no one can
see.

END SCENE

chapter 16

My body drags around the track Friday afternoon. I was up half the night waiting for Alice to sneak back in from wherever it is she goes. I cross the finish line, still 1.5 seconds behind the time I need for state. Coach asks me if I'm doing my home runs on the weekends. I lie. He doesn't need to know about the heart-pounding episodes. I'll get my times down. That's all that matters.

On the drive home, my phone dings:

> **Sam:** why'd you leave practice so fast? And can we PLEASE hang out tonight?
> **Lily:** can't. Working on the project
> **Sam:** please tell me that "working on it" is some sort of lurid euphemism
> **Lily:** Mind. Out. Of. The. Gutter.
> **Sam:** another day? I miss your face
> **Lily:** definitely. Just been busy

Trying to fix my brain
my sister
everything.

Sam: we're all busy, Lil. *You* are MIA.

I don't know why I don't tell her about Micah and his muse-recovery plan. Probably because she'd go into graphic detail about his paintbrush again. But it's not like that. It *can't* be like that. Not with Alice and this contest and the 400 meter taking up all the space.

Which is why I show up at his doorstep later that afternoon armed with my favorite book and a determination to squash any sort of skin-buzzing, twitterpated-girl antics before they start. Focus on the project. That's *all.*

So the lip gloss is for the project, then?

I shush the monsters and knock. His house is small, with a freshly mowed lawn and purple sage bushes in full bloom out front. The walkway up to the front door is covered in chalk drawings like the ones from the 100-acre-wood. Micah opens the door, his hair and clothes semi-rumpled. His hoodie has a picture of Bob Ross that says GOOD VIBES ONLY, and his socks match, with little Bob Ross heads floating in a sea of black.

"You're just in time," he says.

"For . . ."

"Tamales!" Micah rubs his hands together as a woman in blue scrubs scurries from the kitchen and practically tackles me in a hug. She rocks me back and forth so forcefully, I'm afraid I'll snap in half.

"Lily, my mother. Mom, this is Lily," Micah says.

I say hello from deep inside the woman's voluminous black curls.

"Que linda," she says, putting her palms on either side of my face. Then she wraps her fingers around my upper arm, shaking her head and clucking her tongue. "But too skinny. All you girls these days. You need to eat. Need to grow. So you can have babies."

"Mom!" Micah's face flushes pink as he shoots his mom a *shut up—I'm serious* look. I relish this rare moment of Micah mortification. His mom rumples his black curls like he's a toddler.

"This one, embarrassed by his own mother."

Micah pulls her hand off his head and holds it between his. "Oh, I'm sorry. Please, oh please, talk more about making babies in front of pretty girls I bring home."

His mother smiles at me like we're in on a secret. Now it's my turn to be embarrassed.

"Okay, okay, *mijo.* I'll be quiet," she says. "You work; I cook."

His mother hums softly to herself as she fills corn husks with meat and the house with the aroma of spices. Micah pulls out a chair for me at the kitchen table. "All right, poet laureate of Ridgeline High, teach me. Mold me. I am putty in your hands."

I put my favorite book, *The Bell Jar,* on the table with a thick black permanent marker.

"So, poetry is about putting emotions into words in a way that surprises the reader, and maybe even the poet. So we're gonna do an exercise I did once in creative writing, just to kind of get the juices flowing." I open to a random page. Micah scoots his chair over, his black hair dangling in front of his eyes. I focus on the assignment rather than the nerve endings where his arm touches mine.

"Basically, it's not about the words we cross out," I say, dragging the black marker along a line of text, leaving only one word revealed. "It's about the words we keep."

"Whoa, whoa, whoa," Micah says. "We're going to *draw* in a *book*? That's a very coloring-outside-the-lines thing to do."

"Didn't know about my wild side, huh?" I try not to laugh. "Plus, I may or may not have three copies of this book at home."

Micah laughs and picks up the marker.

"I don't know, seems like a gateway drug. Today it's scribbling in books; tomorrow it's not using a planner. Where will the madness end?"

I shove him slightly, and he shoves me back, until his mother gives us a knowing grin while she folds a tamale.

Stop being an idiot.

Focus.

We take turns finding words we like, dragging the black marker in lines until the page is covered except for tiny windows of white.

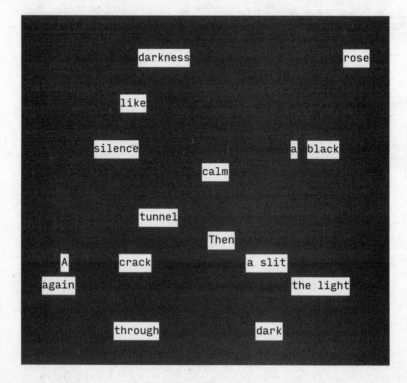

Micah clears his throat and reads the blackout poem out loud.

"Bravo!" His mother cheers from in front of the stove. "An assignment for school?"

I tell her about the project, and before I even finish, she has turned to Micah, her hands on her hips. A string of quick Spanish words spills from her mouth, and Micah replies just as rapidly. They talk so much faster than my Spanish teacher, but I pick up that Micah has not told his mother about the summer college program, and she is *not* happy about it.

In the end, his mother throws her hands into the air, stomps to the counter, and then returns with two plates of steaming tamales. She shoves them in front of us.

"Lily. Talk to my son."

She tosses her apron onto the counter before walking out, still muttering in Spanish. Micah runs his hands though his hair, leans his head back, and groans lightly.

I blow on a bite of tamale. "Flustered looks good on you, Micah Mendez."

"Har-har. Well, I'm glad one of us enjoyed that."

"Oh, I did."

"Well, you'll love this, then. My mother shares your opinions about college being *the* path. The only path."

I chew the tamale, the warm deliciousness exploding in my mouth.

"I *knew* I liked her," I say. "Tell me again why you're so against it?"

Micah stabs at his food with his fork. "She already works *all* the time. I think she took out a loan for Fairview. I'm not about to ask her to pay for college, too." He pops a bite of tamale into his mouth without waiting for it to cool. Steam escapes from his lips as he talks.

"And say I do go to college? What if I relapse and it's all for nothing?" His eyes follow down the hallway to the bedroom door where his mother disappeared. "I've put her through enough. It's better if I get a job, start pitching in. Dad would want me to take care of her. Keep this family together."

I understand the feeling. After Mom died, Dad was left trying to do it all on his own, and even as a six-year-old, I felt that burden. It was like there was no more safety net, no breathing room. I knew our family was more fragile without Mom, and even though it wasn't my fault she was gone, I believed that if I was good enough—did enough—I could keep us from cracking.

Behind Micah, a picture on the wall shows a schoolboy version of him standing next to a thinner version of his mother and a man with slightly lighter skin but the same dark hair as Micah's. And even though I know exactly how Micah feels, I also know his art is incredible, and throwing away this chance would be a waste.

"I think your parents would want you to go as far as you can with your art." I finish off my tamale. "And maybe this is just a classic case of safer not to try than fail."

Micah shoves me again playfully. "Hey. No using my own wisdom against me." He picks up my plate, shaking his head. "Here I invite you to my home, make you a delicious—and authentic, I might add—Mexican dish, and you repay me by dumping on all my life choices."

I clear the silverware and glasses and follow him to the sink.

"Oh, I'm sorry, you're right. Unsolicited life advice is really more *your* area of expertise."

Micah's eyes crinkle up as he smiles and takes the silverware from me, our fingers grazing one another as he does, and he's looking at

128

where we touch and then looking at me like he did on the cliff, and there's no ocean or sunshine to blame, just *him* buzzing under my skin.

I drop my hand, and he starts washing dishes, trying to ignore the awkward tension in the room.

"So, speaking of unhealthy family dynamics." He side-eyes me while soaping a dish. "Did you ever talk to Alice? About bipolar?"

I pick up a towel and start drying. "You don't understand, Micah. It's like—it's like I've lost her."

She didn't die that night, but a part of her did—the Alice who was always trying something new, who treated life like her personal choose-your-own-adventure book. The Alice who made me believe I was a fearless ocean explorer and helped me swim back to shore.

"She's not the same person anymore."

Micah turns off the water. "No, she's not. When you get to a place where dying seems like the easy way out, that changes you."

He hands me a dish. His wrist faces up, and I see the semicolon tattoo, and as much as I'm fighting it, I want to know why it's there. Did he get to that place, too? Did he get past it? And why can't I stop wondering about this boy with his rumored past and visible scars?

Tears prick my eyes. I haven't told anyone the way I feel about Alice. Dad's too busy pretending everything is better now, and Sam wouldn't get it. But Micah? He does. "You want to hear something truly terrible? Sometimes I don't even *want* to talk to her. It's like I'm so mad at her because now I can't slip up, not even a little bit, because Dad can't take one more letdown. I know it makes me a jerk, but sometimes I hate her for what she did."

Micah nods, his eyes drifting down the hall again. "She hates herself for it, too. Trust me."

"Maybe," I say. "I wouldn't know. She never tells me *anything*. It's like I haven't even met this new Alice."

He hands me another dish, and our fingers meet again, and this time we let them linger a second more than we should. I let go of the dish first, but he keeps my eyes.

"Maybe you should."

chapter
17

After Alice turns out the light that night, I lie in the dark for an hour, gathering my courage.

I try to decipher her breathing. Is she awake? Do I dare violate the Treaty of Bedroom Silence? Maybe Micah's right—she's still in there, somewhere.

"Alice." I whisper so quietly that there's no way she can hear me. I take a deep breath and try again, for real this time.

"Alice."

"Sleep. Now," she mutters.

"I just—I just wanted to talk to you about something. You know your medicines?"

Alice sits up, her eyes accusing me in the darkness. "You're snooping around in my medication?"

"It's right there in the bathroom."

"And you just *happened* to read it?"

Off to a bad start.

"Look, that's not the point."

"Then what *is* the point?"

"Well, what if—I mean—I was just wondering how you think they're working. Like, do you feel better?"

She falls back onto her bed and stares up at the glow-in-the-dark stars on the ceiling that she put up during a short-lived space-themed room redecoration.

"Why are you asking about this?"

"It's just. Well, you seem—"

"What? What do I seem, Lily? Please, tell me, with all your expert medical knowledge, how I seem."

"Actually." I clear my throat. "I've been doing some research on bipolar—"

"Oh, here we go." She sits up in her bed again, and I can feel her staring at me through the dark. "Look. I don't want to talk about my medicine. Or Fairview. Or have some sisterly heart-to-heart about this. So can you please just drop it?"

A long, heavy silence presses down on me. Can't she see that I want to help her? That I'd do anything—everything—to bring her back? Beneath the sheets, I pick off a scab. I make one final attempt.

"It's just, maybe I could help you. Maybe we could fix—"

Alice groans. "I don't need your help," she says, rolling away from me to face the wall. "And you can't fix this, because *this* is me."

Alice pulls the cover over her head so I can't even hear her breathing.

You blew it.

Again.

Silence fills the room except for my heartbeat, whooshing in my ears, and the lingering echo of Alice's words. I tuck my own words somewhere deep inside my chest and retreat to the bathroom. Sitting on the lip of the tub, I stare at the tinge of blood that stains the grout. Maybe she's right: I'm trying to fix the unfixable.

Poking around in old wounds can't do anything but hurt.

Friday, 11:30 pm

LogoLily: Well, that went over like a fart in an elevator.

100-acre-wood: Umm . . . you *really* need to work on your sexting skills.

LogoLily: I'm serious! I tried to talk to Alice.

LogoLily: Total crash and burn.

100-acre-wood: Sorry.

100-acre-wood: I have something that may cheer you up.

LogoLily: Alice's medical records?

100-acre-wood: No. Better. Meet me Monday in the art room after school?

LogoLily: Aye, aye, sir!

100-acre-wood: Also, in re: the sexting earlier. I'm totally not into that.

100-acre-wood: I mean like TOTALLY not.

100-acre-wood: probably wouldn't even respond

LogoLily: Good night, Micah.

100-acre-wood: G'night, Lily. Sleep well.

Not a chance.

Margot tiptoes in after midnight, *Harry Potter* clutched tight to her chest. She wants to know why we were fighting.

"Honestly, Margot, I have no idea." I'm staring at my empty notebook by the light of my cell phone so I don't wake Alice, trying to see if Micah's muse rediscovery program is working, even a little bit. Spoiler: it's not. "But I do know it is *way* past your bedtime."

"I'll be soooo quiet," she pleads. I'm no match for her puppy-dog eyes.

"Fine, but I have a ton of work, so No. Talking." I wag my finger at her. "Deal?"

She hops into my bed, snuggles up next to me, and positions her book into the light from my phone. She turns the pages of Mom's book slowly. It's the one Mom was reading to us while she was pregnant. Before Margot was born, Mom was working her way through the whole collection, reading them to us in bed every night. We'd huddle up, all three of us and sometimes Dad, in one little bed. I don't have a lot of clear memories of her, but I can remember the smell of her lavender lotion as I snuggled in, the sound of her laugh

134

filling all my empty places, her words keeping me safe and warm in the dark.

When Margot came home from the hospital and Mom didn't, I never picked up the books again.

Margot sits up suddenly, pointing to a passage.

"I think I may have found something," she whispers. "I've been thinking about what you said about Alice's brain. You know, how it's not working like it used to? And I think it's like Dementors, these super-scary demon things. Basically, they kiss you and suck out your soul. Well, not your soul exactly, but they take away all your happiness and mess up your brain so you just keep replaying all your saddest and scariest moments over and over again. Maybe *that's* what Alice has."

Her eyes are wide, animated, like middle-grade fiction has just cracked the code to mental health.

"Margot. That's a story."

"Well, yeah, I don't mean *actual* Dementors, but maybe it's *like* that. I'm gonna do some more research." She pats the book. "I haven't gotten to the part yet where they actually fight the Dementors, but the good guys *always* win."

"Margot, I really don't think *Harry Potter* is going to have the answers to—"

"But it might. We can't just do nothing. All for one, right?" she says, using the slogan Dad used to say after Mom died, when he'd call us the Four Musketeers.

"Right." I want to point out how delusional she's being, but it's not like I've got a better plan.

Margot sticks her icy toes beneath my legs. Pretty soon, she's snoring, her mouth gaped open, one hand flung across my chest, the other cradling her book, confident she'll find the magic we need to turn back time.

If only we could all live in her fantasy world.

From across the room, Alice tells me to turn off the light so she can sleep. This from the girl who keeps me up most nights, waiting for her to sneak back in from wherever she goes.

Ping!

Sam: the she-witch is at it again

She sends me a link to Kali's latest post, a close-up black-and-white photograph of herself with the caption: **PORTRAIT OF AN ARTIST—my partner and I are KILLING this project. Be ready to be blown away!**

"Seriously, Lily!" Alice says without even turning around. "Sleep. Now."

I turn off my phone and the light and sit in the dark thinking about Margot's magic plan and my own dead ends to bring Alice back or shut off the monsters in my head. At least I still have a shot at winning this poetry contest.

Which is why, whatever Micah has planned on Monday, it *has* to work.

Because this room is running out of oxygen.

And I'm running out of time.

2:45 a.m.

You shouldn't be messing around with Micah.

3:07 a.m.

You need to be shaving off 1.7 seconds
or sleeping (ha!) or writing a poem (double ha!)
or helping get Alice back.
Why can't you write it?
Why can't you sleep?
You must be doing something wrong.
Maybe you're doing everything *wrong.*

4:00 a.m.

You're bleeding again.
Seriously
what's wrong with you?

chapter
18

After school on Monday, the art room is hopping. And loud.

Way too many decibels for my pounding head. Alice snuck out around two a.m., meaning I was up on Alice-watch until she crept back in at five this morning. And while I waited, I picked my stomach raw.

The hallway's more or less empty, but I worry Damon will walk by any second armed with more psycho jokes, or that Sam will see me and offer more stress-busting sex tips. Just standing here, watching from the door, I have to shove my hands into the pockets of my jeans so my fingers don't scrape at the scabs on my waist. Little imperfections screaming to be picked.

A speaker on a bar stool fills the room with a heavy bass beat. Using his paintbrush like a slingshot, Mr. Friedman flicks hot-pink paint onto a massive canvas hanging from the ceiling. In the back corner, Micah sits on a long, black-topped table, laughing with a group of fellow artists.

You do not belong here.

I'm sure everyone else is thinking the same thing about me. A girl wearing cutoff shorts over ripped tights whispers something to the guy with the dreadlocks next to her. The girl is pretty, like model pretty. Micah probably likes her. Which is fine, because who cares who Micah is into? Not me, that's who.

Friedman spots me standing awkwardly by the door.

"Come in, come in! All artists welcome." He waves me in. When I say, "Oh, no, I'm just watching," he practically pushes me into the room. "You don't *watch* art," he says. "You *do* art. Now come. Do."

Micah nods at me and hops off the table, sticking a paintbrush behind his ear. He plunks a roll of tape and scissors down in front of me, along with a huge stack of magazines.

"So I was thinking about that blackout poem, and I thought you could find more words in these." He pats the stack.

Around us, other students are deep in their work, painting, drawing, sculpting a butt out of clay with a putty knife. This place is weird.

You shouldn't be here
wasting time you don't have.

"I don't think arts and crafts is the answer here," I say, my skin itching. "It's been two weeks, and my muse is nowhere to be found. What exactly are we doing? What's the plan?"

"You know my philosophy on plans."

"I mean it, Micah. We should have thought of a project by now. I don't think this whole muse thing is working."

You knew *Micah wasn't taking it seriously.*

He shakes his paintbrush at me. "No quitting until it's done, remember?"

Friedman flips off the music. A few students moan in protest.

"Sorry, ladies and gentleartists. You don't have to go home, but you can't stay here. Let the muse rest."

Micah and I walk into the hall, and he hands me the magazine stack.

"Give it a little more time," he says, and our fingers touch again like they did in his kitchen, and I leave them longer than I should because Micah's giving me that smile of which I'm becoming problematically fond, the one that makes me forget my best-laid plans. And as hard as I'm telling my skin not to buzz where he touches me, I can't stop it. And maybe I don't want to.

But just as I'm thinking that, Damon turns the corner, and he stops, a sinister smile on his face. I jump away from Micah, pulling my hand from his like he's a leper.

"Told you. Freaks flock together," Damon says. He leans in closer as he passes me. "Don't worry, Lil. I won't tell."

"Nothing to tell," I spit back, looking at the ground instead of Micah.

When Damon's gone and I finally look up, Micah says nothing, just stares at me, his face soured. He starts to say something, but then just shakes his head, shoves the stack of magazines at me, and walks back into the art room, leaving me in the hallway, wishing the floor would swallow me whole.

Sam is already stretching on the track by the time I get there. When I start lunging next to her, she turns and offers me her hand.

"Oh, hello," she says. "Have we met?"

After the awkward moment with Micah just now, I'm not in the mood for whatever this is, but I take her hand and play along.

"Yes. My name is Lily. You may know me from such roles as your best friend."

She shakes her head. "No, that can't be right. From what I understand, best friends spend time together. Or at least return each other's texts."

I give her shoulder a shove.

"You know I've been busy."

She plucks my phone from my track bag and turns it toward me, showing a series of texts from her over the last few days. Nothing monumental, mostly just checking in, lamenting about this project, memes making fun of Coach Johnson's red face. I didn't realize I hadn't replied to any of them.

"For real, Lil, what's going on?"

> ~~I don't have a project~~
> ~~and I was just a total jerk to Micah~~
> ~~and Alice isn't Alice anymore~~
> ~~and maybe I'm not me~~
> ~~because there are holes in my skin~~
> ~~and holes in my brain~~
> ~~that I can't fix.~~

"It's just, this poetry contest has me running in circles," I say.

Kali chimes in from where she's stretching and not-so-covertly eavesdropping on the grass with the tennis team.

"Tell me about it. And *so* much is riding on it." She stands up and pulls her leg behind her in a quad stretch. "Lucky for me, my partner is basically a genius. Speaking of partners, how's it going with *your* handful, Lil?"

A lump lodges in my throat when I think about the way I just jumped away from Micah in the hall. Luckily, Sam responds for me.

"Kali, you have as much chance of beating Lily as you do of removing that pole up your ass without surgical intervention."

I can tell by the fire in Sam's voice that we're going to be okay, even if I have been a craptacular best friend lately.

A craptacular everything.

Kali scoffs and sprints off, purposefully swinging her ponytail extra hard in our direction. Sam links her arm through mine.

"I just miss you, that's all."

"I know. As soon as I figure out this project, I'm all yours. Burgers and shakes on me and we'll catch up."

"How dare you ply me with strawberry shakes! My one weakness!" Sam shakes her first toward the sky. "And you're still coming to my concert, right?"

Sam takes my phone again and creates a new event in my calendar in about three weeks: *7 p.m.—SAM SLAYS HER SOLO!*

"Now you have no excuse, even if you *are* too busy to reply to me."

"I wouldn't miss it for the world," I say, and the guilt eases slightly in my chest.

See how easy it is?

To be normal?

To be nice?

Keep it up.

"Now, since the she-witch brought it up, how *is* your mysterious partner?" Sam says, her usual mischievous smile resurfacing. "Any news on the brooding-artist front?"

I roll my eyes. "Did you not just hear Kali? She's basically waiting for me to fail. And between this poetry thing and the state finals and Alice walking around our house like a disgruntled zombie, I have absolutely zero space in my life for anything else." Tears fill my eyes, and I don't even really know why, except all I can see is Micah's face in the hallway when I yanked my hand away, terrified someone might know that the Boy on the Verge is more than just my partner. He's someone I can talk to, someone who gets it—gets me. "And the worst part is, she's totally right. Micah and I don't have *anything* that even resembles a project yet, which means no summer program, which means maybe no Berkeley ever, and—"

"Whoa, whoa, whoa. Calm down." Sam holds my shoulders. "You're really spiraling, huh?"

I nod.

"First of all, Kali is like the most basic bee-yatch at this school. And second, you're going to win. It's what you do. It's who you are."

Sam hugs me before joining her relay team, and I jump up and down on the rubbery track, swinging my arms across my chest. I try to shake Micah and the summer program and Alice out of my head. Coach says races come down to focus. *One-millionth of a second of distraction, and you've already lost.*

But while I wait for my heat, my fingers find a small, fresh scab on my stomach. It's a tiny one, but right now it's can't-think-about-anything-else huge.

It shouldn't be there.

Get rid of it.

And just like that, I'm gone. Trapped behind the glass, watching me dig into my skin.

I dig, and dig.

Until I pick off the bump.

All the way to the root.

And I can breathe again.

"Lily!" Coach yells. "Care to join us?"

I slam back into my body in time to hear Coach ask me where my head's at today, and I tell him it's here, and I'm ready.

~~Oh, and there was this weird bump on my stomach,~~
~~and you know how sometimes you get a bump and~~
~~it's ALL you can think about until you scrape it out~~
~~and the world makes sense again? No? Just me? Cool.~~

I take my spot on the starting blocks, head down, butt up, feet pushing back. The track, warmed by the spring sun, radiates heat up at me. I close my eyes and picture myself kicking off, rounding each turn, sprinting across the finish line. When the buzzer sounds, I rocket forward, muscles flexing, eyes ahead, body moving down the track.

Coach clicks his stopwatch and tells me I've added .3 seconds to my time.

"Do you want state or not?"

"I'm having an off day."

~~An off year.~~
~~An off life.~~

But he doesn't want to hear that.

So I tell him I'll fix it.

I'll be better.

I'll win.

Because if I don't—who am I?

My brain and heart are still sprinting even though my race is done.

The familiar tingling starts down my arms. If only I were alone,

144

I could pick more of the scabs on my stomach. I could stop the tsunami rolling through me.

It's happening again.

I can't breathe.

I grab my bags and sprint off the track, into the school, where I end up on the floor of a bathroom stall. Again.

Is this my life now? A revolving panic attack carousel? My fingers have crept under my shirt, searching for skin.

"No!" I yell, pushing my hand away.

I need a distraction.

Something, anything.

I read the words on the stall walls. Permanent-marker declarations that apparently Mr. Bronson has done unspeakable things to Señora Garcia. And Tom Day loves Sharon Goodman. FOREVER. And this gem: *There are three things I hate. 1. Vandalism. 2. Irony. 3. Lists.*

But there are also smaller ones, written in pencil, so faint that I have to lean in close to read them.

I'm pregnant
I have no friends
my dad has cancer

And in thin, almost imperceptible strokes in the grout above the trash can:

when will I be fine?

I picture the people who wrote these confessions. Were they like me? Alone? Panicking? Etching out their truth anonymously on a bathroom stall.

Hidden people.

Hidden words.

The thought burns a sadness inside me, just behind my rib cage, where I keep all the words I don't say, either.

Get it out or it festers. That's what Micah says.

Get the words out.

And before I even know what I'm looking for, I'm pulling out his magazines from my backpack and flipping through them, frantically. Anything to keep my mind, my fingers, off my skin. I cut out headlines and sentences and words from articles telling me how to LOOK GREAT IN SKINNY JEANS and CLIMAX YOUR WAY TO BETTER SKIN!

I cut and cut and cut and then lay out all the words in rows on the tiled floor.

One by one, I tape them onto the back of the stall door.

be brave

be smart

beUtiful

be

the

best

do it right

do it now

do it better

just

do

it

stay sweet

stay out of trouble

stay focused

stay

on

track

I stand back and read the words.
Not mine.
Not exactly.
But they're a start.

chapter
19

I don't tell anyone about the poem. But it's there—a real piece of me.

The only person I would tell is Micah, but he's been absent for three days with no word from the 100-acre-wood. Not that I've been checking my phone like a certifiable addict or anything.

Friedman and Gifford do their usual pep rally about our "poetic dance through the human mind" when we meet for collaboration in the art room at the end of the week. Micah walks in ten minutes into their song and dance, slings his backpack onto the bar stool next to me, and sits two seats away without so much as a glance in my direction.

He hates you.

"Art connects us," Friedman says. "Every time we put our story out there, even a small, seemingly insignificant piece, we are that much closer to seeing that it's not a bunch of little stories. It's one big story. The *human* story."

As always, he tells us to "Go, create!" His slingshot canvas is gone, and in its place, a pile of junk. Odds and ends from around the school—ancient DVR players, chairs with missing legs, and all sorts of other remnants of classrooms past—that Friedman intends to give new life through art.

"Nothing is ever truly broken," he says, surveying his pile.

Micah is drawing in a sketch pad with long, swooping strokes.

"Where have you been?" I ask.

He answers without looking up.

"Mental-health sabbatical."

I open my mouth to tell him I'm sorry for jumping away, that it's not him, it's me, but I stop short, unsure how to start or if it's even true.

He looks at me sideways while drawing. "Is it just me, or are you being weirder than usual?"

"I—I just wanted to say, about the other day, in the hallway—"

Micah holds up his hand. "Gonna stop you right there. That one's on me. Think I misread some signals."

"Micah—"

"Seriously. Message received. We're project partners. That's it."

Before I can tell him I have absolutely no brain or heart or calendar space to give, Kali trots over, an accusatory finger pointed in my direction.

"Do you know who it is?"

"Who what is?" I answer.

"The guerrilla poet?"

"The what now?"

She rolls her eyes like I'm an impossible moron and turns her phone to show me today's edition of the Underground. There, front and center, is a picture of my bathroom stall poem with a post: **RANDOM ACT OF POETRY BY MYSTERIOUS GUERRILLA POET.**

"So far, it's just this one, and all we know is that this so-called poet is a girl," says Kali. "It's really not you?"

I shake my head.

"Then we both have a *huge* problem," she says.

Micah cranes his neck to look at Kali's phone, then cocks a knowing eyebrow at me. "How do you know it's a girl?"

"Because it's in the *girls'* bathroom," Kali says, annoyed. "And now people are, like, posting other stuff in there, too, and someone showed Gifford and she's been going on and on about how public art is *so* inspired. Like sticking something on the bathroom wall is so hard. It's basically graffiti, and the poem isn't even that good." Kali points her bony finger at me again. "Anyway, heads up. Looks like someone else is in it to win it."

Kali trots off, ponytail swinging, and Micah narrows his eyes at me.

"A poem made of magazine clippings. You wouldn't know anything about this, would you?"

I smile, and Micah is already up and headed for the door. We practically run to the bathroom.

"Excuse me? Where are you going?" I point to the sign with the little girl on it when he starts to follow me inside. "See the dress?"

"Huh," Micah says, smiling. "I always thought that was a cape."

He puts both hands out in front of him like a flying superhero. I roll my eyes.

"All right, Superman, but let's be quick."

When I give Micah the coast-is-clear sign, we hurry into the bathroom stall and lock it behind us. The back of the door is covered with words. Some written in marker. In pencil. On neon Post-its, stuck to the door next to my *stay on track* cutouts.

go to college
ace the test
snap out of it
don't mess up
why are you like this?
try harder

"This was you?" Micah says.

"Not all this." I touch a note that says *be someone better.* "Just the clippings. And they weren't *my* words, exactly."

"But you breathed life into them."

Micah is face to face with me in the tiny stall, his black curls grazing my nose, and I can smell wintergreen gum on his breath. The same electric energy pulses between us as on the beach, in his kitchen.

This time, *he* pulls away from *me,* and I don't blame him one bit. I'd steer clear of me, too, after the way I treated him in front of Damon. But his eyes hold mine, the little gold flecks dancing.

"This should be our project."

"Bathroom stall graffiti?"

"No. Well, yes. Words that mean something to people our age."

"Right. 'Cause the world needs more angsty teen poetry?"

"Nope. The world has enough noise. It needs more truth. More real."

"The world can't handle my real." I look at my magazine clippings again. "*I* can't handle my real."

"Write it anyway."

He scans my face in a way that makes me feel totally naked. Like he sees the *real* me, which may even be more terrifying than being stark raving nude in front of the entire school.

"You still want to work with me?" I say.

"Don't have much choice," he says, with a hint of a smile. "It's in the official rules: No quitting until it's done."

I jump at the sound of footsteps. The bathroom fills with girls' voices as I peek through the slit in the door.

What if you get caught in here?

"Hey," Micah says, his hand on my arm bringing me back to my body, to the electric zaps where his skin touches mine, zaps I'm desperately trying to ignore. "Come back to me."

"But they're gonna see us," I whisper.

Micah frowns. "So what?"

He thinks this is about him again, and maybe it is (a little), but it's more about my words. If people know they're mine, they'll know about the Lily I've tried so hard to hide.

"No one can know I wrote this." I peek through the gap once more. "Whatever we do with this project, it has to be anonymous, okay?"

"You mean until we turn it in?"

"Right . . . well . . . I'll figure that out later, but for now, promise me. A-non-y-mous."

"O-k-ay," he says, dragging out his letters to match mine, and then, before I can stop him, he flips the lock on the door.

"What are you doing?" I whisper, panicked.

Micah sighs. "When are you going to start trusting me?"

Without further explanation, he strides out like he owns the place. A girl by the mirror squeals, "What the hell, pervert?" Through the crack in the door, I see him walk to the entrance of the bathroom, turn, and loudly declare, "Ladies, B-minus for cleanliness, but A-plus for reading material. Keep up the good work!"

He shoots them a thumbs-up, and with all eyes on him, I slip out of the stall undetected. As I wash my hands at the sink, I see my flushed face in the mirror. A girl next to me whispers about "that weird rehab kid."

"If you ask me," I say, tossing my paper towel into the trash can, "the world could use more weirdos."

Between Micah's eyes and my poem on the wall, my heart is jumping all day.

During track practice, the rhythm of running works its magic for the first time in forever, an idea forming with the thud-thud-thud of my feet. Friedman's words come to me. *Art connects us.* Makes us feel less alone.

The pieces start clicking together. The puzzle isn't fully formed, but the energy of an idea surges through me. I don't even care that Coach barks at me, "Pick up the pace, Larkin! Keep daydreaming, and you can kiss state finals goodbye!"

I even engage at dinner when Staci's telling us about how she's decided to go back to work, teaching a few days a week at the yoga studio. I tell her that sounds cool, and Dad smiles at me and gives me a wink across the table. Alice answers yes-or-no questions about her online courses. Yes, they're going fine. No, she doesn't need help. But my mind is too alive with possibilities for this project to fall into the Alice black hole tonight.

After dinner, I almost run to my room to message Micah.

LogoLily: I know how we can share our project AND keep me anonymous. At least for now.

100-acre-wood: Do tell.

LogoLily: Meet me Sunday night? School parking lot. 1 a.m.

100-acre-wood: Why, Lily Larkin, are you suggesting we break a rule? Clutching-my-pearls emoji

LogoLily: Just be there.

100-acre-wood: Aye, aye, Captain.

LogoLily: And bring your chalk.

100-acre-wood: Double-high-five emoji. Can't wait emoji. Excited to meet rule-breaking Lily emoji

I shut off my phone and sit alone with my thoughts.

What if this doesn't work?

And the project tanks?

My breath starts to catch in my lungs, so I find a scab on my stomach. It would be so easy to scrape it off. Reset my brain with the mindless motion.

But I stop my fingers.

And pick up my pen.

My Monsters

At night
the monsters come.
One
by
one
by
one.

They sit on my chest
laugh in my ear
steal my breath
whisper words I don't want to hear.
They crowd me out.

Go away, I say.
But my voice is tiny
and no match for monsters.

chapter 20

I wait until 12:45 a.m. to slip out.

Margot has crept into my bed again, so I have to ease out. Alice is cocooned across the room, thank goodness. Didn't want to have an awkward hey-you're-sneaking-out-too moment.

I walk to the school through a springtime fog that gives the night an eerie sheen, the smoky billows blanketing the houses and the path ahead. But I've run these roads so many times, I know the curves by heart. I wind my way down the loop toward the school and the shore, and tonight the memories from the Night of the Bathroom Floor leave me alone.

As I get closer, the rhythmic breathing of the ocean fills the world. I inhale deeply, filling my own lungs with the cool night air. Micah is waiting in the parking lot, doing figure eights on his orange bicycle. Seeing him there, ethereal through the fog, waiting for me, makes my heart jump slightly. Not in a pending-panic-attack way, but in a way that tells my body to wake up, to be ready, to take everything in.

"So what's this grand plan?" he asks, hopping off his bike.

"Okay, so I was thinking about what Friedman said, about connection." My idea falls out of me, fast and excited. "So, what if the words aren't mine, or yours, or anyone's? What if the words are *everyone's*?"

I hold up the bucket of chalk sitting in the parking lot by Micah's feet. "We take my poetry and your art to the people, and leave space for them to add to it."

Micah nods along.

"I like it. *Very* Bob Ross of you," he says. "So where do we create this masterpiece of the masses?"

I look around. "Parking lot?"

He shakes his head. "Auto-ped liability."

"Side of the building?"

"Vandalism."

Both our eyes land on the massive sidewalk right in front of the main entrance. Micah looks at me through the fog.

"Bingo."

We start without a plan.

I write out my monster poem, line by line in front of the door. Micah stands behind me, watching the words form on the sidewalk.

He's gonna think you're a head case.

He'd be right.

"I haven't edited it or anything," I say, feeling again like I'm standing naked in front of him, exposed by my words. I have to restrain myself from erasing the poem, running home, and hiding my notebook under my mattress. "It's a rough draft. Definitely a work in progress."

Micah kneels down on the ground next to me, reading my words, his lips moving as he does, which is so adorable I can barely stand it.

"Well, it's real," he says. "And, by the way, we're all a work in progress."

He taps a piece of chalk to his chin and then starts drawing next to my poem: a girl with demons perched on her shoulders, yelling into her ears. Her eyes are shut tight, and one of the monsters is covering her mouth. It's dark and moody. But it's also beautiful, a mix of light and dark, just like Micah. He makes the girl come alive, shading here, lightening there, until she pops off the sidewalk, fully formed. Her monsters look like they, too, could leap into reality.

He asks me to help him shade in the rest, and we work side by side like we did on the beach, in comfortable silence, putting ourselves—our art—into the world. And I don't know if it's Micah's arm brushing mine or writing my words on the ground, where everyone will see them, but an electric chill rocks through my body.

Micah's eyes focus fiercely on the chalk, the muscles in his arm flexing as he draws.

Stop staring at his biceps, you weirdo.

You're just project partners, remember?

You made that perfectly clear.

He looks up through his curls.

"What's up, creeper?"

I turn back to the sidewalk, thinking about the way his face fell in front of Damon in the hallway. I can't let that happen again. I can't lead him on.

"You've got chalk on your face," I say, standing without looking at him, because if I look, I'll see that scar on his eyebrow. I'll wonder

158

where it's from. I'll wonder about this boy and his past, and he'll take up more space in my brain. Space I don't have to give.

He swipes at his cheek but totally misses the bright blue swatch. "Just looked like you might be coming awfully close to violating the whole just-partners policy."

"You're one to talk," I say. "With that little raised-eyebrow smolder in the hallway."

The corners of his lips fight a smile. "I'm sure I have no idea what you're talking about."

"I think you do."

"Am I doing it right now?" he asks, jumping up next to me. "I mean, I'd hate to be walking around, inadvertently smoldering at people."

I fake punch him, and he grabs my wrist, igniting electricity where he touches me.

"Fine," he says. "For the sake of our partnership, I will try to rein in my natural sex appeal."

"How generou—"

"But you"—he points at me—"have to stop doing that thing where you bite your lip when you concentrate."

"I do *not.*"

"You do, and it's *very* distracting." He clears his throat, rocking back on his heels. "Speaking purely from a partnership standpoint, of course."

"Of course." I crouch down so he can't see the heat in my cheeks, because holy crap, are we talking about my mouth right now?

I add a final line beneath my monsters poem: *My greatest fear is . . .*

I leave the bucket of chalk right next to it, and we stand back to admire our work.

"I guess this concludes the first official meeting of the guerrilla poets of Ridgeline High," I say, trying to draw the attention away from sexy smolders and lips.

"Not so fast." Micah dusts his chalky blue hands on his pants. "First you have to answer. What's yours?"

"My what?"

"Greatest fear."

I laugh, and my voice rings out in the empty space. "Just one?"

"Yep. Greatest. Numero uno."

How do I narrow my list? I fear Alice hurting herself again, and me not stopping her. I fear my brain betraying me. Not getting into Berkeley. Not being all that Dad wants.

"Then I guess"—I crouch to pick up a piece of chalk—"letting everyone down."

Micah squinches up his face. "Who have *you* ever let down?"

"Alice," I say before I censor myself. "I'm *still* letting her down."

I've made zero progress on my make-Alice-Alice-again plan, which means I'm just as useless to her now as I was the night she reached out for me in the bathroom. Micah takes a step toward me, like he's going to hug me or touch me, but then stops, and looks about as awkward as I feel, so I quickly say something.

"Your turn. What does the great Micah Mendez fear?"

His chest expands, then empties slowly. "It's hard to explain."

"Nuh-uh. I told you mine. Now spill."

He smiles, tapping his finger to his chin. "What if I show you instead?"

I wipe the blue streak off his cheek.

"What exactly did you have in mind?"

chapter
21

Micah rides his bike toward the ocean with me perched on the handlebars.

He pedals fast, the night air rushing past me eagerly, whipping my hair. It hits Micah in the face and he laughs. I laugh. *Aren't we normal? A boy and a girl on a ride down the coast. Look at us! Happy and laughing and moonlight in our faces.*

Micah pulls off above our cove, the sand that held—briefly—our art. He leads me by the light of his cell phone down the steep stairs to the beach and across the sand to a rocky point, jutting out into the water. The waves crash onto the rocks, rough and hard, spraying plumes of frothy white into the air as we make our way over slick stones.

Ahead of us, the ocean sprawls out to the edge of nowhere. To the right, Deadman's Cliff looms, large and immovable. At the base of it, Micah sits on the edge of a big, black rock, half-submerged in the water, misting us with each wave. All around us, sharp, angular rocks poke up from the water—a lethal landing pad.

I sit next to him, the rumors about Micah bouncing around in my head. The picture of him on the Underground, teetering on top of the cliff. He was going to jump. Isn't that what people say? That he almost let the ocean suck him away?

Is that why he brought me here? To lay all his secrets bare? How do I react? Shocked? Sad? What's the right response to something like *this*?

He turns his hand over, his semicolon tattoo barely visible in the dark. My stomach tightens.

"Do you know what this means?"

I nod. "It means—it means you tried to—" I can't find the words.

Micah runs his fingers over the ink. "Last year—"

"Micah, you don't have to—"

"I want to." He looks out at the cliff again. "The first time, it was pills. Mom sent me to Fairview. For a while, I was better. Until I wasn't. I was going to do it again."

"But you didn't."

He shakes his head. "Because of art."

"Art?"

"I had this art teacher at Fairview, and he told me to stay. Stay and take all the hurt and the sad and the numb and put it into my drawings. So I did. And the more I poured into my art, the easier it was to stay. 'One more day,' he'd say. Then one more. Until I didn't have to remind myself to live. And the art saved me. One day at a time."

"Is that why you're always sketching?"

He nods.

"I'm glad you stayed." The words sound stupid leaving my lips, but they're all I have. He looks to the north, and I follow his gaze to where the cliff stands silhouetted against the milky moonlight. The picture of Micah flashes into my mind again. So close to the edge. "Do you still—are you still—" The panic takes hold in my gut, quick and sharp. I stand up on the rocks. "Is that your biggest fear? That one day you'll go through with it?"

Micah pulls me back down to sit. "No, no, wait. I didn't finish. I don't go up there to jump. I mean, if I'm being honest, yeah, I think about it. I'm not sure I will ever *not* think about it. My biggest fear is that no matter what I do, all people will ever see is the boy who *almost* jumped. The boy from rehab. And maybe that's all I'll see, too.

"So I come here to remember that I'm alive. That I'm more than *Manic* Micah. That I have a choice." He turns his hand palm up, and without thinking, I reach out and outline the semicolon tattoo on his wrist with the tip of my finger. "This doesn't mean I almost died. It means I chose to stay."

His heartbeat pulses up and down, his blood blue and full of life through his skin.

"That my story isn't over," he says, offering me his hand. "Come see."

I let him pull me to my feet and guide me across the rocks. The tide is coming in, soaking my shoes as we make our way toward Deadman's Cliff.

"But they closed the path," I say, my mind already creating headlines for tomorrow's news. *Two teens found at base of cliff.*

"Don't need a path," Micah says. The wind almost carries away his voice, but I can see the determination in his eyes. We *are* going to the top of that cliff. At the base, he stops and takes off his shoes. "You'll have a better grip barefoot."

I neatly stack my tennis shoes under the earthy overhang. He has me go first, telling me where to step and where to grip as I scale upward, step by step, only seeing a foot ahead of me in the dark, the rocks sharp and uneven beneath my feet. When I get almost to the top, Micah pushes my butt from below. He heaves himself up behind.

We walk until we run out of earth. From the edge, darkness and ocean and nothing reach to infinity, the moonlight spilling onto the water. On the horizon, the sky's so black, I can't tell where the ocean stops and the night begins. Looking down, I get the same feeling I did when Dad took us to the Grand Canyon. *What if I jumped? Would I fall? Or would gravity release me? Let me fly?*

"I want to show you something," Micah says, standing behind me. He puts both his hands on my waist, just above my hips. His fingers graze under my shirt, near my scabs. I freeze and instinctively pull away before he can feel them.

"Sorry. I—" he starts.

"No, it's just . . ." I tuck my shirt into my jeans. "Your fingers were cold."

I grab his hands and put them back on my waist. Micah pulls back on me, slightly.

"Lean forward."

I shoot him my best *not on your life, buddy* look.

"You still don't trust me, do you?" He's staring at me earnestly, and even though I'm standing on a cliff where a man died, with a boy who just told me he almost did, too, the funny thing is, I do. I trust him. Slowly I lean forward. Micah's hands hold me by the waist like a tether, anchoring me to the earth.

"This is all very *Titanic*," I yell back at him over the roar of the waves crashing below.

"Right? And we haven't even reached the nude drawing portion of our evening."

"Don't make me laugh!"

I let my weight fall forward, Micah's hands holding me steady. Below, jagged rocks splinter waves into a million pieces. The darkness swallows me.

"Don't look down." His voice cuts through the night. "Keep your eyes on the horizon."

When I do, the world disappears: Micah and the cliff and the waves—vanished. Just me and the sky and the water, and the feeling that I'm soaring, weightless through the air. The wind rushes by my ears. My fingers tingle. Every nerve of my body is alive, going berserk. Every inch of my skin is connected. Awake.

"This is wild!" I scream.

Micah's hands pull me back from the edge, and I turn to face him, our noses almost touching, only an inch of night between us.

"And what is wrong with me that being centimeters from certain death is the most alive I've felt in a long time?" I whisper.

"Nothing," he says, brushing my hair out of my face. "Absolutely nothing."

With those gold-speckled eyes piercing mine, I almost let myself believe him.

chapter
22

In the shower, my heart's still racing. Not in a bad, panic-attack way but in a good, feeling-alive, soaring-over-the-ocean kind of way. I think about the way he looked at me, the way he talked about his brush with death. And even though *that* rumor may be true, I still can't believe the others, that the boy I know could hurt someone, *has* hurt someone. I'm lost in thoughts about the Boy on the Verge when I open the door to Alice leaning against the frame, her arms folded, blocking my exit. All the beauty of tonight blows out with the steam.

"Where'd *you* sneak off to?"

I want to tell her. About the cliff and the chalk poetry. How Micah's hands on my waist tonight sent shivers down me, my body short-circuiting in the best way. Alice and I could jump into bed, pull the sheet over our heads like we used to when we'd stay up giggling and chatting and swapping secrets in the dark. But we're not those girls anymore. Our secrets are stored, not shared.

Margot is asleep in Alice's bed, so I whisper, "Maybe we should start with where *you* go at night."

Alice looks away. *Busted.* "You know about that?"

"Of course I know. We share a room."

~~And nothing more.~~

"You don't need to worry about it," Alice says.

Suddenly all the hurt of having her, my louder-than-life big sister, act like a stranger sears into my chest, makes my words wobbly.

"Of course I do. You're my sister. But I swear it's like you hate me."

She crumples slightly, her shoulders falling along with her face.

"I don't hate you." Her voice has lost its edge. "Things are just different now."

Normally I'd let it go, just keep my mouth shut, but something about tonight—writing my words, Micah sharing his tattoo with me—propels me forward.

"Why? Why are things different?"

~~Why are *we* different?~~

She stares past me at the reddish stain on the tile floor but flicks her eyes away just as fast. We've never actually talked about that night, like the memory of it doesn't exist inside us.

"They just are."

Her eyes plead with me to stuff this conversation down with all the other unsaid things.

~~Is it because I didn't stop you?~~
~~Didn't save you?~~

She steps past me into the bathroom, her face twisted. She wipes a tear from her eye before it falls, and when she does, her sleeve rides up slightly, revealing thin pink lines on her wrist that intersect. A raised, dark purple scar slicing upward from her palm.

I want to wrap my arms around her, tell her I love her, tell her I'm going to make it better.

"Alice, you can talk to me," I say. "I have no idea what's going on with you, or what happened at Fairview or what you're thinking—"

"You want to know what I'm thinking?" She cuts me off, her voice shaking. "What goes through my head every single time I look at you?" She points to the floor, to the spot where I found her. "I'm thinking about how you looked at me that night."

"I—I was scared." How can I possibly explain how it feels to find your sister with a blade to her wrist?

"Exactly. And *I'm* the one who scared you." She takes in a heavy breath and lets it out slowly. "And I saw that look again on your face—on Dad's face, on Margot's face—the other night when I missed curfew. I just keep hurting people. Which is why it's best for everyone if you just stick to your life, and I'll stick to mine."

She doesn't wait for an answer—just closes the door.

chapter
23

No one notices the words.

Like a herd of cattle, they walk over them, stomping their way into school as Micah and I watch from my car. But then, finally, a girl stops, picks up a piece of chalk from the bucket, and crouches down.

"She's writing something!" I say, hitting Micah, who's half-asleep in the passenger seat. He probably got as much shut-eye as I did last night. It was almost dawn by the time I fell asleep after my confrontation with Alice, which means I slept through strength training this morning and my head is foggy. I chug an energy drink like my life depends on it.

"Go guerrilla poets of Ridgeline High," Micah says with his eyes closed, weakly fist-pumping.

A few others have stopped now, looking at the ground.

"Do you think they like it? They probably hate it," I say. "Maybe they don't hate it."

Micah turns sideways in the seat and props his backpack like a pillow underneath his head.

"You're a roller coaster of emotions, Lily Larkin," he says. "Remember, art is putting a piece of yourself out there and saying, 'Look, world. Here I am. Like it or not.'"

Still, knowing they're reading *my* words makes my head a little woozy, my heart a little erratic, like I'm standing on the cliff again. The warning bell forces us from the car, and we walk toward our artwork.

Micah groans, throwing up his hands. "Oh, come on, seriously?"

Someone has sketched a crudely shaped, and egregiously enormous, penis next to our art. He rubs the addition with the side of his hand. "It's official. We go to school with imbeciles."

"Well, it's a good thing we don't care what they think," I say, smiling, although my mind is not really on the penis. It's on the new words, scrawled in chalk next to *My greatest fear is . . .*

Principal Porter
my parents
not being enough
rolling the dice on a fart
spiders
oblivion—RIP, Augustus Waters
being alone

Micah has managed to eviscerate most of the phallic chalk, and he stands next to me, mouthing the words.

"Well," He says, "it's not exactly Shakespeare."

"True." But people read my words. They connected. I take a picture of the chalk art and all the new words. "But it's something."

* * *

170

"Is it you?"

Sam's staring at me in the orchestra room where we meet up before track, her violin perched on her shoulder, her bow pointed accusingly at me.

"Is what me?"

"The chalk poetry. Kali swears it's not her. And she asked me if it was you, and not like I would tell Kali *anything*, but you would tell *me*, right?"

She's waiting for me to answer. Of course I'd tell her. Under normal circumstances. This is Sam. Sam who knew about Alice and didn't tell. But these are not normal circumstances. And what I wrote in that poem is stuff I've *never* told Sam—or anyone else.

What if she doesn't understand?

What if she thinks I'm nuts?

What if

What if

What if

The what-ifs push her away from me.

"It's not me," I say.

"Well, Kali is capital-*P* pissed about it. And I guess part of me secretly hoped it *was* you just to stick it to her." Sam packs her violin into her case and flips the little silver locks into place.

"How's the solo coming?" I ask.

Sam groans and rolls her eyes. "Terrible. I can't get the timing right, and rumor has it, there may be some college scouts in the audience. My parents only mention it fifty-six times a day."

"You're a shoo-in for first chair," I say, linking my arm through hers as we head to track. "Seriously, Sam, there's no one better."

"You *have* to say that. It's in the best-friend handbook," she says, laughing, and my guilt for keeping secrets lifts slightly off my shoulders.

Coach puts it right back on.

"You missed training this morning," he says.

"I know. I'm sorry. I had—"

"I don't need excuses, Larkin. I need someone I can count on, and frankly, I'm seeing a bigger commitment from some of the other runners." He looks at me intensely, like he's trying to show me how serious I should be taking this. And I am. Of course I am. I've been training to win state since freshman year. I'm not about to lose it now. "If I'm going to put you in the qualifier, I need to be able to count on you."

"You *can*."

He looks me dead in the eye. "Whatever else you have going on, stop thinking about it. You've got to give a hundred percent here, or I can find someone who will."

After practice, I watch from my car as more people add words to the sidewalk in front of the school. So even though Coach's warning makes it hard to breathe and makes my fingers want to reach for my skin, I reach for my notebook instead.

All in My Head

Relax.
Calm down.
Just
Don't
Think
About
It.

Ask me not to breathe.
For the blood to halt in my veins.
Not to exist.
Not to be me.

Isn't that what you mean?
Be someone different.
Someone better.
Someone who
Isn't
All
Wrong.

chapter
24

I sneak out to meet Micah again a few nights later, armed with poster boards, tape, markers, and an idea. He follows me to the track, where I lay the boards on the ground and start writing my latest poem, a line on each poster.

Be someone different.

Someone better.

Micah watches for a minute and then gets to work on his own poster board. He draws a man, a smoky whisper of a being, all black strokes and billowy form being stripped away into nothing. Then we set up the hurdles on the track, evenly spaced all the way around, and on each one we hang a poster board.

Micah reads the last line of my poem out loud, "Someone who isn't all wrong."

"It occurs to me"—he pauses while ripping a piece of tape with his teeth to stick the poster on the hurdle "that there are two Lilys. The Lily who writes these poems, and the one you want people to see."

Uh-oh.

Here it comes,

the you're-crazy-and-I-know-it conversation.

Frankly, I judge him for not saying it earlier. It's been a week since he saw my bathroom-stall poem, and he hasn't run away screaming or done any of the things I'd expect someone to do after getting a glimpse into the chaos of my mind.

"This from the king of enigmatic double lives," I say, deflecting about as hard as I can. Micah looks at me through the dark, opening his arms wide.

"I'm an open book. All you have to do is ask."

"Okay," I say, thinking about the rumors on the Underground about his expulsion from his past school. "Where did you get your scar?"

"Playing catch with my dad as a kid. Baseball broke the skin, and it kept busting open so many times, my eyebrow never quite grew back." He walks toward me in the dark. "But that's not really what you want to know, is it?

"You want to know if the rumors are true. If I'm the guy they say I am. The kind of guy who could hurt someone." He's within a foot of me now. "What do *you* think?"

I remember how he looked when Damon soaked his sketch pad. The darkness in Micah's eyes. Damon definitely deserved to get hit, but Micah stopped.

"Honestly?" I say. "Jury's still out."

"Well, I eagerly await the verdict." Micah smiles. "And the answer to the question you didn't actually ask is yes, I am that kind of guy. Or at least I used to be. For a long time, maybe even since my dad died, my depression didn't exactly look like depression. It looked a lot like me being pissed off at the world. And this kid at my old school said something about my dad, and I just—lost it."

Through the dark, I can see the outline of him, the bright socks and T-shirt with a big yellow smiley face on it. This is not a boy with anger issues.

"So when did you go from *that* guy to the one who subscribes to the dorky-sock-of-the-month club and idolizes a make-love-not-war icon like Bob Ross?"

"I told you, when you get to the point where dying seems like the answer, you have two choices: change or fade away. I chose to change." He looks down at his legs, at the zebras on the bright green fabric. "And the socks? I guess they help me remember I'm still here. Living out loud. Still screaming into the void." Micah holds up his poster board, eyeing the smoke man fading into nothing. "Sometimes, though, the void still wins.

"Plus," he continues, "living out loud has the extra awesome benefit of pissing off people like Damon. People don't like unpredictable. They want to put you in a box. I'm the depressed kid. You're the A-plus student. It makes people nervous when you're not what you're supposed to be."

I read my words that loop around the track. The loop I've run a million times. Always pushing to be the best. Because that's what I'm supposed to be. That's *my* box.

"So is that the point of the Hundred Acre Wood? Bears and pigs and tigers who don't fit into boxes. A bunch of weirdos against the world?"

Micah shakes his head and laughs. "Keep guessing."

He tapes his drawing to the final hurdle and then lies down in the grass next to the track, his hands behind his head as he stares up at the night sky. I lie next to him, inhaling the sweet scent of the April orange blossoms. Without the sun, the night air has a nip, and when I shiver, Micah scoots closer.

"Don't get any ideas," he says. "Just don't want my partner freezing to death before our project's done. Now your turn. Why the two Lilys?"

I don't know if it's the obscurity of the night or the track where I've spent so much time chasing a better time—a better me—but I don't stop the words.

"Because I'm afraid," I start. "Of losing control. Of becoming—"

"Like Alice?"

I nod, ashamed.

"There are worse people to become," he says.

I pick at a blade of grass on the field.

"I just—I just don't need people knowing about the monsters in my head."

He leans up on one elbow, giving me the same look as on the cliff, the one that makes it hard to remember that I have no time for boys.

He taps my leg with his foot. "I know, and I'm kind of okay with you."

"Yeah, but you're different."

His smile pierces through the dark as it spreads across his face.

"Oh my gosh. Stop throwing yourself at me," he says. "What part of *just* partners do you not understand?"

I kick him lightly in the shin, and Micah laughs, a rich, genuine sound that fills the empty track. We pick up our supplies and leave the field, walking over our sidewalk chalk art. My words and his monsters are smudged and fading. He pulls his bike upright and nods toward the handlebars. I hop on, and he starts toward my house.

"I go to this therapy group a couple times a month," he says while we ride. "Just some Fairview friends and indigestible refreshments, but you could come. If you want."

"You think I need therapy?"

"I think *everybody* needs therapy."

I turn my head to look at him in the dark. "Because I'm a head case."

"No, I just—"

"You're just ruining guerrilla poetry with this therapy talk, is what you're doing." The last thing I need right now is therapy. Someone with a degree on the wall diagnoses you, and suddenly that's all you are anymore. One more box, one more label. "I am not about to lie on some overpaid therapist's couch while looking at inkblots that totally are all penises, but you can't say they're penises or you'll be diagnosed as a grade-A sicko who wants to murder puppies or whatever."

"Wow. So that's a no to therapy. But you *should* talk to someone. What about Alice?"

"Told you—not gonna happen," I say. *Stick to your life, and I'll stick to mine,* she said.

"Still shutting you out?"

We're almost to my house, and Micah pulls over to let me off.

"And sneaking out at night. Ignoring me. So can you please just drop this?"

"Yes."

"Thank y—"

"In exchange," he continues, "for an evening of your time."

I cross my arms, trying to figure him out.

"Do you ask *all* your project partners out on dates?"

"I'm officially horrified that you think I'm capable of something so conventional." He starts pedaling away into the night but yells back at me. "Tomorrow. Pick you up at seven!"

The Ridgeline Underground

260 likes

The guerrilla poet strikes again! The track this time. Anyone know who it is??

72 comments

No idea. But I love it!

Wish I'd thought of it

The drawing kind of looks like something I saw on that Micah kid's page

Ummm . . . his partner is Lily Larkin

LOL never mind. She's about as deep as a kiddie pool.

Maybe one of his friends does the poems.

That guy has friends?

chapter
25

When Micah pulls up Saturday night, he hands me a single white lily in full bloom. He's wearing a collared shirt and enough cologne to clear my sinuses.

Not a date, my ass.

"Thank you," I say before trying to jump into the car he's driving and get this show on the road, or at least away from my father, who has been informed (by me) that I'm going to a study session.

"Whoa, whoa, whoa. Isn't it customary to say hello to the parents?" Micah says, holding out his hand and pulling me back out of the car. I trudge back to the door and call for Dad. He comes out of his office, taking off his reading glasses, clearly in a book daze.

"Micah, Dad. Dad, Micah," I say.

Micah wipes his hands on his pants—is he sweating?—and reaches out. Dad takes his hand, eyebrows knit together in confusion.

"He's my partner on the English contest," I say, jumping in. "For the Berkeley summer program."

Dad's eyes go back and forth from me to Micah, and then to the lily in my hand.

"And I know Alice from Fairview," Micah says. "You've raised two amazing daughters."

"Three, actually," Dad says, stiffening and crossing his arms over his chest while narrowing his eyes. "So you were at Fairview?"

Micah rakes his fingers through his hair and undoes the top of his button-up shirt.

"Yes, sir."

A little piece of me wants to die. Two pieces, actually, one for me and one for Micah, who is standing up so straight and smiling so hard that I worry he'll break his face. Seeing Micah, the boy from the 100-acre-wood who doesn't give one flying flip what the world thinks, trying to impress my dad makes me want to laugh—or cry, I'm not sure which.

I grab Micah by the arm. "Well, we should go."

Micah shoves his hand out again. "A pleasure to meet you, sir."

Dad doesn't even uncross his arms, just tells Micah I'll meet him by the car.

"I need a word with my *amazing* daughter."

As soon as Micah's out the door, Dad looks from the lily in my hand to the shirt I'm wearing that shows a little more collarbone than he's used to, and whispers, "Are you *seeing* this boy?"

"He's my partner."

Dad takes his glasses off and pinches the top of his nose. "How well do you know him?"

"Well enough to know he's not going to murder me in a dark alley."

"I'm serious, Lil." Dad puts his hands on his hips, trying to look stern. It doesn't suit him.

"Dad," I say. "Micah's a good guy. Trust me."

"Oh, I trust *you.*"

Margot has heard us whispering and has sidled up next to Dad, along with Staci, who has just come in from teaching yoga.

"Lily has a *date,*" Dad explains, as if he's just announced I have leprosy.

"It's not a date."

"Oooh . . . ," Margot coos, not helping at all.

Staci leans in close and whispers to match us. "Last time I checked, Lily was almost an adult who has never given you a reason to worry."

Dad puts his glasses back on, studying me.

"Well, yes, but—"

"Okay, then," Staci continues, stroking his arm. "Is it fair to assume she's going to do something stupid now?"

He shakes his head as Staci's particular brand of magic works on him, and he gives me a hug and tells me he loves me before going back into his office, where he blatantly opens the blinds to watch Micah.

"Thank you," I mouth to Staci.

She takes the lily and gives me a hug, whispering, "I'll stick this in water. If you need anything, anything at all, text me."

Micah's waiting by my open car door, staring up at the darkening sky.

"So, your dad hates me."

"*Hate* is a strong word." I duck into the passenger side. "Accurate. But strong."

Micah slumps into his seat, one hand gripping the wheel so

hard, his knuckles turn white. Is he fighting the anger he told me about?

"The Fairview factor strikes again," he says, more to himself than to me.

He drives in steamy silence down the Pacific Coast Highway. Deadman's Cliff is a distant silhouette. I wish we were back on it, where we could breathe, pretending our monsters and pasts don't exist.

He pulls into a parking lot next to a massive warehouse, and sits for a minute, contemplating the steering wheel.

"It's just, I have this vision, you know? A world where your diagnosis doesn't define you, and getting help doesn't make you weak or dangerous or *other*. And sometimes I forget that the world isn't there yet."

"I thought you didn't care what people think of you."

"I care what *you* think about me." He clears his throat again. "It's just—I mean, the thing is—it's important for a partnership. The respect, that is, mutual respect and all."

He stumbles over his words in such a non-Micah fashion that I can't help but laugh, and he laughs, too, which breaks up the darkness in his eyes.

"I assume, then, that you give *all* your project partners flowers on your non-dates?" I ask.

Micah shoots me a serious look. "Partnership bonding is *very* important." He walks around and opens my door and offers me his hand. "If you were thinking this was anything more than that, I'm sorry to disappoint you. Tonight is *strictly* professional."

* * *

Inside, the warehouse is not a warehouse at all but an enormous interactive art display. A rainbow-colored crocheted netting stretches between the walls and all the way to the ceiling, creating geometric shapes and patterns and tunnels in vibrant hues. On the nets, people are walking, crawling, climbing like it's a massive indoor playground.

"Shoes off," Micah says, kicking his into one of the cubbies by the door. He has on purple socks with avocados.

"Glad you're still you under that collar," I say, and Micah's off running like a little kid, jumping onto the netting, with me right behind him. It sways beneath my feet, but we keep climbing until we reach a rope tunnel filled with hundreds of plastic white balls. Micah's pushing through ahead of me and then disappears.

A second later, he pops up by my side. "See—art can be fun!" He laughs, and it's so infectious, I can't help laughing, too, as I swim through the balls, slipping and falling every few steps.

"I'll save you," he yells with mock heroism. "Hop on."

I jump onto his back, and he crawls with me through the rest of the tunnel that ends in a large spiderweb. We tightrope-walk on the web's threads until we reach the center and lie down on what is essentially a huge hammock, and we're both breathing hard from battling the balls, and his arm is touching mine, and I'm aware of every inch of my skin touching his.

But then he's up, and he's pulling me up, and we're tightrope-walking again and shooting down a slide that empties into a small, quiet room with white walls covered with red-and-white rectangular name tags that say HELLO I'M. In each blank, people have written words: *a superhero, trying my best, hyper, in love, the future.*

Micah tosses me a pen and starts writing. I'm—

an artist

a work in progress

alive

And before I can overthink it, I write, too. I'm—

a guerrilla poet

terrified

never enough

He looks at my tags—my confessions—but doesn't comment, just walks into the next room, and I follow. The dark space is lit only by small white lanterns hanging from the ceiling. As we walk in, other lights blink on—bright, flashing strobe lights—and music plays.

Micah starts dancing around, waving his hands and jumping.

"It's motion activated!" he says as the electric lights get brighter and faster, flashing reds and blues and purples across the room as the music picks up speed. And before I have time to tell myself how stupid I'll look, I'm dancing, too. And then Micah is grabbing my hands and we're moving together in what can only be described as chaotic lurching, and we're spinning in a circle, daring the lights to keep up with us. But they can't because we're moving too fast, and all I can see is Micah's face illuminated in the darkness, laughing as we spin and spin and spin.

"You're nuts!" I scream over the sound of the music.

"So they say!"

But then his usual smile fades, and he's slowing down, and I'm slowing down, and the music quiets and the lights dim, and it's just me and him and the darkness between us, and we're swaying to the slowing music, my hands still in his, his body pressed against mine, his chest expanding into me, still breathing hard. My own breath catches inside me because the lights from the hanging lanterns are just bright enough that I can see his eyes, and they're serious—and looking at my lips. And I think he may kiss me, and, perhaps more alarming, I think I want him to.

He leans his forehead against mine, still swaying.

"Lily," he says, half question, half declaration, and 100 percent longing, the same kind surging through me that makes me want to erase any sliver of space between us—to know the texture of his lips, the taste of him.

But some kids come in and start jumping around, and the lights flash again, breaking the spell. Micah looks at our intertwined fingers, his jaw muscles clenching and releasing, like he's trying to say something or trying *not* to say something. But then, like he's flipped a switch, he lets go of my hands, and his serious look vanishes along with whatever he was going to say, replaced with his usual, mischievous smile.

"Ready for the second portion of our partnership-bonding non-date?" he says, completely and abruptly brushing over the hand-holding, slow-dancing near kiss.

"There's more?" I say, following him out of the room while playing along, as if nothing out of the ordinary just happened.

"Oh, there's more." Micah slips his shoes back on at the exit. "There's someone I think you should meet."

We walk four blocks, the backs of our hands brushing against each other, my mind silently wishing he'd reach out and wrap his fingers around mine again. But he doesn't, because of course he doesn't, because I've made it very clear I can't or won't or shouldn't go down that path. Except, right now I can't quite remember why.

We stop in front of a hole-in-the-wall café called Tony's with a chalkboard sidewalk sign for OPEN MIC NIGHT! Micah has that look in his eyes, the one that makes his eyebrow arch up and my stomach drop, as he opens the door. We enter a dimly lit space—half bar, half restaurant—that's loud and what Dad would call artsy-fartsy, with mind-trippy paintings on the walls and disco-style lights hanging from the ceiling. A mix of smoky cigarette stink and sickly sweet vapor hangs in the air where people are packed around square tables, chattering loudly.

And like in the art room, I instantly feel like I don't belong.

People are staring.

You're dressed totally wrong.

You *are totally wrong.*

Micah holds my hand to guide me to a crowded table near the corner.

"This is Lily," Micah says. "Lily, the gang."

They say their hellos and ask me how I know Micah, and he jumps in to make it clear we're just partners on a school project, but he gives me his signature eyebrow lift that undermines his words and takes me right back to the way he exhaled my name in the dark.

"We won't bite," Micah says, pulling out a chair for me. "Not hard, anyway."

His easy, genuine smile keeps me in my body, even though I feel the familiar tingling in my fingertips. Even when, from across the room, fully makeupped and staring at me like I've grown a second head, Alice walks right toward us.

chapter
26

"What is *she* doing here?" Alice glares at Micah.

"I should go." I scoot my chair back. It screeches across the ground, and everyone turns to stare at me. Micah puts his hand on my arm.

"Stay."

He and Alice are having some sort of silent eyebrow battle. Apparently she loses, because she huffs into a chair and murmurs to a girl next to her. A man in an afghan-style poncho with his hair wrapped into a man-bun steps up onto the small stage at the front of the room. I laugh when everyone else does, except I'm not really listening, mostly deliberating ways to implode into stardust each time Alice shoots me serious side-eye.

But now the poncho man is saying Alice's name, and she stands up and walks to the stage. Micah's smiling at me, mischief in his eyes as Alice takes the mic.

"So, I want to talk about being crazy," she says, her voice slightly unsteady. "And no, I'm not talking about that one jerk who always says he's bipolar when the word he's looking for is jackass."

The room titters with laughter. What is going on here? Since when does Alice do stand-up?

"But I was crazy before crazy was cool." She looks down at me and hesitates. "I'm bipolar. When my doctor told me my diagnosis, I said, 'I don't know whether to laugh or cry.' And she said, 'Exactly.'"

The room busts into laughter. I do, too. Alice smiles, wide and bright like the big sister of my childhood, and she stands a little straighter. She paces across the stage, easy, like she belongs up there. When the spotlight catches the waves in her hair, she looks exactly like Mom.

"I spent some time recently at a treatment center, which usually makes people feel sorry for me. But maybe *we're* not the crazy ones." She stops midstage and taps her finger on her head. "Three meals a day and all the craft glue and glitter you can eat? Sign me up!"

She's incredible. Working the room like so much clay in her hands. Micah looks at me, eyebrows raised like *What do you think?* I shake my head to say *I can't believe it.*

"And you want to feel like the best stand-up comedian in the world? Give your show in front of a bunch of girls hopped up on happy pills. Instant. Ego. Boost. I mean, really, there's a lot of great things about being bipolar. Like one time, my boyfriend said, 'We're breaking up. I don't love you anymore.'" And I said, 'Wait ten minutes. I'll change!'"

The guy behind us laughs so hard, water comes out his nose.

"On a more serious note," Alice says, lowering her voice. "Mental illness affects one out of four Americans. So think of your three closest friends. You picturing them? Now, if they all seem stable, I hate to tell you this—" She holds the mic close, breathing into it ominously. "You're. The. One."

She waves to the audience. "Thank you all. You've been great."

The crowd claps wildly as she steps down. The girl at the table squees and side-hugs her. Part of me is jealous of the girl, hugging *my* sister. But another part, a much bigger part, is mesmerized.

Because for the first time in forever, Alice is . . . Alice.

We end up driving home together, thanks to some tricky carpool maneuvering by Micah. As I'm getting into her car, I whisper to him, "It's not going to work."

He feigns innocence. "I have zero idea what you're talking about."

"She does *not* want to talk with me about this."

"Then don't talk about *this,*" he says. "Just talk."

In the car, the Alice from the stage has vaporized into the universe, her laugh bouncing somewhere along the Milky Way, her jokes sucked into a black hole. At a stoplight, she turns toward me, her face tight.

"Why did you come?"

"Micah brought me."

"Look. You're hanging out with Micah, fine. But I don't need you coming into *my* world. Into the one place where I can be myself."

"You can't be yourself around me?"

"You're joking, right? I see the way you all dance around me. You're always watching my every move, playing mental-health detective from across the room. Dad wants to, like, cocoon me in Bubble Wrap, and Staci thinks she can yoga me better. But with my friends—I'm not broken. I'm just me." The light turns, and she slams her foot down hard, lurching us forward. "But now Mr. Fix-It Micah and his compulsive need to meddle in people's lives has gone and messed it all up."

"Is this where you've been going at night?"

"You got it, Sherlock. My friends from Fairview have been helping me practice my act."

I have so many other questions I want to ask now that the topic is out there, ripe for the picking.

What does bipolar feel like? Do you have panic attacks? Circling thoughts? What about scratching your skin until you bleed? Is that part of it?

Or is that just me?

What's me and what's the disease

and what's you

and what in the hell is normal?

But Micah's voice repeats in my head: *Just talk.* So even though I want to spew my questions at her rapid-fire, I choose my words carefully.

"You were amazing up there."

"Thanks," she says dismissively, pretending to be enormously interested in a left-hand turn.

"How did you learn to do that?"

"We had a performance club at Fairview."

"Well, seriously, you were hilarious. This guy behind me literally spewed water out his nose. I'm not even kidding."

"I saw that!" She un-tenses slightly but still doesn't look at me. "I could barely keep it together."

"You couldn't tell. You were a pro. And you seemed really happy up there."

"It's a pretty big rush."

Alice sneaks a quick glance in my direction. "That's it? That's all you want to know?"

"Yeah. I know you didn't want me there, but I'm glad I got to see that."

We drive in silence until we reach the house. Alice pulls the car into the garage, and neither one of us makes a move to get out. We sit until the lights blink off.

"I guess—I guess I didn't want you to see it because I thought it might be strange, hearing me make jokes about it after, well, what happened. But it helps me, I don't know, deal. But maybe that's weird for you."

"Alice." I turn in my seat to face her. "Things couldn't possibly get any weirder between us."

She fiddles with the keys on her lap, not looking at me. "I've kind of been an ass since I got back, haven't I?"

"No." I shove her softly in her shoulder. "You were an ass *way* before you left."

She laughs a big, boisterous Alice guffaw, and as soon as I hear it, I realize how much I've missed it. She shoves me back.

"Well," she says, "as much as it pains me to admit it, I guess it wasn't so bad having you there tonight. Not that I will *ever* tell Micah that."

I laugh. "Oh, trust me, I have a pretty strict policy to never tell Micah he's right."

"Right? Cockiest bastard I know. And remind me again, you and he are—"

"Project partners," I say, even as the memory of how he looked at my lips tonight, the nearness of his body, rockets through my nerve endings. Alice nods like she's buying it, but I know she can see right through me, because her face turns somber.

"He's one of the good ones, you know?"

I nod. "Yeah. I think I do."

And even though there's still a million miles between us, the distance feels smaller somehow. Afraid this moment of candor will end when we open the car doors, I add, "Alice, I just want to say, seeing you up there, it was like . . . like . . ." I can't find the right words, but I try anyway. "I've just missed you, that's all."

Alice smiles at me through the dark.

"I've missed me, too."

Breathe

Through the waves
she
reaches
me

I didn't know
how far I was
or how long I'd held
my breath

until
she
finds me
grabs me
holds me

and I can breathe again

chapter
27

Two nights later, I wake for another guerrilla poets rendezvous, to find Alice teetering on top of her desk in pajamas, pulling the glow-in-the-dark stars off the ceiling.

"What are you doing?" I whisper as I fumble for my socks, trying not to wake Margot next to me.

"Redecorating." She hops off the desk and stands, hands on hips, surveying our room. "This place is in desperate need of a makeover, and I found this *amazing* paint color—seafoam green."

Alice steps into my side of the room for the first time since she got home, pressing a greenish-blue paint sample to the wall.

"It's going to look incredible." She eyes the shoes I'm lacing up. "What are *you* doing? Don't think I haven't noticed you sneaking out lately in the dead of night."

"I learned from the best," I say, and Alice smiles, and I try not to get my hopes up too high that she's really back, the old Alice I've been searching for. She's been waking up more and more since her comedy show, but tonight she seems particularly original Alice. "It's for this art contest."

"It has to be done at night?"

"Yeah."

She cocks her head to the side like she's trying to understand my intentionally vague answers. "Could this have anything to do with Micah?" She smiles the most Alice-like smile she's given me in a long time as she holds up another paint sample to the wall, and I decide I agree with her: a fresh start is *exactly* what this room needs.

I finish tying my shoes and hold a hoodie out to her. "Do you want to, maybe, come?"

She's dressed in two minutes flat, like she's as eager as I am to resurrect the old Alice, the girl who was *always* up for adventure. We tiptoe down the stairs. Alice recoils when her foot sets off the creaky wood. She covers her mouth, eyes smiling. Suddenly we're eight and ten again, sneaking down on Christmas morning to shake all the presents before Dad gets up.

We walk the fog-filled streets toward the school, the eeriness of the one a.m. silence surrounding us. We don't talk, but it feels nice not to walk alone, the heady smell of jasmine in the air. Micah is already at the school, lying on the grass next to his bike, looking at the stars. He hops up when he sees us.

"What's this? A visitor?"

"Yes, but to what, I'm still not sure," Alice says, looking from me to him and back again. "What's this all about?"

Micah opens his arms wide.

"This? Why, this is the nightly meeting of the GPRH!"

"The what now?" Alice says.

"The guerrilla poets of Ridgeline High!"

I lower Micah's arms. "The name's a work in progress."

"I've said it before, dear Lily. We are *all* a work in progress." He smiles at me, and it sets off a storm of butterflies in my stomach. We haven't really talked since our date-not-date or addressed the way our bodies swayed together, or how every time I close my eyes, I can still feel him against me.

"Wait," Alice says, looking at the chalk in Micah's hand. "*You're* the anonymous poets?"

"How do *you* know about that?" I ask.

"Ridgeline Underground, of course. A girl's gotta keep up on the local gossip."

Micah elbows me. "See. We're famous."

I shake my head. "Nope. Nope. Nope. Not famous. *Anonymous*. And that's how it has to stay. Agreed?" I turn a finger to Micah and then Alice, waiting for each to nod in agreement.

"Well, whatever. I just can't believe it's you guys," Alice says. "Who writes the poems?"

"I do."

"*You* do?" She leans back slightly, eyes narrowing like she doesn't quite believe it. "Huh."

Micah holds up the bucket of chalk. "Shall we?"

He's also brought a bunch of magnetic poetry strips to scatter anywhere they'll stick. Alice goes to scope out magnetic hot spots while Micah and I start on the chalk outside the front doors, since our original art has faded away. I write my latest poem about Alice saving me in the ocean—*Through the waves she reaches me*—while he draws two hands clasped together.

"So about the other night," he says, clearing his throat. "I don't usually make a habit of slow dancing with my project partners."

I focus intently on the chalk pressing into the pavement as he continues.

"And maybe it was nothing, and I definitely don't want to misread signals again, but for a second there, it felt like—I don't know—it felt like *something*."

He scans my face.

"Or maybe . . ." He clears his throat again, looking away from me. "Or maybe we were just high on art and had a moment of artistic indiscretion?"

He says this like a question. One I'm supposed to answer. And the answer is that it was NOT a moment of indiscretion—it was a moment of truth. I know what friendship feels like, and this is not it. You don't know the outline of your friends' jawlines, or feel a jolt when you see his name on your messages. You're not aware of *exactly* where a friend's body is in relation to yours, and you definitely don't lie in bed replaying the hungry way he said your name in the dark, the voracious way he looked at your lips.

But that's not part of the Plan.
You have to focus
for your family
your future.

So even though I want to tell him I felt a spark in the darkness, too, I don't. I can't.

"Totally an art high," I say. "Bad case of guerrilla poets gone wild."

"Totally," Micah says. I know his face too well to believe it.

Alice returns, clearly sensing the awkward tension, but she

launches into a full report on bleachers and light poles where the magnetic poetry will stick. She watches as I finish my poem.

and I can breathe again

"It's about us," I say. "About that day at the beach? When we swam out too far?"

Alice nods. "And when we made it back to shore, Dad hugged us so hard, we almost broke."

"He probably wanted to kill us for going out so far. But you were fearless, making up stuff about being explorers."

She smiles absently, as if she's caught up in a memory of her own.

"I don't remember feeling all that fearless." She surfaces from her memory and looks around the school grounds. "So you only do it outside?"

"Mostly, and usually at night."

She studies the school building, and for the first time since she got home, she has a true Alice spark in her eyes.

"What if I knew a way in? I mean, wouldn't it be totally badass to take your guerrilla poetry inside?"

Micah shakes his head. "No way."

"Hold up, hold up," I say, my brain zapping with possibility, the same way it did when I first got this whole random-acts-of-poetry idea. "If we go in, we could do something big. Like a guerrilla take-over."

"Lil—"

But before either of us can say any more, Alice is off, running toward the school. She disappears around the side of the building, and then reappears on top of the roof thirty seconds later.

"It's open!" Alice's voice reverberates in the night. She beckons us from the roof, her eyes lit up so bright, I can see them from here.

Micah stares at me. "Your call, Larkin."

I think out loud, half trying to convince Micah, and half myself.

"Something like this could be just what we need to win."

Plus, Alice is looking down at me, eyes wide. She looks alive and wild like the Alice from my memories.

"I know it's crazy," I say. "But then again, who isn't a little nuts in the Hundred Acre Wood?"

Micah looks at me again, trying to act stern, but the upturn of his lips gives him away.

Part of me thinks this is the worst idea ever. But another part of me, one that is making my heart race, wants to go on another adventure with my big, brave sister.

I toss the chalk into the bucket.

"Let's do it."

chapter 28

Alice claps excitedly as we climb the metal ladder on the side of the school. She's standing on the edge of the flat roof, holding open a huge service hatch.

"And you knew about this how?" I say as we scale down the rabbit hole on an even tinier ladder.

"It's how all the seniors get in for their pranks," Alice says. "The janitor leaves it unlocked for his secret smoke breaks."

We come out in the boiler room. The massive equipment heaves and belches and hisses.

"The underbelly of Ridgeline High," Micah says like we're on a horror show. "What torrid tales this room could tell. Naughty children being tortured. Librarians making out with janitors. Terrified freshmen hiding from wedgies."

Alice laughs. The sound of it calms me. Stops me from turning around. From slipping out of my body.

We exit into a dark and deserted senior hallway. Our footsteps echo against the walls.

"Creepy," I whisper.

"It doesn't even feel like the same place," Micah says.

Without all the people, it seems less, somehow. Less daunting, less chaotic, less final without the teachers and the tests and the shoulds and should-bes taking up all the oxygen. Alice's fingers beat out a dum-dum-dum rhythm as she drags them against the lockers, rattling the locks.

"Everything seems so small," she says.

"You've only been gone a year," I say. "It's a little soon for a nostalgic montage of your youth."

"A year and a lifetime," she says. "And it's definitely not nostalgia. I hated this place."

"I think you're supposed to hate high school. It's like a rule," Micah chimes in. "The only ones who like it are the kids who are peaking at seventeen, and that's just interminably sad."

"Besides," I add, turning to Alice, "in case you forgot, everybody *loved* you in high school. Girls, guys—especially the guys, as I recall. Trust me, I know. I was the little sister to wild, popular, funny Alice Larkin with the best smile in the senior class. She's a hard act to follow."

She stops for a second, looking back at the empty hallway. "Smiles can hide a lot."

Micah finds a switch, and light floods the hallways, filling all the dark spaces. My stomach tightens when I notice the security camera in the corner.

Micah follows my eyes. "You want to turn back?"

I shake my head. "We're already in. Might as well do what we came to do."

"Who *are* you tonight?" Micah asks.

I shrug, trying not to smile.

We get to work covering the school with words. On each classroom window, I write a poem in dry-erase marker. Alice writes prompts on bathroom mirrors:

I wish . . .

I won't . . .

I want . . .

Micah draws sketches on whiteboards.

We make our way around the building, leaving a stream of words and art in our wake. When we get to the main lobby, I pause, the muse whispering in my ear. Every student passes through this lobby at least once a day. Walks past the enormous eagle-mascot painting on the wall and the oversized poster spelling out the school rules with a cheesy acronym: SOAR—Safety, Optimism, Accountability, Respect. *Keep your hands to yourself. Use your words. Speak in inside voices.*

"Micah," I say. "You don't happen to have access to some black paint, do you?"

He looks at the poster, and without a word, he takes off down the hall toward the art room. He comes back with brushes, jars of paint, and a huge roll of paper and tape.

"Alice, help me." I toss her a paintbrush and show her which words on the poster I want to keep. Then we black out everything else. Micah tapes up the paper next to us on the wall and gets to work on his own idea, which turns out to be two massive eagle wings rising out to the left and right, with just enough space between them for a person.

When I'm done blacking out words, Micah reads what's left.

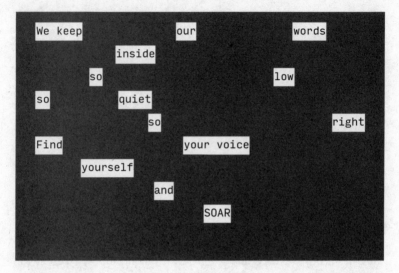

We keep   our   words
          inside
      so   low
so   quiet
              so   right
Find   your voice
    yourself
        and
              SOAR

Micah adds one more touch to his painting, writing, *SAY SOME-THING* between the wings and *#mywords #mystory* below them.

"What?" he says with a Valley girl accent and a flip of his hair. "You *have* to have a tagline. Everyone who's anyone on the interwebz has one."

"But we are not *on* the interwebz," I remind him.

"Not yet."

He tapes more paper all around the lobby, plenty of space for everyone in the school to *say something.* When he goes to return the supplies, Alice flips through my notebook.

"You really wrote these?"

"Yep."

"I had no idea."

"Yeah, well, that's kind of the Larkin family way."

"Well, they're . . ." She pauses.

Ridiculous?

Frightening?

Insane?

"Brave."

I exhale.

"Don't get me wrong," she says. "They're also super dark and twisty, but I wish I could put myself out there like that."

The far-off hallway light haloes her hair, which has grown out a little since she first came home. It's not traditional-Alice wild yet, but it's getting there.

"Hello? You've always been the brave one."

She scoffs. "Right. What is it I'm supposedly doing right now? A work-study project? I'm hiding in my own life."

She shakes her head like she's shaking off the thought, and holds up my notebook. "So, these monsters?" She points to the poem I wrote about the voices in my head. "Did they get worse after— I mean, when you"—she pauses, swallowing hard—"found me that night?"

"Yes." My voice is small, the images leaping to my mind, fresh and raw. Alice's blood. *Help me.* I don't know how.

She starts to say something, but stops, tugging the sleeves of her shirt down farther over her wrists. She picks up a pen and writes on the paper next to the eagle.

I'm sorry

Then she whispers, "I wasn't trying to kill myself, you know."

Her voice falters a little, but then her words come out in a rush, like they've broken a barrier. "I just wanted to feel something. Something real. I saw the razor and I was so numb, and when I cut into myself, it felt—better."

She laughs, but it sounds forced—fake—as it echoes in the empty hall.

"That probably sounds crazy, huh?"

205

I touch my scarred stomach. All the times I've dug into my body, made myself bleed. For what? A distraction? A release? A momentary fix. Something, anything, to quiet the voices in my head.

"Not crazy at all."

She sighs heavily. "It's just, sometimes I feel so big. Like my body can't contain me. Other times, so small I could disappear. Too big, too small, and sometimes, too nothing at all. It's exhausting, you know, never fitting in your own skin."

She groans. "There I go again, making it all about me. What I'd really love is to not have it be about me for one freaking second. And I know I haven't been much of a big sister lately, but I'm feeling more like my own self every day."

"Just like that?" I ask.

"Not exactly." We start walking down the dark hallway to meet Micah. "Can you keep a secret?"

I nod.

"I stopped taking my medicine."

I pause midstep. "Alice—"

"Don't do that. Don't do the voice."

"What voice?"

"The Alice-you're-being-an-idiot voice." She turns to me, her eyes boring into mine. "The meds were killing me, Lily. Maybe not all at once, but pill by pill, I was disappearing."

"What do your doctors say?"

"Those doctors don't know what I need. *I* know what I need. I know my own body, and it wasn't working."

"I have to admit, you do seem more you lately."

"I am. I really am. I'm getting better."

"Well, that makes two of us," I say, and it sounds exactly like the

206

truth. No recent panic attacks. I haven't woken up with blood on my fingers since our first night of guerrilla poetry.

"Promise me you won't tell Dad about the meds?"

"Alice, I—"

"Promise me," she says sternly. "He just wants me to be better, and this *is* better for me. I *know* it is. So promise me."

She looks at me like she did when we were young, swapping secrets beneath the covers.

"Fine," I say, even though in my gut I know I'm being stupid. "But same with my poems."

Alice crosses her heart, buttons up her lips, and kisses her fingers like when we were little. She loops her arm through mine and we walk down the dark hallway together. For an instant, we're two fearless explorers again making our way in the world with nothing but each other. And even though that world may be crumbling around us, for a moment, we are not bloodstained floors and scars peppering my stomach. We are matching Hello Kitty lunch boxes and snuggles before bed and frolicking in frothy waves. We are limitless possibilities and invisible worlds unfolding before us.

We are whole.

When we've sufficiently guerrilla-poetried the crap out of Ridgeline High, we head back to the boiler room. We crawl up the small ladder, and barely make it out onto the roof before a loud, male voice barks at us from the sidewalk below.

"Hey! You! You can't be up there."

Micah mutters obscenities as he ushers us to the ladder on the side of the building. We fly down, stepping on each other's fingers as we go, and hit the ground as the security guard turns the corner of the building. We barely make it to Micah's bike, with the guard yelling at us to stop, but Micah hops on and Alice sits on the handlebars while I run alongside, and we zoom out of the parking lot, leaving the poor guy doubled over in the dark.

Alice laughs, and I'm laughing, too, and Micah is whooping into the night.

And my brain is firing a million little zaps through my body. *Aren't we happy? Aren't we normal?*

Micah winks at me as I run, and even though my heart is in my throat and my lungs are gasping for air, I'm here and Alice is here and our laughter fills the dark spaces.

I wake to Alice's phone in my face.

"Say 'Good morning,' Lily!"

"Too early," I say, rolling over and covering my face with the comforter.

I don't know how Alice is this bright-eyed at seven a.m. after last night, talking about a new idea that is apparently going to "change everything."

"It's because of *you*, Lil!"

I force my body out of bed and head to the bathroom. Alice follows me, still talking while I brush my teeth.

"I just keep thinking about the guerilla poetry. How you put it all out there. And how that's so brave, and I have all these thoughts and feelings that I never share, and like, how sad is that? And so I was thinking about your poems and what's going on in your brain, and how I never talk about what happened to me, and the point is—" She takes a big breath. "I don't want to hide anymore."

I spit into the sink.

"And the videoing comes in where?"

"I'm starting a YouTube channel! Gonna talk about Fairview. About being bipolar. All of it."

"You know people watch YouTube, right? Like, real, live people."

"Yeah. That part is slightly, all-consumingly terrifying, but like Micah says, it's not brave if you're not scared."

I point to the paint samples scattered across her desk. "Maybe you should finish the redecorating before your YouTube career?"

Alice laughs like I'm hilarious. "I can do both! I'm an excellent multitasker." She's gone back into the room now, and I can hear her plucking posters and décor from the walls. "Maybe the redecoration will be my first video! I mean, home decor isn't really about mental health, but people always love a good before-and-after montage, right?"

Alice pops her head into the bathroom, scaring the snot out of me.

"Oh!" she half shouts. "And text me. I want to know how everyone responds to the guerrilla takeover! Man! What a rush. Are we going again tonight? I can bring my video camera!"

"No cameras," I say. "Anonymous, remember?"

"Right. Right. You're the boss. But I want in!"

She's off again, humming from the bedroom as she continues prepping the walls for the seafoam green. In the medicine cabinet, her nearly full bottle of pills stares back at me. Maybe she's right: she's better off without them.

And I'm better, too.

Aren't I?

My skin is starting to heal, and I'm not up Googling all night, and I haven't even posted on my Word of the Day in forever because I'm writing poetry instead.

At night, when the thoughts are circling, I pull out my pen.

I get the words out.

And the monsters get a little quieter.

And the random acts of poetry are a hit, which means I'm that much closer to UC Berkeley and the win my family needs. And Alice is becoming more Alice every day. We're almost normal again.

Things are definitely getting better.

Ridgeline High is awash in words. Ours, plus more, so many more. The white paper in the lobby slowly fills throughout the day:

I wish my parents were still together. I'm in therapy. Nobody sits with me at lunch. I love Meredith Iorg. I hate the way I look. Someday I'll travel the world. John Dougherty is a manwhore. I cry at chick flicks. Does God even exist?

Gifford is beside herself.

"It's wonderful," she says, and I swear she gets a little misty-eyed. "To be surrounded by words. Just wonderful! But, guerrilla poets, whoever you are, one word of warning. Principal Porter is concerned that these random acts of poetry are bordering close to vandalism. I pointed out that no actual school property was harmed besides a poster, and I've offered to buy a new one. Push the boundaries, my dear poets, but don't overstep."

She looks in my direction so briefly that I'm sure no one else catches it, but I do.

She knows.

I wonder if Principal Porter personally reviewed the security footage tape with her. Did she convince him to look the other way in the name of art? I make sure to give her an extra-big smile on my way out of class.

"Just wonderful," she whispers so that only I can hear.

Even Sam is caught up in it.

"Let's go add something," she says, pulling me by my sleeve toward the lobby before track practice. She plucks two pens from her backpack and hands me one, then starts writing in an open space under Micah's SAY SOMETHING.

"Such a cool idea," she says as she draws a small violin. Next to it, she writes: *sometimes I want to smash my violin to pieces.*

"You do *not*," I say, not sure if I should laugh or take her to the counselor's office. Sam has played violin since we were in elementary school. I can't even picture her without her black case in tow.

She shrugs. "It's a love-hate relationship. I love playing it, or at least I used to, but I hate that it's taken over my life. Between practicing for my solo and track and homework, I have zero social life. Not like you're ever free lately anyway." She nods toward her violin case. "But yeah, sometimes I fantasize about just going all rock star and smashing this puppy into a million little pieces. Except my parents would just buy me a new one and ground me for life, so it's not a totally solid plan."

She nods to the blank space in front of me. "You didn't write anything."

"Oh, I—"

She lifts up my hand with the pen and laughs. "You can do it, Anxiety Girl. It's not *actual* graffiti. You won't get in trouble."

Micah walks past just then, giving me his signature *we've got a secret* grin, and I guess now we do. I know some of his. He knows some of mine. And we share the guerrilla poets.

Sam elbows me, bringing me back to the crowded hallway.

"People are talking about you two, you know."

"About who two?"

"You and Micah." She click-clicks her pen and sticks it behind her ear. "I told people there's nothing going on, because if there were, I'd definitely know about it."

"Who are these *people*?" Probably Damon. Probably started spreading rumors the second he saw me jump away from Micah in the hallway weeks ago.

"Just people. Dumb gossip." She picks up her violin case, and we walk to practice. "You know, if there were something between you two, you could tell me, right? I'm Sam, best friend extraordinaire, remember? I don't care what people say about him, only what *you* say about him, but if you *do* have some secret love affair and don't let me live vicariously by sharing every juicy detail, then I *will* be pissed. 'Cause if my parents have their way, the only relationship I'll ever have is with Tchaikovsky."

"I hear those Russians can be wild in bed," I say, because I'm nothing if not a master of deflection, and what I'd really love right now is to take all the attention off me, especially when I'm standing in a hallway surrounded by my words while simultaneously being totally unable to tell my best friend that they're mine, or even something as simple as how I feel about Micah, how I feel when I'm with him.

When I look back, Micah's standing with his art posse across the lobby, writing on the paper like he wasn't the one who hung it there. It's better this way. Him in his world. Me in mine. And us? We're in a good place. We're over the awkwardness of the hallway jump-away. We're killing this project. Why mess with it?

Micah and I add more words and art all week.

We do it in broad daylight this time, leaving small random acts of poetry throughout the school when no one's looking. Post-it notes with small sketches surreptitiously stuck around the school. Index cards with poems slipped into locker slats. I even pen a short and admittedly terrible haiku in Spanish and tack it to the NOTICIOS bulletin board.

Micah brings more magnetic poetry and slaps it onto the lockers casually as he walks down the hall. We do it quietly, slowly, so no one knows it's us, but over one week, we've scattered random acts of art and poetry through the school.

And we're not the only ones. People write words and poetry on the windows. Leave small sketches on the whiteboards. In the halls, rhyming couplets and long strands of magnetic poetry materialize, along with the occasional *blow me* imbecility, the letters constantly rearranging into something new.

In the girls' bathroom, someone has written messages on the mirrors:

you are beautiful
you are unique
you are loved

During one of our last in-class artist-poet collaborations, the other partnerships are buzzing with rumors of the identity of the guerrilla poets. Micah and I are sitting on the floor of the art room because

Friedman has decided we all need to give his junk-to-masterpiece theory a whirl.

"Just thrown out. Can you believe it?" Friedman says after showing us a Frankenstein-level atrocity he's made out of a broken guitar and a busted lamp.

I'm creating some sort of microwave-utensil mash-up, while Micah's scrolling something on his phone. He turns his screen so I can see: in little digital squares, pictures of all the poetry people are making or finding. Snippets of random acts written under a desk. Sidewalk chalk drawings. A row of books in the library, their spines lined up to create a short and sweet poem:

THE HATE U GIVE
EVERY LAST WORD
I'LL GIVE YOU THE SUN
ALL THE BRIGHT PLACES
EVERYTHING, EVERYTHING

Each picture is tagged with #mywords #mystory.

"You're a hit," Micah whispers.

"*We're* a hit," I correct him. "And we're hardly viral."

"Maybe not, but look at these comments."

He holds up the latest Ridgeline Underground, where someone has posted a picture of my blackout poem in the lobby.

13 comments

THIS. So much this.

Wow. Get out of my head, guerrilla poet!

Love this. Give me more!

"Are those all from secret accounts you have or something?" I ask.

"Nope. These are bona fide people, reading *your* words." He puts down his phone and picks up a couple of cheap forks from the pile of junk. "So. Would you say the method was a success?"

"Definitely. I'll be posting my Yelp review tonight."

"Excellent. So then this is the part where I get to say I told you so, right?"

"Only if you're sure you want to play the jackass card this early."

Micah taps a fork to his chin. "Nah. I'll save it."

"For what?"

"For when we win."

"We?" I say. "I thought you weren't making too many plans for the future."

"And that is still my official party line," he says. "But I may or may not have looked into some art programs."

"And what, may I ask, caused this change of heart?"

He leans in close, pretending to reach for something in the junk pile, his breath tickling my skin just like it did in the motion-sensor room at the art exhibit. And just like then, all my own plans become a blur because all I can see are his lips.

"Word on the street is that Lily Larkin, perfect student extraordinaire, broke into the school, plastered her deepest fears on the walls. I can't just let her be the only brave one, now, can I?"

"No, you definitely cannot."

The same electric energy pulses between us as on the beach, drawing in chalk at night, standing on the cliff.

"Am I interrupting something?" Kali's voice drives us apart.

"Just some project planning," Micah says, bending one of his forks against the edge of a desk.

Kali looks from him to me and back again, trying to figure us out. She's probably heard the same rumors Sam has.

"Well, we're all just going for second place at this point anyway, right? Like anyone could beat these freaking guerrilla poets. 'Ooh, look at me, I wrote on the walls.' It's all so juvenile, and honestly, I'll tell them right to their faces when they turn in their project."

Micah scoffs. "I'm sure your disapproval will break their hearts."

Kali huffs as she walks away, and Micah chuckles again to himself, but stops midlaugh when he sees my face. "Whoa. What's up? You look like you're about to have one of those panic attacks you don't have."

"I guess—I guess I just never really thought about what happens when we have to turn the project in." I lean in close to Micah to whisper. "Everyone will know it's us. They'll know the poetry is mine. They'll *know.*"

"And this is just occurring to you now?"

In the back of my head, I knew there was a deadline, a moment when all this anonymity would end, but I was so eager to get my muse back, to win, that I didn't think it through.

"Maybe Gifford will let us turn it in but not share it. We could convince her the anonymity is part of the whole idea?"

Micah raises his hand, and I tug at his sleeve, whispering for him to "Stop. Never mind. It's a bad idea." But Friedman nods at him, and Micah asks—*in front of everybody*—if anonymous submissions are allowed.

Friedman and Gifford exchange a glance across the classroom, and then shake their heads.

"As Matisse says, 'Creativity takes courage,'" Friedman says. "So

217

I'm afraid not, Mr. Mendez. Once created, art belongs to no one—and everyone."

Micah shrugs at me. "Well, there you go."

"What the hell was that?" I whisper to him, scanning the room to see if anyone is looking. "Are you *trying* to out us?"

Before Micah can answer, Damon walks behind him, discreetly dropping a putty knife from the supply closet into Micah's lap. As he walks back to his seat, Damon makes wrist-slashing motions to Micah. I fight the urge to huck my microwave at Damon's head.

"When did he start pulling this crap again?" I ask.

"Never stopped." Micah tosses the putty knife into the junk pile. "In fact, there's been an uptick in his efforts ever since he saw you and me in the hall that day."

"Micah, I had no—"

"It's fine," he says, waving off my concern.

"It's not *fine*, Micah. You need to tell someone."

He ignores me, focusing extra hard on whatever he's doing with the tines of his bent forks. "Trust me. Better to lay low." He holds up his creation, the forks wrapped around each other, tines overlapped so that they look like two hands clasped together, the handles curving into a heart above them.

"How do you do that?" I ask.

"What?"

"*See* things like that."

He shrugs. "I don't know. I just see what something could be instead of what it's been." He puts his pointer fingers to his temples and closes his eyes. "Like right now, I'm seeing you and me, standing in front of everyone, telling them we are the guerrilla poets. They applaud. They carry you on their shoulders! They worship you as the poet queen!"

"Micah!" I almost yell. "You seriously want me to spew my most personal secrets to strangers, and you won't even tell anyone that Damon is straight-up harassing you?"

"Touché." He hands me the fork heart. "But where's all your bravery from the night we broke in?"

I toss the microwave back into the pile of junk. I can't see the potential in used-up appliances like Micah can. Across the room, Damon's banging together two pieces of junk from the pile, looking particularly apelike. Part of me wants to strangle him for tormenting Micah. The other part wants to make sure he never knows that *I'm* the girl with the monsters in her head. The thought of everyone knowing makes me want to rip into the still-healing scabs on my stomach.

"But that was at night, with no one around. I'm a different Lily there. I'm—I'm guerrilla poet Lily—and in the daytime, in front of everyone, I lose her."

Micah grabs my phone from next to me, flips open the calendar, and taps a few times. He turns the screen to me. POETRY PROJECT DUE is in big, bold letters.

"Well, then, according to the almighty planner here, you've got about two and a half weeks left to find her."

Unspoken Haiku

Just behind my ribs
deep by my heart, lies a trove
of words unspoken.

I hide my scars, too,
because no one wants to see
the truth that is me.

Will they want to stay
if they see the wounds and hear
all the words I keep?

The Ridgeline Underground

220 likes

These random acts of poetry are amazing! It's about time we had some positive messages in this school and on this hell site.

85 comments

I wrote, like, four magnet poems today!

Seriously. So awesome.

Yeah, but also kind of sad that everyone has all these secrets!

Right? Someone wrote in the lobby that they have an eating disorder no one knows about.

So sad :(I wish people felt safe sharing that kind of stuff.

I know! And also, has anyone thought about how whoever is writing the poems is kind of messed up?

That shit is dark

I just want to hug them! When they turn in their project, I will!

Hug them? I want to get them some help.

Definitely mental.

And you wonder why no one shares, assholes.

1:30 am

LogoLily: Have you seen the Underground?

100-acre-wood: Imbeciles.

LogoLily: *This* is why no one can know.

100-acre-wood: As someone who is no stranger to the public lashings on the Underground, I assure you, it's not so bad.

LogoLily: They'll crucify me.

100-acre-wood: Lily. Those words are yours. Be proud of them. Be proud of what we've done.

LogoLily: I am.

100-acre-wood: Then stop hiding.

chapter 30

The rumors roll on. The Ridgeline Underground is full of speculation about the true identity of the guerrilla poets, and it's not pretty. Someone posts a list of the top five students most likely to commit suicide. Micah makes the cut. Someone else makes a mock GoFundMe to collect donations for therapy for the poets once they're revealed. It's a mental-health witch hunt.

On my bed, I scroll through all the accusations while Margot recites multiplication facts from the math flash cards she's spread on the floor, and Alice plays YouTube videos as research for her new channel. I'm glad she's returning to the land of the living and all, but with her videos and shuffling the furniture around for her redecoration extravaganza, she's been nonstop since she joined us as an honorary guerrilla poet.

I end up on the UC Berkeley summer English program site. Maybe I don't even need this sponsorship. I could just not turn anything in, and no one would know I'm one half of the infamous guerrilla poets. I'd apply on my own, and I'm sure Dad would pay for it if it means I could be a Golden Bear. And I'd still make the connections, get that leg up on admission.

But you'd fail the project.

And so would Micah.

I slam my computer shut. Between the noise of Alice and the noise in my head, I need to get out.

I need to run. But that's a big, fat no—I'm trying to *calm* my body, not induce a panic attack. I turn to the almighty Google yet again, hoping to find something that can actually stop the chaos in my brain. What I find is—drumroll, please—yoga.

Depression? Try yoga!

Panic attacks? Yoga, baby!

Hangnail? Yoga with a goat!

So, instead of running, I find myself standing outside Staci's bedroom door in hot pursuit of peace. When I walk in, she's lunging in a particularly commanding position, one hand pointing toward the back wall, the other pointing at me, her eyes focusing down the length of her arm.

"Warrior pose," she answers without me asking. "The ancient warrior Virabhadra stood like this as he drew his sword to cut off his enemy's head."

"I thought yoga was about inner peace," I say, inching into the room. I haven't spent much time in here since Dad and Staci became newlyweds last year. Which means sex. And lots of it. So I've avoided the place where all the magic happens because, well, eww.

Bachelor Dad's only décor was books, dog-eared and coffee-ring-stained. Now there's fresh flowers in a tall vase on the nightstand. The room smells like orange blossoms, and the bed is not only made but has six bedazzled throw pillows on it.

Staci has turned the corner of the room into her own mini yoga studio, with an essential oil diffuser on the dresser and a mat in front of a mirror. She shifts her arms, stretching them toward the ceiling.

"Sometimes," she says between long, loud breaths, "you have to fight for peace."

Her steady in-and-out breathing fills the room as she stands up straight, brings her hands together in front of her chest like she's praying, and does a small bow to the mirror, before turning to me.

"What's up?"

"Oh. Well. I—" I stumble over my words because I've never actually asked Staci for anything before, a fact I've prided myself on since she moved in and took over the nightstand and the pantry and Dad. "Could you maybe, uh . . . teach me?"

"What? Yoga?" She does a double take.

"Yeah."

She wastes no time getting me onto the mat, showing me how to dip my head down and butt up in something called a Downward Dog, while plinky-plunky rain sounds play on her phone.

"Now, breathe in through your nose, pulling the air deep into your lungs," she says. My chest cracks open when the air fills it. "Let go of all the bad; inhale only good. Clear your mind. Focus on your breath. Your body. Listen to what the silence is telling you."

But the silence only leaves gaps for my brain to go wild (like full-on parents-out-of-town kegger). It replays all the Underground rumors about the guerrilla poets.

Dark.

Messed up.

Mental.

Thankfully, my hands are holding me up, so I can't claw at my side, even though all I want to do is rip into myself. Quiet the monsters by picking myself clean.

After a thirty-minute session where I fall over at least five times, we namaste and bow, and she crouches down to roll up her mat.

"You okay? You've seemed a little, I don't know, in your head lately."

"Got a lot going on at school."

"I'm here, you know." She turns off the diffuser and the rain sounds. "If you ever need to talk. Whatever you're going through, you don't have to go through it alone."

Then she hugs me, which is kind of gross because she's in a tank top and sweaty, but I let her and I nod like I understand, but here's the thing: I *am* alone. I'm the only one who can hear the monsters, feel the panic. I'm the only one who can feel the urge to pick at myself drumming through me like an unstoppable rhythm. When the problem's in your head, no one can carry it but you.

Around midnight, Dad notices me pacing around the house.

"What's up, Lily pad?" he says from his office.

"Can't sleep."

"Must be something in the water. I can't seem to turn off the old noggin, either." He opens his drawer and holds up a small white medicine bottle. "Don't know how I'd function without these babies."

He pours a blue pill into his hand, pops it in his mouth, and chases it with water.

"Now, this Berkeley summer program? Did you say it was paid for?"

"Yeah. Why?"

226

He thumps his pen on the lip of his desk, looking at his computer screen.

"Just doing some budgeting." He says this with a smile, the kind meant for my benefit, but Dad's not that good an actor. His pen taps the desk and his leg vibrates the floor—whap-whap-whap. Dad pinches the top of his nose, right between his eyes. It's a gesture he's done a thousand times—when he's grading a particularly terrible paper or worrying about Alice.

"Is something wrong?"

"Nothing your old man can't handle." He plops a stack of papers into his top drawer, closes it, and then adds, smiling, "But I wouldn't say no to a scholarship."

He turns off the computer, stretches out his arms wide with a yawn, tilting back in his office chair. "And luckily, I happen to be the proud dad of the most talented kid at that school." His voice is back to its normal, steady assurance as he stands up and puts his arm across my shoulders, pulling me into my spot. He flicks off the office light as we walk out. "Alice seems better, doesn't she?"

"Much."

"And you?"

"Good as ever."

As we leave the office, he squeezes my hand—once, twice, three times.

"Don't know what I'd do without you, kiddo."

Once I'm sure Dad's in his bed, I tiptoe back downstairs into his office and open his drawer. I flip through the papers, which are mostly printouts of online pages with titles like *Tips for Parenting a Bipolar*

Child and *Learning to Live After a Suicide Attempt.* Underneath, I find bills from Fairview with enormous dollar figures on the TOTAL DUE NOW line at the bottom.

No wonder Dad asked about scholarship money. Is this why Staci's working at the yoga studio again? Why Dad's teaching extra classes?

I don't know how he's affording it, but I do know this: my apply-to-Berkeley-on-my-own plan is out. I can't ask Dad to shell out more money right now, mostly because I know he'd find a way. Take on more classes. Work himself sick. Add more bills to his already over-filled drawer of worry.

I stuff everything back into the desk and creep upstairs. Alice is struggling to move her dresser out from the wall.

"Oh good," she says. "Help me?"

I step over the cans of seafoam green paint stacked in the middle of the room and pick up a corner of the dresser.

"Your multitasking is going to kill me," I say.

She just laughs, inching the dresser to where she wants it. "You'll thank me when our room is featured on HGTV."

Her plans for the room spill out. New shelving and two-tone paint and something called shiplap that apparently is all the rage. Suddenly I'm having flashbacks to all the other times she's re-decorated our room. Spoiler: it never ends well. Two years ago, we had a half mural of a tree on our ceiling that she abandoned after a few weeks. Then there was the time she plastered the wall with inspirational quotes from magazines. They fell off one by one when she moved on to her next big idea.

"How are you paying for all this?" I ask, mentally tabulating all the improvements she has planned.

"Dad. He said as long as it's making me happy and keeping me busy, open tab." She holds up a thin, silver MacBook. "Even bought me supplies for the YouTube channel."

She lowers the computer, and I feel the anger rising, just like it did when she stayed out past curfew. She says she doesn't want everything to be about her, but it is. It *always* is. This whole last year. And now she's spending Dad's money like it's going out of style, totally clueless that her Fairview visit (which didn't seem to do *anything*, by the way) has already drained us dry.

"Oh, unclench, Lil. I swear you and Dad are going to get your faces stuck like that one day."

"Stuck like what?"

"You know, your worry face." She tightens up her jaw and purses her lips in a ridiculously overdramatized way, and then busts out laughing.

"I do *not* do that." I relax my face muscles, which I didn't realized were tensed so tight.

"Seriously, though, you okay?" she asks.

"Fine."

But I'm not. Nothing's fine. Dad *needs* me to win this summer scholarship to make up for what Alice has cost us. But winning will cost something, too. Everyone will know, once and for all, the Lily I've worked so hard to hide.

1:30 a.m.
How did you not see this coming?
What exactly was your exit strategy here?

229

2:00 a.m.

You should have just done the project on your own
rather than finding your muse with Micah
or playing guerrilla poet.

2:20 a.m.

100-acre-wood: You up?

I don't message him back.

Instead, I lie in the dark, trying to figure out a way to keep my secrets while also winning this contest. After an hour of trying not to tear into my own skin while also ignoring the sound of Alice's YouTube research, I sneak back downstairs, take a blue pill from Dad's drawer, and swallow it.

Something—anything—to turn off the noise.

chapter
31

My fingers find my still-healing scabs in my sleep.

I wake with blood caked on my stomach and a pounding head-ache. When the sleeping pill finally kicked in, it hit me hard, so even though I slept for the first time in weeks, my body aches and my head is fuzzy.

"What's wrong with you?" Margot asks when I almost speed through a red light on the way to her school. I slam on the brakes and stick my arm out to stop her from flying forward. She's got her fingernail between her teeth, chewing off a hangnail.

"Just stressed."

Like I'm going to tell my ten-year-old sister the truth. *Guess what? Your second sister is losing it, and everybody is about to find out. Plus, bad news, Fairview cost a small fortune and Alice is using up what's left on projects she'll give up on in a week. Good luck at school today! Not that it matters one flying rat's ass.*

Instead, I slap on my everything's-going-to-be-fine face (I learned from the best, after all) and practically peel out when the light turns green. As I pull into the school drop-off lane, Margot tells me how the key to fighting a Dementor is something called a Patronus. "Alice *does* seem better, but we need a plan," she says. "Just in case the Dementors come back."

Without thinking, I tilt my head back on the headrest and groan. "Margot! Enough with the Hogwarts!"

My regret is immediate, as is the hurt on her face. "I'm sorry. I didn't mean that. It's just—let's talk about it after school?"

"If you have time," she says. "I know you're busy."

She hops out of the car and slams the door behind her.

I don't even see Micah coming.

I'm lost in my thoughts as I walk the hallway, when he comes out of nowhere, grabs my shoulders, and pushes me through an open door. I catch a flash of his smile before he slams the door behind us.

"This is it, isn't it?" I say in the darkness, which is can't-even-see-your-hand-in-front-of-your-face black. "This is the part where you kill me?"

Micah laughs. I tune into the sounds around me. His breathing. The sound of a boiler hissing nearby.

"Where are we?" I whisper.

"Janitor's closet."

"I don't think we're supposed to be in here." (As if there aren't enough rumors about us flying around already.)

"You didn't message me back last night."

"I know. I—"

"No worries," he continues. "It's better this way. I can tell you in person."

"Tell me what? What's going on, Micah? You're freaking me out."

He inhales deeply and takes my hand in the darkness, rubbing the side of my palm with his thumb, his touch setting my skin on fire.

"Artistic indiscretion?" I say, whispering now because whatever is happening here has sucked all the air out of my lungs. He moves closer to me, and my heart speeds up like it did on the cliff, dancing with him in the art exhibit, like it does whenever we're together, no matter how hard I try to deny it.

"Not this time." He erases any space between us. "A few days ago, I told you to stop hiding. But I've been hiding, too, because I'm scared to say how I really feel. Because I don't know if you feel the same, and we both know I've been wrong before, but I think you do. And what is all this about, this whole project, if not facing your fears? Putting yourself out there? I guess what I'm trying to say is, I know you're scared, and I'm scared, too, but I also know that if you let the world see the real you, they'd love her. Myself included."

Heat rushes to my face. "You did *not* just confess your love for me in a janitor's closet."

"I did not." His black curls graze my nose. "I confessed that I *know* you."

He takes my other hand in his and pulls me closer, and I let him, and our hands are intertwined and I can't see him in the dark but I've spent enough time trying not to think about him to know the curve of his jaw and the exact location of his lips. And he's holding me against him, chest to chest, cheek to cheek, and he smells like pencils and paint and beach and sunshine.

"You *know* me?"

My pulse speeds up as his breath warms my face. "I know you can rock a planner like nobody's business."

He presses his lips to my forehead softly.

"That you want to take care of everyone."

He brushes his mouth down my cheek.

"That you have a lot to say, even if you're scared to say it."

My other cheek.

"And you want to be perfect."

My nose.

"And you're funny."

His breath traces down my jaw.

"And smart. And already . . ." He pauses, his hand under my chin, his thumb pulling down my bottom lip slightly. "Perfect."

He's going to kiss me. I *know* this as surely as I've known anything in my life, and all my misgivings about him—about us—give way to the feel of his breath on my skin and the roller-coaster-drop feeling lurching inside me as he leans in.

And for all of two seconds, my mind is quiet, out-screamed by the sound of a thousand explosions erupting in my chest, my mind, in every nerve ending. His body presses into me, and his hands wrap around my waist. He tugs me even closer to him, his fingers hooked into the top of my jeans, and the tips of his fingers graze my skin.

The skin you picked in your sleep.

He'll feel the scabs.

What if he's not okay with all your secrets?

And just like that, the monsters worm back in.

What are you doing?!

234

More rumors is not *what you need right now.*

Are you seriously this much of an idiot?

THIS IS NOT PART OF THE PLAN.

I pull away.

"I'm sorry. I—"

I can only vaguely see the outline of Micah, but I can hear him exhale, hear him take a step away from me, too. He swears under his breath.

"I'm such an idiot," he whispers.

"No, you're not. I—"

"You're what, Lily? Because I thought—I thought you—"

"I do. I just—can't."

"Can't what?" His voice is louder now, with an edge I'm not used to. "What is it? What are you so afraid of?"

~~Everything?~~

~~Ev~~

~~er~~

~~y~~

~~thing.~~

~~That if I lose focus for one millisecond,~~

~~I'll let everyone down~~

~~and my crazy will be out there,~~

~~real,~~

~~clear and large and undeniable.~~

"This." I gesture between us, but he can't see me. "Us. The contest. I can't do any of this, Micah. I've been trying to tell you."

The silence in the darkness is unbearable.

After an eternity, Micah speaks. "Are you more scared of people knowing the poetry is yours, or that you have feelings for me?"

235

Why did you let it get this far?

"You don't get it, Micah. I'm the good one. The one who holds everything together. It's one thing to write these poems at night, when no one can see me. No one can know these are *my* thoughts. You've seen what they do to people on the Underground."

"Who cares what they think?"

"I care, Micah! *I* care. Aren't you listening? None of this is part of my plan. And now I find out, I *need* to win this summer sponsorship more than ever, but winning it means that Dad, everyone, will know I'm a mess, and I—I just should never have done any of this. I've worked too hard to hold everything together, and if people know about me, about my poetry, about us, I'll . . . I'll unravel. And so will my family. It's just not as easy for me as it is for you."

Even though I can't see him, I feel him pull farther away from me, feel the space between us grow wide.

"You think any of this is *easy* for me? Having you ignore me in the halls? Like we're super-secret friends no one can know about?" His voice wobbles. "Reading what they write about me on the Underground? Hearing what people say about me every single day?"

"But it's different for me, Micah. People like you—"

"I'm sorry. People like me?"

"That's not—what I mean is—"

"It's pretty clear what you meant," Micah says, his voice like poison. In the dark, I hear his hand turn the doorknob.

"Wait, wait, wait," I say. "This is coming out all wrong. I just mean, this is serious for me. I don't have time—"

He throws open the door. The light floods the room, illuminates the sharpness in his face that's turned him into someone I hardly recognize. But worse than the anger in his clenched jaw is the hurt in his eyes. The hurt I'm causing.

"You know, they say when people show you who they are, believe them the first time," he says, his eyes dead level with mine. "So, really, this is my fault. And you know what? *I* don't have time for people like *you*."

chapter
32

Micah's gone.

He's not at lunch with the Artists in their usual corner of the courtyard. I watch the door, willing Micah to walk through it. I imagine how I'll run up to him and tell him he's right, and I'm ready to tell everyone that the poetry is mine, their judgments be damned. And he'll be so proud of me, and maybe I'll be a little proud of me, too, and our classmates will hoist me onto their shoulders and parade me through the halls shouting, *Hooray, Lily Larkin, poet laureate of Ridgeline High!*

Of course none of that happens because (a) this is high school and no one applauds hypothetical epiphanies, and (b) I've screwed everything up.

Lily Larkin—destroyer of happiness.

Micah doesn't return all day. He's not in the halls. Isn't in the art room when I casually stroll by at the bell, although I'm not sure what I'm hoping for. That he'd be there, paintbrush in hand, thrilled to see me?

Oh, Lily, so glad you could come! I've totally forgotten what a mon-

strous B you were earlier. Let's draw! Let's create! Let's wander through the glory of our imaginations in search of your muse. Huzzah!

As I run the track after school, I watch the Artists leave together. No Micah.

When he's gone the next day, too, I check the 100-acre-wood so much during Spanish that I totally mess up an oral exam, which is awesome because I've already tanked a quiz in Spanish and one in math because my brain can't seem to focus on anything.

Sam sits with me during project collaboration. Her partner has taken over their entire project.

"I don't have time for it anyway, so if she wants to do all the work, fine by me," she says, nodding to her partner, who is painting some sort of modernist piece with sharp angles and bright colors that makes absolutely no sense. The other artists see me looking and whisper to each other.

Did you hear what she did to Micah?

Total cock tease.

Don't know why he's into her anyway.

Her?

Isn't that hilarious?

Principal Porter is here, too, talking hotly in the corner with Gifford and Friedman because people have started writing on the actual walls with permanent markers since the paper in the lobby is running out of space. Before he goes, Porter gives the class a stern warning about "taking things too far."

"While I wouldn't dream of interfering with the *artistic process*—" he says, with a look toward Gifford. Then, I swear he looks straight at me, and I scrunch down in my seat. "—acts of vandalism in any degree will *not* be tolerated. And our security cameras don't lie."

He totally knows it was you.

Even if you don't turn in the project, everyone could still find out.

I breathe in and out like Staci taught me, trying to unravel the knot of nerves in my stomach. Freaking Damon takes it upon himself to sit on the other side of me after Porter leaves, a smirky grin on his face.

"So, where *is* Señor Loco? Suicide watch?"

I burn holes into my paper, staring at it so hard, wishing he'd go away. When he doesn't, I reply without looking at him.

"Seriously, Damon, are you in some sort of competition to insult the most people with the fewest words?"

"What can I say?" He leans back, getting too comfortable in the chair next to me. "Your boyfriend just brings it out in me."

"He's not my boyfriend."

Not your anything.

"Not what *I* heard," he says.

"Well, you heard wrong."

Damon leans in closer but talks louder. "I heard you two were getting cozy in the janitor's closet."

Sam's eyes shoot to me.

"It was about the project." My words come out shaky. My face burns and my heart flip-flops in my chest. I breathe in and out slowly, trying to stall the panic.

Damon smirks again. "Riiiiiight." Then, with fake concern, he adds, "Just be careful. The guy's a menace."

I slam my notebook shut. Mercifully, the bell releases me and I shove my books into my backpack and wait for Sam outside the classroom door.

"Is it true?" she says as we walk side by side down the crowded hall, me searching for Micah, hoping to see his neon in the sea of normal.

"Is what true?"

"What Damon said."

"Damon's an idiot. Micah is *not* a menace."

Sam opens her locker and chucks her books in so forcefully, they clang against the back. "Not that." She pulls her violin out just as violently. "About you and him. In the closet."

"No. Well—yes."

Sam closes her eyes in exasperation. Magnetic poetry on the locker next to hers says DANCE IN THE RAIN, SING IN THE SUN.

"So which one is it?"

"Yes, we were in the closet, but it's not like—"

She puts up her hand to stop me. "You know what, Lil? Forget It. You don't want to share anything with me? Fine. Don't. But you can't have it both ways." She slams her locker, hoists her backpack on, and looks me square in the eye. "Either we're best friends or we're not. Do me a favor and make up your mind."

Ridgeline Underground

315 likes

Anyone else hear that Micah Mendez got suspended?

112 comments

Yeah. For stealing art supplies.

For banging a girl in the janitor's closet

I think it was Lily Larkin

No. Way.

chapter
33

The rumors spread like an ever-evolving virus through the student body. Sam basically ignores me for two days, and Micah doesn't re-surface at school.

They're both sick of your crap.

In the lobby, the word wall is still growing, people adding their words, their stories every day. But in the 100-acre-wood, silence.

I reread our last message thread. I don't type anything new. The last thing he wants is to hear from me.

You'll just end up hurting him more.

He'll be better off without you.

I fall asleep each night (thank you, magical little blue sleeping pills) replaying the way Micah looked at me in the closet, trying to understand me. But he can't. *I* don't even understand me.

And each morning, I wake to Alice going nonstop between her YouTube and redecoration projects. I mentally add up all the money she's spending.

"Good morning, sleepyhead!" Alice says one day, crouched by the baseboards of our room, armed with a spray bottle of disinfectant and a roll of paper towels.

"What's with the cleaning blitz?" I ask as she attacks a baseboard with a towel.

"I was going to start painting, or at least do the primer, but then I saw how nasty these baseboards were. Like, so gross. And I can't redecorate until this place is clean, like really, really clean."

"What time did you go to bed last night?" I ask.

She pauses, like she's doing a quadratic equation in her head. "I think I lay down for a little bit. But I honestly don't know if I ever actually slept."

She launches into a description of her latest video for her You-Tube channel—interviews and retrospectives and maybe even a tour of Fairview.

"If they'll let me. I bet they'll let me. Don't you think?" Her words spill out so fast and furious that I can't keep up. Partly because she's jumping from idea to idea, but partly because my own brain is elsewhere.

"Have you heard from Micah lately?" I ask, changing the subject and trying to sound like I didn't stay up half the night imagining worst-case scenarios involving cliffs.

Like he'd do that *over you.*

Alice shakes her head. "No, why?"

"He hasn't been at school."

"I wouldn't worry too much. He does this sometimes."

"Does what?"

"Disappears. At Fairview, we called it his depression cave. Just give him time." She looks at me like she's waiting for something else. "So what do you think?"

"About . . ."

"Are you even listening? My video ideas!" She points to a series of Post-it notes on the wall. "I had to start writing them down just to keep track."

The bright pink of the Post-it notes, lined on the wall like they used to be before the Night of the Bathroom Floor, makes all my other thoughts stop cold.

When did this *start again?*

"Are you feeling okay?" I ask, eyeing her cautiously.

"Never better."

Is she wearing the same clothes as last night?

How long has it been since she slept?

"Oh! That reminds me!" She jumps up to get something from her desk. "I found this under your bed."

She carries a box over to me and flips open the lid, revealing all the razors and pencil sharpeners and various don't-let-Alice-hurt-herself paraphernalia I hid away. She stares at me, waiting for an explanation.

"I—I was—"

~~Terrified.~~

She hands me the box as I stammer for words. "Keep 'em if it makes you feel better. But I mean it, Lil, you don't have to worry about me anymore."

She scuttles out of the room, leaving a whirlwind of energy and disinfectant in her wake. I want to believe her. She's better. I'm better. We're better. Right?

Isn't this what you wanted?

For Alice to be Alice again?

It's never enough for you, is it?

Still, the symptoms of bipolar mania tick through my head.

Decreased need for sleep.

She darts back into the room and grabs the blue painter's tape from the pile, jumps onto her desk, and yanks out a long strip where the ceiling meets the wall. Seeing her up there, her eyes wild with ideas, her words coming in a long, rambling string, makes my stomach tighten.

Increased activity and agitation.

My fingers start picking at a scab on my stomach.

No!

I'm not doing that anymore.

Normally I'd write something, but my brain can't focus on anything but the buzz of energy vibrating from Alice's direction. Or I'd message Micah, tell him how Alice is acting.

But he loathes you now.

I need something to stop my mind and fingers from turning on me.

"Can I help?" I ask.

She chucks a roll of tape at me and I tape around a light socket, but it ends up wonky. So I rip it off and start again.

And again.

And again.

"Doesn't have to be exact, you know." Alice laughs. It's too high, too shrill.

Unusually elevated mood.

I tell myself she's fine. She *has* to be. I just got her back. I can't lose her to the pills again.

I ignore the uneasy feeling in my gut, rip the tape off, and try it again.

Once, twice, six times.

Until it's perfect.

chapter
34

Four more days of silence in the 100-acre-wood. Four days of me watching Alice, trying to decide if she's careening toward disaster or just being Alice. Four days of people adding their secrets to the wall I created even though I'm too much of a coward to claim my own words or my feelings about Micah.

Alice says I'm brave, but I can't even bring the real Lily into the light.

It's also been four days of cold shoulders from Sam, who thinks I'm hiding some spicy janitor's-closet affair, when nothing could be further from the truth right now. At track practice, she's stretching before our scrimmage against the high school from Riverside. She straight-up ignores me when I lunge beside her.

"Sam," I say. "Come on. I'm sorry, okay? I promise there's nothing going on with Micah. It's just this contest. You know how important it is to me."

Sam doesn't look at me. "Yeah, well, I thought I was important, too."

"You are. Of course you—"

She turns to me now, her eyes a mix of anger and hurt. "You missed my concert."

"No, no, that's not possible. It's not until next week." I grab my phone from my bag to check my calendar. Right there, last night: *7 p.m.—SAM SLAYS HER SOLO!*

"Did you text me?" I ask.

"I shouldn't have to remind you about the most important night of my life."

"I know, I know." I'm out of excuses. I can't even tell her where my brain has been, because I haven't told her about Micah or the guerrilla poets or Alice acting strange again. "Things have been so crazy—"

~~I've been so crazy.~~

"Save it," she says, putting her palm up to me. "Don't give me the I've-got-a-lot-going-on speech. We've all got a lot going on. Do you even know that I've been up, like, every night, worried that if I miss a note or a beat or a millisecond of perfection, then I'll let everyone down? No, you wouldn't know that because you don't ask, because this friendship has become so one-sided, it's embarrassing. I told you the other day: either we're friends or we're not. Your choice is pretty clear."

"You're right, you're right. I'll fix it. When's your next concert?"

Sam yanks my phone away and tosses it forcefully onto my track bag. "I'm not an item on your to-do list, Lily. You shouldn't have to pencil me in."

And then she turns and joins a pack of senior girls running the warm-up lap. Maybe I should run after her, tell her everything that's going on in my head, and she'll take pity on me. Give me another chance. But she shoots me a *don't even try to make things right* glare from across the track, so I warm up alone, my brain racing.

You should have been there.

You should have told her

about Micah

about Alice

about you.

You should have been a better friend.

You should

should

should

have been better.

When my heat is called, I ignore the fluttery feelings behind my rib cage and line up on my spot. In autopilot, I dig my toes into the rubbery track and push my heel up against the starting block.

I close my eyes and try to center, envision myself bolting down the lane.

The race starts and time slows.

My body pushes off the block instinctively.

My thighs propel me forward with pure muscle memory. But my brain won't behave.

Sam hates you.

Micah hates you.

Your grades are down.

Your race times are up

and Dad's counting on a scholarship you're too chickenshit to win.

You're on quite the sucktastic roll, aren't you?

My mind focuses on the monsters a millisecond too long, and in that one millisecond, the girl on my right passes me. I dig in, trying to catch her. But she's a full body length ahead now, and my chest is tightening and the pulse in my neck is flip-flopping, and someone has dropped a sledgehammer onto my lungs.

I slip out of my body just in time to see her cross the finish line.

I see me finish fourth.

I see Coach's mouth moving at me. He wants to know what's going on in my head.

Well, Coach, what's going on is, my mom died when I was six and we lost our safety net, and then my big sister almost offed herself a few months ago. But now she's back, and she has pills she's not taking, and Dad has little blue pills that I'm taking, and maybe I should have my own pills, but I don't. Because I can't. Because pills mean you're sick. Broken. And I'm Lily. I win races. And scholarships, because apparently I have to win scholarships. But my brain is leaking, or maybe it's clogged with memories of Alice on the floor and the voices of monsters that never quit.

I see Coach telling me I'm *this close* to losing my spot in the qualifier.

I see me, nodding.

Me, walking away.

Me, alone.

I find myself inside the school, staring at a group of freshmen taking their pictures with Micah's eagle. The wings spread out on either side of them, transforming them into birds. All around them—around me—are words and art and pieces of truth. The pieces of themselves everyone has left here.

Because of *my* words.

Because of Micah.

251

Micah, who didn't care if I won or lost.

Who brought me into the 100-acre-wood, and knew my flaws—
and stayed.

But I pushed him away.

I pick up a pen someone has left on the floor by the word wall,
and find a small open corner, and write four words: *I'm tired of hiding*.

Then I turn and walk quickly, flanked by my words on the walls
as I head straight to the boy who helped me find them.

I end up on Micah's doorstep with a Hey-can-we-forget-everything-I-said? gift from the drugstore. Standing on his front porch now, his chalk drawings beneath my feet, I second-guess myself.

He doesn't want you here.

I breathe in through my nose.

Good in.

Bad out.

In.

Out.

The monsters quiet slightly. Not gone, but enough to let me knock.

Micah answers the door in sweatpants and his rumpled GOOD VIBES ONLY hoodie. His hair is matted against his head on one side, and his cheek bears deep blanket wrinkle lines. No whimsical socks today; he's stripped of his brightness.

He squints into the angled afternoon light, keeping the door semi-closed, his face expressionless.

"Yeah?"

He rakes his fingers through his hair, staring at the ground. I want to grab his face and make him look at me. Make me feel the electricity that lit up the dark of the custodial closet.

"I—I just needed to see you."

"No need to waste your time worrying about people like me," he says, the same edge to his voice. My heart sinks.

"Micah. I . . ." I pause. How do I make this better? "I'm sorry. I was a total jerk, and I probably shouldn't be here, but I need to know you're okay. Are you? Okay?"

"No."

"Oh. . . ."

"Is that not that answer you wanted?"

"No. Maybe. I don't know."

"Well, do you want the truth, or do you want to ask the question so you can check it off your list?"

I force myself to look at him, even though I'm embarrassed to be here and horrified at how I treated him and scared by the hurt in his usually bright eyes.

"I want the truth."

Micah leans against the doorframe, arms folded protectively across his chest.

"Well, the truth is, if I were okay, I wouldn't be asleep at four in the afternoon. I wouldn't have spent the last week in bed, trying to stay unconscious. I wouldn't have to muster every molecule in my brain to be having this conversation right now because looking at you makes me—"

He stops, like the thought of how I treated him hurts. It hurts me, too.

"So, no, I'm not okay, and if that makes you uncomfortable, then maybe you shouldn't be here."

He looks me in the eyes now, intensely, daring me to say something. Daring me to walk away.

"I—I don't know what to say. I don't even know why I'm here, exactly." I shush the voice in my head that's yelling at me to stop. To turn away. To leave before I screw this up like I do everything. "All I know is, I wish I could take back what I said, and all I've wanted all week is to see you, and I want to tell you some things that I should have told you already, and I know there's absolutely no reason for you to trust me, but if it's all right with you, I'd like to be with you. I'd like to stay."

Micah scratches his head, considering me as he uncrosses his arms. "I'm pretty shitty company right now."

"Perfect," I say. "That's kind of my entire brand."

Micah's gaze lands on my hand. "I'm sorry, but I cannot continue this conversation until I know: Is that a Bob Ross bobblehead?"

"Oh, yeah. For you." I hand him the box. He shakes it, bouncing Bob's head back and forth.

"This is the most amazing and strangest gift anyone's ever given me." His eyes are still dull, but the anger has softened somewhat. "Perhaps the perfect metaphor for us."

Us. My brain rolls the word. Polishes it until it sparkles.

"Well, I'm nothing if not strange," I say.

The corners of his mouth lift, only slightly, and he opens the door wider, leaning against it like he's half-annoyed, half trying not to smile.

"Well," he says. "You coming in or what?"

chapter
36

The inside of his house is dark, even though the sun is still sharp. The curtains are drawn and the house is quiet as I follow him down a tiled hallway into his room. His floor looks like a fast-food grave-yard, with empty cups and bags scattered across the floor. Yeah, a teenage boy has for sure been holed up in here for a week. He mutters an apology and clears away a small stack of dishes by his bed and a McDonald's bag on his floor before he takes Bob Ross out of the box. He pushes the audio button, and Bob dispenses a one-liner: "You have to have dark in order to show the light. Just like in life."

He puts Bob and his bobbling head on his nightstand next to the copy of *The Bell Jar* I gave him. When I flip it open to our blackout poem, I notice dog-eared pages.

"You're reading it?" I ask.

"It came highly recommended by this cool girl," he says. "We were working on this project together, but then she, like, grew horns and started breathing fire, so I'm not sure it's going to work out."

He smiles, but it's still strained. Still unsure.

"Well, I, for one, am a firm believer in second chances," I say. I'm putting the book back when I notice a bottle of pills—aspirin— sitting on a ripped piece of paper with scrawly handwriting: *Do us all a favor.*

I pick it up. "Micah—"

"A little love note from Damon," he says dismissively.

I shake the pill bottle. I knew he was an ass, but this is next-level asshattery.

"We have to tell someone. An admin or something."

He smirks like I'm a toddler announcing she wants a unicorn for Christmas. "Yeah, I'll get right on that."

"Seriously, Micah, this is not okay."

"And you think Principal Porter is going to believe the transfer kid with a history of violence who just skipped a week of school?" He chucks the pills and the note into a trash can. "Not a chance. Now, if you'll excuse me a second."

Micah heads back down the hall, and I can hear an electric tooth-brush whir to life, followed by the sound of gargling. While I wait, I pick a sketchbook up off a huge purple beanbag. On the open page, a wispy, black demon squats on top of a man, a natural extension of his shoulders.

"Much better," Micah says, coming back into the room, his hair somewhat tamed and his breath minty fresh. He plucks the sketch-book from my hands and flops backward onto his mattress, the bed-springs creaking beneath him.

"So shall we keep going with the small talk, or are you ready to say what you came to say?"

He gestures for me to sit in the beanbag, and then waits for me to start. Where do I even begin? How do I articulate what's going on in my head? How do I explain *me*?

I sit up straighter, the beanbag shifting loudly beneath me, and I take a deep breath. "Could you maybe—close your eyes?"

He gives me an *Are you serious?* look but closes his eyes, his elbows propped on his knees, head in his hands.

"I—I—think there's something wrong with me," I start. "Maybe like what's wrong with Alice."

"You think you're bipolar?"

"Maybe. I don't know. All I know is, my brain is . . ." I search for the right word while picking at a loose string on the seam of the beanbag. If I pull it out, will the bag unravel? Will all the insides gush across the floor? Would we ever be able to stuff them back in? ". . . off. Like, I have all these thoughts. It feels like . . . like . . . like my brain is broken. Like a busted laundry machine that's stuck, and it keeps going around and around. And then my body goes haywire. I can't breathe and I think I'm dying and it's—terrifying."

I don't mention the scars on my stomach. Talking about this is one thing, but actually seeing it etched in my flesh is another. Micah's nodding like he understands.

Could he? Could anyone?

"It's like there's this voice," I continue. "Not like I'm hearing voices—it's *my* voice. And it knows all my worst fears and insecurities and it uses them against me. Constantly. And it's usually the loudest voice in the room, always telling me I'm wrong, and sometimes it makes me think"—I take a deep breath—"I'm crazy."

As I say it, out loud, part of me, the part behind my rib cage where I keep all the unspoken words, cracks open slightly. I envision my words flying like butterflies, leaving their perch inside me, floating into the air. They travel through the space between us, and land on Micah. His face twists slightly under the added weight of my confession.

He doesn't say anything. The silence gnaws at me as I wrap the unraveling beanbag thread around my finger. "I shouldn't have told you. I came over to check on you. I'm supposed to be helping *you*."

"I think," Micah says, opening his eyes, "we're supposed to be helping each other."

"But I sound mental."

"You sound scared. But just so you know, I already knew you were a total weirdo."

I throw an empty McDonald's cup at him. He dodges it and laughs. "Joking, joking!"

"Okay, jokester, your turn. Where have you been since last week?"

Micah stares at the ceiling, where he has stars scattered like the ones Alice put in our room years ago. Micah keeps his eyes on the stars as he talks—slowly, quietly—so different from his usual sarcastic bravado.

"I know what they say about me, you know. That I'm a psycho. That I'm dangerous. It's all very sensational and intriguing, except it's all shit. *This* is depression." He gestures to his room, the discarded food, the rumpled sheets, the funky smell. "This is what it is. It's like, like I wake up sometimes and—nothing."

"Nothing?"

Micah springs off the bed and switches off the overhead light.

"So right now, your pupils are dilating, yes?"

I nod. The room comes back into view slowly, illuminated with just enough light from the cracks around the drapes to let me see the shape of Micah in the dark.

"Sometimes it's like I can't dilate. I can't see the light, and I lose hope that I'll find it again." Light floods the room when he flicks the switch back up, and my mind shoots back to when the lights came on in the janitor's closet.

"Was it because of me? Did I . . . cause it?"

Micah gives a short, small, forced chuckle, like what I've said is funny, not in a ha-ha kind of way, more like a life-sucks-doesn't-it kind of inside joke.

"*It* as in depression?"

I nod.

"You can say it out loud, Lily. You won't summon it." His eyes meet mine. "But no, it wasn't you. Or maybe it was you. I don't know. It just *is*. It's part of me. People always ask, *Why* are you depressed? But the boring truth is that nothing is wrong. I feel nothing. I am nothing. When I look into the future, nothing. It's the nothing that destroys me."

Is that how Alice felt on her meds? Was the nothing chipping away at her? Micah picks up the demon drawing on his desk again, studying it.

"People always talk about mental illness like it's a heroic war with a monstrous disease. But the fact is, we're fighting ourselves. Just a bunch of smaller battles. Getting up, every day, facing down the beasts because I can never beat them. Because they *are* me. The best I can do is—"

"Make friends with the monsters," I say, not even aware I'm saying it out loud until Micah nods.

"Exactly."

Behind him, my eye catches a drawing of all the characters from Winnie-the-Pooh standing on a cliff overlooking the ocean, their arms around each other. I bolt up out of the beanbag.

"Acceptance!"

"Excuse me?" he says.

"The Hundred Acre Wood. It's about acceptance."

He's watching me, and for the first time since I got here, a real smile plays at the corner of his lips.

"I'm listening. . . ."

"Piglet and his anxiety. Rabbit with his OCD rows of carrots." I point to each character, thinking it through as I talk. "Dyslexic owl and ADHD Tigger. Eeyore and depression. Oh, and don't forget Christopher Robin, the boy whose stuffed animals *talk* to him. Hello, schizophrenia!"

Micah's face is all weird, and I'm not sure if I've nailed it or totally offended him, but I keep going. "And they all know Piglet's gonna freak out about the wind. They expect Eeyore to be a dud at the picnic. But they invite him anyway. They help each other, but nobody tries to fix anyone. You're just you and they're just them and that's okay."

I flop back into the beanbag. "I'm right, right? I'm totally right."

Micah looks from me to the drawing and back again. "Sorry, kind of in shock here. You're the first person to ever figure it out. Or care enough to try."

"I guess that makes me pretty special, then."

"Yes, Lily Larkin, I guess it does." A true Micah smile finally appears, and he motions for me to move over. He squishes next to me in the beanbag.

"For the record," I say, turning to him, "I do care. A lot."

I reach out and take his hand, separating his fingers with my own. He doesn't say he forgives me, exactly, just slides his palm against mine as our eyes meet. I can tell he's still holding back, though, afraid I'll pull away again. So I lean in close. Closer. His face—his lips—are a whisper from mine.

His curls tickle my forehead, and a rush of adrenaline shoots through me, white-hot and consuming because all I can see or feel or think is him. I'm not even sure who makes the final move, but the space between us disappears and our lips touch, feather light. I lean into him, and his mouth opens, just slightly, enough for me to feel the wet warmth of him.

His lips move slowly, as gentle as a breeze, but the taste of him makes my whole body hum, my brain float. His hand cradles the back of my head, and our bodies, our lips, melt farther into each other, and all my plans and reasons and worries fade away, and the only question I have is, Why haven't we been doing this since the first moment he walked into my life?

When we pull apart, he smiles, and even though all I want to do is keep kissing him—maybe forever—he leans back on the beanbag, his cheeks slightly flushed.

"You have *no* idea how long I've wanted to do that," he says.

I scrunch next to him as he puts his arm around me, and I cuddle into his chest.

"I have a pretty good idea."

His weight settles into mine as we fall farther into the beanbag, into each other. It feels good, our bodies, leaning in, supporting each other.

"I could almost fall asleep like this," he says, his eyes closed. "And that's coming from someone who *never* sleeps."

"Sleep is for the weak."

"Yeah, who needs it?" Micah says, midyawn.

"Not a couple of weirdos like us."

His heartbeat is steady against me, his body warm against mine. We fall into silence, but not the kind of heavy nothing filled with unsaid words. Our silence is easy, the kind of quiet that says nothing, and somehow—everything.

"Hey, Lily?" Micah says, his voice slow and slurry.

"Yeah?"

"Thank you."

"For what?"

The last thing I feel before falling asleep are his fingers sliding deeper between mine.

"For staying."

chapter
37

My brain yawns awake in the dark. Micah's eyes are already open.

"Best. Nap. Ever," he says.

"Crap. What time is it?"

His hair sticks out at inexplicable angles as he rolls over to grab a cell phone off the floor.

"Nine-forty-five."

"P.m.?"

I practically jump out of the bag.

Dad is going to kill you.

Micah stands up, still shaking off the sleep.

"Slow down."

"Can't. Got to leave. Now."

I grab my keys and phone. No missed calls. No texts. Maybe Dad thinks I'm at study group. Or a track thing.

"Hey—" Micah grabs my wrist, pulls me close to him, so close that I can feel his heart beating through my own chest. "Slow. Down."

For a second, I forget that I'm toast for being so late, and all the homework I have to do. I forget about everything but his body against mine, his hands holding me tight against him. And even though I know I should go, I don't.

"'I took a deep breath and listened to the old brag of my heart,'" he whispers into my ear, starting the first line of my favorite Sylvia Plath passage from *The Bell Jar*.

I finish it: "'I am, I am, I am.'"

"You know what I think our friend Sylvia needed?" Micah asks.

"What's that?"

"Some time screaming into the void."

We walk to the beach from his house, and Micah's hands lead me to the cliff, but I pull myself up this time. One foot in front of the other, until we reach the top.

And then he's yelling at the sea.

Not words, just sound. Raw and guttural. Feral.

And I'm screaming, too.

And the ocean swallows our voices.

Takes them and rolls them like stones.

Smooths out their rough places.

And I'm laughing

and he's laughing

and we're wet and salty.

I can taste it on the air.

I can taste it on his skin, on the spot right above his collarbone, when he pulls me close on top of the cliff where he didn't jump.

And for a minute

I forget

about the what-ifs,

about the monsters in my head

because there's no room for them here

in this moment

with his hand around my waist, the one with the semicolon
tattoo

that says he lived

he stayed

he's here.

We both are

and we're broken

and beautiful

and screaming into the wind.

And we're so

high

high

high

that we'll never come down.

And then we're back on the sand and we're running toward the
ocean. Micah flings his shirt over his head and I'm shimmying out
of my pants, and I don't take a moment to even think about whether
this is smart or stupid, because I know if I stop, the what-ifs will push
out this euphoria, this mad rush of energy and hope and *feeling*.

Because suddenly I want to feel it all. The sand beneath my toes.
The water on my skin. Micah on my skin.

All of it.

So I keep moving, kicking off my pants and laughing as Micah
tries to pull his off while standing on one foot and ends up in the

sand. And I'm taking off my shirt, and I stop short, before Micah can see the barely healed places on my stomach.

He's bare except for his boxers. Bare and exposed and beautiful.

And I want to be, too.

I take off my shirt slowly.

I cross my arms in front of the little red and pink telltale marks on my skin, just above my underwear.

"When I get worried, I—"

Before I can finish, Micah puts his finger on my lips.

"You know that voice in your head—the one that tells you to apologize for existing? That says you're not enough?"

I nod.

"It's lying." He leans in closer to me, his breath warm on my face. "You are enough. Right now. Just the way you are."

He moves my arms and drops to his knees in the sand. His lips touch my stomach, each wound, each scar. My hands are in his hair and his hands are around my waist, pulling me into him as his lips graze each wounded piece of me.

And then he stands and presses his lips to mine, and if our first kiss was a gentle breeze, our second is a hurricane. He kisses me, hard and hungry, like we're running out of time.

"Lily," he whispers in a half moan that sends me over the edge, and I'm kissing him back just as urgently because suddenly it *feels* urgent, like I can't get enough of him or enough oxygen or enough of *this*. For the first time ever, someone knows *all* my secrets and wants me with all my scars.

As we kiss, my hands explore him, the divots in his lower back, the tight corded muscles on his chest. My fingers run through his hair, tugging his mouth to mine. It's warm and wet, and it fills me. He picks me up in one effortless move, and I wrap my legs around him as he carries me into the water.

I taste the ocean on his skin as I press my mouth to his shoulder, his neck, his jaw. He groans, low and guttural, when his lips find mine in the dark.

And for this moment—an ephemeral blip—I'm present.

Feeling the spray, tasting the salt, inhabiting the me that is here and now.

No glass. No monsters.

I'm alive.

I'm here.

I am.

chapter
38

After a million kisses and somehow not enough kisses—never enough kisses—we force ourselves to stop and get out of the water. We pull on our clothes and he walks me to his house and presses his mouth to mine one more time. I drive home, the taste of the ocean and Micah on my lips.

The house is quiet when I creep through the front door and close it softly behind me. I almost make it past Dad's office without detection.

"That you, Lily pad?"

"What's up, Dad?"

Did that sound casual? Or guilty? Casually guilty?

In his study, he's sitting in his armchair, buried in a book. The rest of the house is dark, the dishwasher running softly like it does every night after Dad and Staci go up to bed.

"Were you waiting on me?" I ask.

"Of course. Can't sleep until all my girls are home, safe and sound."

"Sorry I'm so late. I didn't meant to worry you."

"That's the thing: I *never* have to worry about you." Dad stands up, stretches, and puts his arm around me. "Late-night study session?"

I nod.

"Those teachers really push you, don't they?"

"Understatement of the century."

"Not that you ever had a problem pushing yourself just fine," he says with a wink. "Speaking of which, I haven't seen you running much. You still shooting for state?"

"Yep."

"That's my girl." He piles a stack of papers with Fairview's letterhead into a drawer.

"Dad?" I swallow hard. "I know about Alice's bills. And I'm doing everything I can to win this scholarship for the summer program, but—"

Dad cuts me off, shaking his head.

"Now, let's not talk about that," he says. "Leave that to me. That's what dads are for."

On his desk, a picture of the four of us at the beach sits next to a stack of student exams. It's from the day when Alice got me to swim out past where the waves break, when I almost let the water take me. But this is earlier that morning, and Dad has Margot on his shoulders, while Alice and I dance in the *sjushamillabakka,* in the in-between where the waves meet the sand.

"Seems like yesterday," Dad says, changing the topic with a happy-sad look on his face. He picks up the picture and rubs the back of his neck. "I wasn't sure I could do it after your mom died."

"Do what?" I ask.

"Raise you girls. All alone. No one really tells you how, you know?"

The quaver in his voice scares me. He's Dad—always trying to make things better, trying to make me happy. Always there, period. I wrap my arms around him from behind.

"You're doing great, Dad," I say. "And you're not alone."

The Post-it notes have taken over.

Dozens of them adorn Alice's side of the room. She looks up at me from where she's scribbling something on a new one, and then she slaps it onto the wall. Her eyes are bloodshot, and the room is a total mess.

"When's the last time you slept?" I say, stepping over the plastic tarp and paint cans. Margot is zonked out, curled up in my comforter, *Harry Potter and the Prisoner of Azkaban* tucked under her arm. I told her days ago that I'd talk Dementors with her.

Worst big sister ever.

"No time for sleep!" Alice says, and then she skips over to me and pulls on my wet hair. "Besides, I'm the one who should be asking the questions, when my little sister comes in at midnight, fresh from what I can only assume is a skinny-dip?"

Busted.

"How did you know that?"

"I'm your big sister. I know all," she says with a wink. "And also, you're wearing his hoodie."

I look down at the sweatshirt Micah wrapped around me tonight. "Oh."

She laughs, the high, uncontrolled pitch I've been trying so hard to ignore.

"Don't worry, your midnight rendezvous secrets are safe with me. So I guess this means you *are* into him?"

271

I nod, the lingering feel of his lips, sending aftershocks rippling through me. "He just sees the world in this beautiful way, and I want to be part of it."

I sit on Alice's bed so I won't wake Margot. Alice studies the sticky note in her hand. "You know he has a pretty complicated history, right? It doesn't bother you?"

"It did. But then I got to know him, and he's *nothing* like everyone says," I say, sorting out my feelings for Micah as I shape them into words. "And it's like his depression, his time at Fairview, it's all part of who he is, and sometimes I think I could fall in love with who he is. And when you love someone, you love all the broken pieces, right? Or maybe when you love someone, those pieces don't seem so broken anymore. They're just part of them."

Alice is quiet, looking at the scars peeking out from her sleeves now. "You really believe that?"

"Yeah. I think I do."

"Secrets!" she yells, snapping her fingers. "I could do a whole segment on the secrets we keep. How we try to protect people. How we protect ourselves."

"Alice—"

"And why we say some things and not others—"

"Alice!"

"What, what? Why are you yelling?"

"I'm trying to talk to you."

She slaps the Post-it onto the wall and laughs. "Sorry, but the ideas just keep coming, like, bam-bam-BAM! I can't write them down quick enough. It's like they're building up inside me, like this pressure, and they're gonna leak out my ears because they're coming so fast, and like, I have to reach in and pluck them out of this tornado before they're gone forever."

I pat the bed next to me, trying to whisper so Margot stays asleep. "Come, sit."

She obeys, but barely. Her butt is on my bed but her eyes dart around the room, her fingers flicking the pen back and forth.

"Alice. I don't think you're fine."

She rolls her eyes. "I told you—"

"No, Alice, I'm serious. Maybe you need to get back on your meds."

All her energy turns angry in an instant, her bloodshot eyes turned on me.

"No! I'm not going back to that place—where I feel nothing about anything. I want to *feel* everything. What I need is for everyone to stop trying to fix me." She points to Margot. "Did you know she thinks something called a Patronus is going to help me? Told me I had to think of my happiest memory. Like she can wave a magic wand and—poof—no more bipolar disorder."

"I'm not trying to fix you, Alice. I'm trying to help you."

"For the one millionth time, I don't need help."

"If the Hundred Acre Wood has taught me anything, it's that *everyone* needs help." I choose my words carefully. "So if you won't take your medicine—"

"I won't."

"Then Micah said he has this group he goes to, from Fairview. What if you went to that? Just once, just to try it. I'd even go with you."

Alice groans and leans her head back. She puffs out her cheeks as she blows out all her air. "This is important to you?"

"It is."

"Fine. I'll go." She points a finger at me. "But not because I need help. Maybe I could help *them*. Maybe I could show them my videos or—" She stands up, scribbling on another Post-it note. "Or maybe I could interview them. A whole segment on life after Fairview!"

She slaps the note onto the wall with the word *THERAPY* in the center.

I change for bed but leave on Micah's hoodie because it smells like him and the ocean and tonight. And even though the symptoms of mania are still bouncing in my head, I can finally breathe in this room.

Because she's gonna get help. She'll be okay.

We all will.

chapter
39

Micah's curls are in total disarray in the morning outside the school.

"You feeling better?" I ask.

"A little."

"And the darkness is . . . gone?"

"Never fully," he says. "But I'm here, and I'm trying." He points to the yellow socks on his calves, dotted with limes.

I smooth his hair down with my fingers, remembering how he kissed my scars last night. How with him, I felt brave and present and free.

"Thank you," I say.

"You're welcome. And may I ask, for what?"

"For being you. It's because of you. The poetry. Talking to Alice. I never would have done any of this without you." I reach out to hold his hand. "And you were right. We have to turn in our project. I can't keep hiding."

I lean in and kiss his lips, the warmth of them transporting me back to the ocean.

"Aren't you scared someone will see?" Micah says.

I keep my hand in his as we walk through the front doors. "It's not brave if you're not scared."

My courage wavers slightly as we walk the halls. Sam stares at our hands, at me, then strides quickly away. If I were still making lists in the small hours of the morning, I could make a whole one dedicated to the times when I've let Sam down lately. I've texted her one gazillion times, trying to apologize for missing her solo, for being a terrible friend.

She hasn't replied to any of my I'll-be-better promises.

Kali spies us from her locker and gasps like she's in a telenovela. She beelines for us in the middle of the hall.

"Is this"—she points back and forth from Micah to me— "a thing?"

I nod.

"It's perfect," she says, although in true Kali fashion, it's unclear if it's a compliment or an insult. "I wasn't sure if it was true or not, but here you are."

"If what was true?" I ask.

"Oh, you know, the Underground. Anyone can do *anything* to a picture, so I was like, are they *together* together? Or just project partners together? Although, not sure what kind of project requires that kind of"—she smiles suggestively like we're all in on a big secret together—"intimacy."

When Kali realizes we have zero idea what she's blabbering about, she turns her phone toward us. The Underground fills her screen, with a shot of Micah and me standing on the cliff, holding hands, screaming into the void. The post says, *A Poet and an Artist: Crazy in Love, or Just Crazy?*

On Micah's locker, someone has taped a copy of the picture.

"Freaking Damon," Micah mutters as he rips it down, but it's too late. Everyone has seen it. Around me, people look at their phones.

At you,

wondering if you are, in fact, crazy?

I start to leave my body.

The tingles in my fingers. The tightness in my gut. My chest. My throat. The overpowering urge to pick myself open.

"Hey." Micah's standing in front of me, staring me square in the eyes. "Look at me."

I do. But I'm slipping away.

"Stay. With me," he says. He squeezes my hand.

Once.

Twice.

Three times.

Micah's eyes take me back to the ocean and the cliff and our words, flying free.

And the bad thoughts clear.

My breathing settles.

I squeeze his hand back.

Once.

Twice.

Three times.

And I stay.

Enough

You say
I am beautiful
I am enough

With my flaws
my monsters
my scars

You see them
—all of them—
and stay.

And so do I.

chapter
40

I stay in my body for a week straight.

Don't float away even once. Even when Sam ignores me in the
halls. When Damon writes *DIE* in magnetic letters on Micah's locker
and tells me he likes girls with a little crazy. I stay when I come in way
behind my personal best at track. "An entire second, Larkin!" Coach
yells at me, disappointment dripping from his voice.

I even stay when Alice's Post-it notes spread across our room. She
talked to Micah, and she's going to group next week. She'll talk to
someone, and she won't disappear. She'll get better.

And each time I write more words, the pull of my body, of the
earth, of the here and now, gets a little stronger.

At lunch, I sit with Micah, since Sam is doing a full-on freeze-
out, and the girl with the ripped tights offers me a slice of clementine,
and the guy with dreads recites a Sylvia Plath poem for my benefit. I
catch Sam staring, dagger-eyed, at Micah's leg against mine. I move
my leg, and she turns away when our eyes meet. Guilt needles me.

But still, I stay.

Micah and I convene the final meeting of the guerrilla poets of Ridgeline High to put together all our poems and artwork and pictures of the random acts of poetry and all the words that followed. Micah has printed out the comments from online, and all the #mywords #mystory posts, too.

Everyone is going to know.

It won't just be a rumor.

"You ready for this?" Micah asks, holding my hand under the lunch table in the courtyard, his thumb stroking mine.

"Absolutely not," I say. Micah leans in and kisses me softly, tugging my lower lip as he moves away. "But let's do it."

I smile, and he smiles, and it melts the icy places in my chest. I'm lighter than I have been in months, so weightless and airy that a strong breeze could toss me into the air and I'd float away.

Gravity finds me on a Wednesday morning. The day before our project is due.

Micah and I stand on the sidewalk, staring at the side of the school. An enormous, black-and-white spray-painted graffiti of #mywords #mystory mars the side of the school.

He looks at me. I shake my head.

"You?"

He shakes his head, raking his fingers through his hair, his jaw clenched.

"There's only two kinds of people who would do this. Someone who is *really* into random acts of poetry . . ."

"Or?"

"Someone who wants to take down the guerrilla poets."

*   *   *

The Underground wastes no time spewing judgments.

Whoever did it is gonna get suspended for sure.

They should. This was too far.

This is why we can't have nice things.

Micah's not in class for our collaboration with the other art students.
Something's wrong.

Waves of panic rollick through me as Gifford makes a plea to the class, except she's staring at me.

"If you come forward now, I can back you up. Friedman and I are on your side."

The class is silent. I conduct a mini-investigation in my head. Kali—too much of a goody-goody. Sam—yes, she hates me right now, but not this much. Right? Damon—definite candidate. He's been out for Micah since the very first day. He'd totally sabotage us.

Principal Porter's voice interrupts on the loudspeaker. The voice from on high beckons Lily Larkin to the office, and Gifford gives me a frantic look.

The class ooooohs as I get up. I walk down the hall, my monsters roaring out of hibernation.

We tried to warn you.

Why don't you listen to us anymore?

Micah is sitting outside the office, arms folded tight, staring at the floor. Before I can talk to him, Porter opens his office door, and there, in the corner chair, face drained, is my father.

chapter
41

It takes all of two seconds to slip out of my body. It happens so fast, I don't even get a chance to feel the weight of the moment—the way my dad is looking at me and somehow not looking at me, the way Porter scowls at me, his face drawn tight, his mouth a perfect little sphincter in the middle of his face.

But I'm above it now. Floating somewhere near the ceiling, watching the play unfold beneath me.

```
    Camera pans toward Porter, his mouth shaped
    like a butthole.


                      PORTER
        Blah, blah, blah . . . trespassing . . .
        unacceptable . . . . misdemeanor.
```

                                    DAD
                      (Looking disappointed. Looking
                      tired. Looking resigned.)
          I don't know what to say.

                                  PORTER
          What do you have to say, Lily?

                          DISAPPOINTING DAUGHTER
                      (Who is not really Lily because
                      Lily is not here right now. Lily
                      has left the body. Please leave
                      a message at the beep.)
          We didn't do it.

                                  PORTER
          Let me remind you that I have
          personally reviewed the security
          tapes, and while we can't identify
          last night's spray-painters, we can
          clearly identify you trespassing
          several weeks ago. Stealing art
          supplies. Vandalizing the lobby.

                          DISAPPOINTING DAUGHTER
          No. No. We used paper.

                    PORTER

The school's paper.

        (Gifford and Friedman enter.)

                    FRIEDMAN

They're artists. They took a risk.

                    GIFFORD

Blame us, not them.

                    PORTER

        (Butthole mouth pinching
        tighter.)

You persuaded me once, but it's gone too
far. Just like I said it would. Someone
has to be punished, or who knows where it
will stop.

            DISAPPOINTING DAUGHTER

We. Didn't. Do. The. Spray-paint.

                    DAD

Lily. Just stop.

                    PORTER

Personal responsibility . . . blah, blah,
blah . . . good academic record . . .
shame to see one mistake knock you off
track . . . two-day suspension.

                              DAD
          (Looking/not looking at
          Disappointing Daughter.)
     I can assure you this won't happen again.

                            PORTER
     I should hope not.
              (Wags finger.)
     You should consider yourself lucky, young
     lady. Your partner in crime didn't get
     off so easy.

I slam back into my body.

"Wait, what? What did you do to Micah?"

"*We* didn't do anything to Micah," Porter says. "He did this to himself. Told us how all of this was his idea."

"No, no, that's not true," I say as panic wells in my throat. Moisture pricks my eyes. "I had the idea first. I was the—"

Porter holds up his hand, dismissing me.

"No need to be heroic, Ms. Larkin. Micah has told us everything, and we've turned it over to the police."

"The police?"

"Trespassing is a misdemeanor."

"But that's not fair—

"Lily," Dad says, a warning in his voice. "Don't push it."

"Listen to your father," Porter says. "You *and* your sister should consider yourselves lucky that he has convinced us to chalk all this up to a youthful indiscretion."

"But Micah—"

"Mr. Mendez," Porter says, cutting me off, "has a pattern of be-havior. This isn't the first trouble he's been in, and it won't be the last. He will be far better off somewhere more equipped to deal with his needs."

Porter dismisses us with a wave of his hand. Dad thanks him. *Thanks him.* I focus all my energy on not crawling across Porter's desk and socking him right in his butthole lips.

In the hall, Micah walks toward his locker, the school security officer escorting him, a crowd of students gathered round, watching, gawking. Damon's got his cell phone up, filming every second. I start toward Micah, but Dad grabs my arm.

"No."

I yank my arm free and run toward him anyway.

"Tell them the truth, Micah." My voice is strangled and strange. "Tell them I was the one who wanted to do it."

"They've made up their minds." He won't look at me. "About this. About me."

He shrugs, and the gesture is so defeated, so un-Micah, that I want to shake him, make him stop this. But before I can, he reaches his locker, where someone has taped a picture of a man with the same black bushy hair and gentle expression from the photo in Micah's kitchen. And a headline: CLIFF CLOSED AFTER MAN JUMPS TO HIS DEATH.

Below, in magnetic poetry letters:

Like father, like son.

My throat pinches almost shut. The man on the cliff. Micah's obsession with going there. I put my hand on his shoulder.

"Micah—"

He shrugs me off, rips the paper down, crumples it in his fist, and, without a second's hesitation, turns on his heel, his arm smashing forward into Damon's smirking face. Damon's hand flies to his jaw, and then he's barreling toward Micah and they're pushing against each other until Micah has Damon up against the locker, and he's hitting him, hitting him, hitting him, and a girl screams and the security guard is yelling at everyone to "Step back, right now!" and he's grappling for Micah's hands and clicking handcuffs into place.

Damon sucker punches Micah in the face before the officer yanks Micah away. Micah's nose is bleeding as the security guard walks him down the hall, and our classmates point and laugh and hold up phones as witnesses. *Manic Micah at it again!*

My dad pulls me away from the blood on the floor, and the officer pulls Micah away

away

away.

And Sam is there, staring with the rest of them, like she has no idea who I am anymore, and a janitor is plucking the magnetic poetry off the lockers as we walk out. He plinks them, word by word, into a trash can.

Dad drives me home in unbearable silence. I wish he'd yell. Say something. Anything. Give me a chance to defend myself. After the longest drive in the history of driving, he pulls into the garage, shuts off the engine, and leans back against the headrest.

"I expect this from Alice. Not from you."

He takes off his glasses and pinches the bridge of his nose. I'm not supposed to make his eyes squint like that, make his forehead wrinkle up as he tries to rub out all the stress.

"Because you expect me to be perfect."

"I never asked you to be perfect, Lily."

"You didn't have to ask!" I'm embarrassed by the waver in my voice, by the emotions bubbling to the surface. "I'm the good girl. Because you need me to be. But I'm not perfect. I'm—"

~~broken~~
~~terrified~~
~~covered in scars~~

"What? You're what?" he says.

"I'm tired."

"I'm tired, too," he says, closing his eyes with a massive sigh, as if he can blow all this away. Maybe me, too, while he's getting rid of stuff. "And the fact that you dragged Alice into this with you. When you *know* it's the last thing she needs."

I don't tell him that breaking into the school was Alice's idea. Alice, with her wild eyes and wilder ideas. He doesn't want to hear my excuses.

"It's just not like you, Lily. Keeping secrets from me," he says. "Obviously, you won't be seeing that boy anymore."

"This wasn't his fault."

He shakes his head. "You've worked too hard to throw everything away for someone like that."

"Someone like *that*? You mean with black hair? Brown eyes?" My voice fills the car. "Or do you mean someone who went to Fairview, because in that case, your daughter is *someone like that,* too."

"Your sister and that boy are *not* the same," he says, his voice loud in the car now.

"But what if they are? And what if I'm like them, too? Are you

going to send me away? Isn't that your solution—ship off the problem and hope it comes back fixed so you don't have to deal with it?"

I've gone too far. I know it the millisecond the words leave my
lips. I wish I could stuff them back in, but I can't, just like I can't
wipe off the look of shock/disappointment/hurt on Dad's face. He
opens his car door and gets out, but leans in before he leaves.

"Who *are* you right now?"

"I guess that's the million-dollar question!" I yell, but he doesn't
hear me before he slams the door, leaving me alone with a lifetime of
words left unsaid.

He doesn't really want the answer.

And I guess, deep down, neither do I.

chapter
42

Wednesday, 6:45 pm

LogoLily: Micah. I'm so sorry.

I wait for a ding for hours.

It never comes.

Alice sits on the edge of my bed, tells me she's sorry. I say it's not her fault. (Even though, maybe it is—a little. For telling us to go inside. For sucking Dad's bank account dry. For leaving no room in this family for me to ever fall short.) She tells me Micah will be fine.

"He's tough," she says.

I nod like the world makes sense. On the dresser, the lily Micah gave me has wilted and browned around the edges, which is just so pathetically sad that I can't look at it, but I can't bear to throw it away, either. Before I pop a sleeping pill, I put on Micah's GOOD VIBES ONLY hoodie and check my messages one more time. Nothing. But I do get an email, a two-paragraph nuclear bomb.

Dear Lily,

I am so sorry, but Principal Porter has informed me that due to the suspension and the incident in the hallway this afternoon, you and Micah will no longer be eligible for the creative arts contest. He feels allowing you to continue at this point would send a bad message.

Lily, dear, you know I've always been a big fan. Please don't let this change your passion for the written word. You have a gift! Also, please know that I am working to see if there is something else we could do to get you noticed by the English admissions team at UC Berkeley. Will keep you updated.

Mrs. Gifford

I toss my phone away like it's poison. It lands on my notebook. Full of words. *My* words. That I thought meant something. Words I thought could get me out of here—out of me.

Idiot

idiot

idiot.

Page by page, I tear up the words. My fingers ripping them out of existence.

How did you think this would end?

That a boy and some chalk could make things better?

Make you *better?*

And then, my fingers turn on me. Find the pink patches on my stomach.

And I rip those out, too.

He would have been better off without you.

Maybe everyone would.

I pick and pick until the blood coats my fingertips, warm and wonderful.

And I wonder why I ever stopped.

LogoLily's Word of the Day

puriderm (v) Cleaning oneself from the outside in, knowing
that if you can just reach deep enough, you can pluck out all
the bad and leave only the good.

From English *purify* + *-derma* (skin)

Ridgeline Underground

600 likes

GUERRILLA POETS REVEALED! Lily Larkin and Micah
Mendez are the team behind the random acts of poetry.
Update: Micah has been expelled! Anyone heard from Lily?

300 comments

The truth always comes out. Thanks, Underground!

Told you that guy was trouble

Sad he took Lily down with him

She probably didn't mind going down

Ew.

What? The mental ones are always the best in bed.

I always knew no one could be *that* perfect! Lily Larkin, what
a hypocrite!

She may be nuts, but her poetry was awesome

Probably plagiarized

chapter
43

I spend my suspension waiting. For Micah to message. For Gifford to tell me she can save my future.

I wait

and wait

and wait.

Across the room, Alice sticks ideas onto the wall for her YouTube channel until she crashes at one a.m. still in her clothes. I Google *Deadman's Cliff* and read anything I can find about Micah's dad. I force myself to look at the pictures, read the words, the descriptions of the wife and little boy left behind. As I read, I pick at my scabs. In fact, I purposefully dig until I bleed. I *like* the sting—I want it—as if pain can pay my penance.

I skip the pre-state track scrimmage on Saturday. I'm sick.

At least that's what I tell Dad. My stomach *does* hurt, but technically, it hasn't stopped hurting since the loudspeaker summoned me to the office and my life started unraveling thread by thread. It hurts in waves—big crashing peaks that overtake my whole body when they hit. I curl into a fetal ball in my bed and wait for the tide to wash back out.

I watch the minutes tick by on my clock during the track meet. They're doing their stretches now. They're on the starting blocks. Crossing the finish line.

They probably don't even notice you're gone.

Dad checks on me, but he stands at my door instead of sitting on my bed. He's barely spoken to me since the principal's office. He doesn't tell me what a massive disappointment I am. I haven't told him that I lost the scholarship.

I don't say other things, too.

~~I'm sorry.~~

~~I'm still your good girl.~~

~~Aren't I?~~

We dance around each other, a silent and deliberate duet of moves and bends and twists.

Alice, on the other hand, won't shut up. She's standing by my bed, wearing a bright pink short-sleeve T-shirt, the brightest color she's worn since Fairview. Her scars are easily visible on her arms—light pink and fading, but still there.

"I'm actually getting kind of pumped about this therapy group next week. I have all these questions I'm gonna ask for my video. Oh! I'm going to do an interview with Micah, too. Have you heard from him, by the way? He's not returning my calls. Should we go see him? I think we should go see him. What do you think?"

My head pounds. "I think that's a lot of questions."

Something dings on her computer, and she's off again, zipping back and forth between helping Margot with her math flash cards and editing her videos.

Margot smiles at me and leans in close. "It's working."

"What is?"

She rolls her eyes. "The Patronus." She eyebrow-gestures to Alice. "Those Dementors are all but gone."

I retreat to the 100-acre-wood. It's empty. All Micah's drawings, deleted.

You did this.

I carve new tracks in my stomach.

My barely healed spots gape open.

Everyone at school knows.

They stare at me in the halls when I come back after my two-day suspension. Whisper as I walk by.

A few people tell me how amazing our poetry was. How sorry they are about Micah. They want to know how he is. I lie and tell them he's fine. The Artists are wearing bright socks with fruit and palm trees and jungle animals on them, in solidarity with what they're calling a total miscarriage of justice—a violation of First Amendment rights.

In the lobby, the paper has been torn down, along with Micah's eagle wings. A shiny new poster full of Ridgeline's code of conduct has replaced the blackout poem. A smattering of Post-it notes and magnetic poetry show up randomly, but for the most part, the words are gone.

I eat my lunch in the bathroom stall where I found my first

words. My poem has been taken down. The wall scrubbed clean like it never happened.

In English, all the other partnerships are still buzzing about the projects they turned in during my suspension. Gifford says they'll pick a winner soon, and Kali doesn't even bother to flaunt her certain victory in front of me. I'm no longer a threat. I sit on the floor in the art room, Micah's hoodie pulled up tight around my ears, as I fumble to make something out of the junk pile. Damon leers at me the entire time.

"I tried to warn you," he says. "Once a psycho, always a psycho."

Sam yells from across the room, "Hey, douche-canoe, why don't you mind your own business for once in your sad little life?"

She smiles faintly at me before turning back to her partner.

She just feels sorry for you.

She's blocked you.

Cut

you

out

from her phone and her life.

Smart girl.

What did you ever do for her?

I pick up a fork and try to make something beautiful, like Micah did, but I just end up with barely bent junk. I want to say something back to Damon, hurt him the way he hurt Micah. Accuse him of doing the spray-paint, but my words fail me. I see now what Micah meant about staying quiet. Everyone would *love* to see me lose it. Validate all the rumors.

As I walk through the parking lot in the afternoon, it's raining, and Damon and his friends make cuckoo calls after me from where they gather around his car. My hand's on my door handle when Damon yells out one last time, and I turn to see him waggling a can of spray paint in my direction, a vicious smirk on his face. Before I can stop myself, I'm running toward him, dropping my backpack on the wet cement, lifting my knee at just the right angle to rack him straight in the nuts. He bends in half, moaning.

"Crazy bitch." He spits the words after me.

I pretend not to hear.

Instead of track practice, I go to Micah's house. The rain and sun have destroyed his chalk creations.

Did any *of it really happen?*

His mother answers the door, in scrubs like before, except the house is dark and doesn't smell like tamales.

"Lily," she says, mustering a weak smile. She steps out onto the porch and closes the door behind her. Her eyes are circled with pink.

She hates you.

"Micah's not feeling so good today. But I'll tell him you stopped by?"

I jam the toe of my shoe into the hard cement and resist the urge to shove the door open and force Micah into the light.

"It's all my fault."

She shakes her head slowly, putting her hand on my shoulder. "Things like this are nobody's fault, *mija.*" The term of endearment guts me.

I walk, defeated, back to my car and convince myself that I see a flicker of the curtain in his room. Maybe he knows I'm here, that he's not alone in the Hundred Acre Wood.

I stop by the track after the team has left. Alone, I stand on the starting line. Click my stopwatch. Force my legs to move.

I sprint around the track
over and over
until the finish line is a blur
and my lungs are gasping for air.
And then, I run it again.

LogoLily's Word of the Day

anginog (n) The sinking realization that you're floating out to sea, and the waves keep knocking you farther out, until the shore disappears and all you can see is the water, relentless and steady and impossibly strong.

From the prefix *an* (not) + Old Saxon *ginog* (enough)

chapter
44

Kali wins.

She posts a selfie of her and her partner grinning from ear to ear, holding up their photography display with an all-caps caption:

UC BERKELEY: WE'RE COMING FOR YA!

I scroll through the congratulations comments and thumbs-up emojis. Well, that's that.

I throw myself into everything I've ignored while chasing this summer program. I'll be lucky if Berkeley looks twice at my college application now that my grades and track times have slipped. I spend the weekend doing extra credit for every class. I outline for next week's history test.

When I finish my outline, I write it again, neater.

And then, once more.

Five times, I write it, making each letter perfect, until my hand cramps and my eyes are weary.

Alice flips on the light. It burns my retinas. Somehow the day has turned to night while I worked.

"You've been studying nonstop for days," she says. "Time to return to life!"

She's wearing her old clothes. The bright ones. The ones that make her look like she should be on 1940s pin-up calendars. Her dress is cherry red, with white spots and a tulle petticoat that keeps it flouncy. She's wearing makeup, too. Bright red lipstick that matches her dress.

Alice burns my retinas.

"I know you're worried about Micah," she says. "But he's not languishing in some jail cell or whatever other worst-case scenario you're imagining."

"You talked to him?"

"Yeah."

"Is he okay?"

"He will be. Had to pay a pretty steep fine and got community service for the fight, but he's home and doing online classes, and he'll be back to wearing those ridiculous socks in no time. I guarantee it."

I try to believe her. This is just a blip, a setback. But I keep thinking about his dark room, him staring at the stars on his ceiling, the way he described the nothingness. Is that what he's feeling right now? Did his mom have to pay his fine? Did he hate himself for it?

"Did you know?" I ask. "About his dad?"

"Yes. You didn't?"

I shake my head. I guess even Micah Mendez keeps some words hidden.

"Was it depression? Like Micah?"

"Micah doesn't talk about it all that much, but yeah, I think so."
Alice scooches next to me on the bed. "I know things suck right now.
But I also know something that will help."

"*Please* don't say *seafoam green*."

"Better!" She claps her hands. "A bonfire party. At the beach. Tonight!"

I shake my head. "I'm pretty sure I'm grounded for life."

"Dad and Staci went to some fancy dinner downtown, and Margot's watching a movie. We'll be back before anyone knows we're gone." She holds out a pair of jeans to me. "And Micah's gonna be there."

It's a dirty trick. I kind of hate her for it. But I take the jeans and put them on.

The party is a huge, weird mix of people dotting the beach in the moonlight. Across the sand, Sam's talking to some guy who graduated last year. She starts toward me for, like, a millisecond before she remembers I'm the worst.

I scan the crowd for Micah, but he's not here, so I take a seat in the sand, half-hidden by the darkness. I lose myself in the flames of the bonfire. Alice is flirting loudly with a guy with a surfer ponytail and an open flannel shirt who looks like a grade-A douchebag. Alice keeps touching his arm. Bro-dude leans toward her, his body language screaming that he's into it if she is. Spoiler alert: she is. She has reincarnated as the old Alice—loud and bright and up for anything. Why did I let her talk me into coming?

She's whispering something in the d-bag's ear, and they're off, racing down toward the beach, shucking clothes as they go. A splash as they enter the water. A guy somewhere behind me calls Alice mental under his breath.

The darkness conceals Deadman's Cliff, but I know it's out there. Did Micah's father think twice when he stood on the edge? Was he scared, taking that final step into the nothing? Or did the ocean call to him, peacefully, like it once did to me?

And then, like a vision, Micah's there, watching me. The firelight flickers on his face, casts bizarre shadows under the eyes I know so well. Except, their usual light is gone. His face is pale and his hair is unkempt, and the guilt needles me. I want to run to him, to touch him, to have him hold me, but I don't know where he is, how he feels about me, about *us,* after everything that's happened.

I jump up, only to stand in front of him, awkwardly. "You're here."

"I'm here." He smiles half-heartedly with one side of his mouth, like he's apologizing for his presence, or mine—hard to tell which. "Alice said my wallowing time was over."

"Me, too." I dig the toe of my flip-flop into the sand. "I came by your house."

"I know." He shoves his hands deeper into his pockets, his eyes watching my toe.

I reach out my hand to him. "Walk with me?"

He takes it, and my chest fills with hope. We head down to the edge of the ocean, somewhere in the in-between, our toes barely submerged in the cold waves. The breeze blows the ends of his curls.

"So, how did it feel?" he asks.

"What?"

"Kicking Damon in the nuts."

Through the dark, he smiles slightly, and it helps me breathe, helps me believe he's still in there.

"Freaking fantabulous."

"I bet," he says. "I know I'm not supposed to say this, but damn, it felt good to hit that guy."

I follow Micah's gaze out to the ocean, where the water meets the night. He's still a million miles away.

"Do you hate me?" I ask.

"No."

"But you got expelled, Micah. It's not fair. It's—"

"It's life." He stoops to pick up a piece of sea glass and chucks it hard. It lands somewhere in the nothingness.

"But I *know* Damon did the graffiti. He still has the spray-paint can, and if we could prove—"

Micah shakes his head. "No one wants to hear it. I'm Manic Micah. I'll always be Manic Micah."

My hope deflates slightly. "Don't say that."

"You thought it once, too."

"But now I know you," I say, trying to bring him back to me. Back from wherever he's gone that feels so far. I grab his hand as he winds up another piece of sea glass.

"I know your lips move when you read."

I kiss him on the cheek, slide my fingers through his, my heart pounding.

"I know that you love your mom more than anything. And you want to make your dad proud."

"Lily, don't," he says, his voice breaking in the wind.

"And that you believe in a world better than this one," I say, standing in front of him, pulling his body next to mine. "And you make me believe it, too."

He pulls away. "I was wrong. And for a second there, I forgot.

I let myself believe that the whole world could see me like you do." He lobs the glass into the black. "And the worst part was my mom's face. Disappointment, but also like she wasn't surprised. That's what killed me—not the expulsion or the police charges or any of it—but that look."

A flash of lightning illuminates the horizon as a drizzle starts, sprinkling raindrops onto his cheeks as he talks. He's staring toward Deadman's Cliff as he hefts a rock from hand to hand.

"My dad's name was Charlie. He married my mom in college. Studied engineering. He was brilliant and sarcastic and had the greatest head of black hair you've ever seen. But do you think anyone talks about any of that?" He shakes his head. "He was the guy who jumped off the cliff. That's all they'll ever see."

I reach out to him again, take his hand. "You're not your dad."

"So I tell myself every time I stand on that stupid cliff. But even if I convince myself, I'll never convince everyone else. My dad will never be anything other than his weakest moments, and neither will I. I should have known better than to think it could ever be different, that I could go to college or be any sort of normal."

The rain wets his hair, and I watch a droplet roll down one of his curls, cling for a second, and then fall.

"So, what? You're just giving up?"

"I don't have much choice here, do I? *This* is why I shouldn't make plans. Because whatever I do, the past gets in the way. And no matter how hard I try, the monsters always find me. Why try?"

The rain's falling harder now, sending people scurrying from the beach. Someone touches my arm.

"You're Alice's sister, right?" asks a girl I don't know.

"Yeah. But we're kind of in the middle—"

"We can't find her."

"What do you mean, you can't find her?" Micah says.

Bro-dude's here now, too, wet and stumbling over his words.

"We were in the water—both of us—you know—messing around"—he shakes water from his hair like he's a puppy—"and, like, she was there and she was, like, talking all fast, and then she was gone. Just took off."

My heart speeds up. The beach is dark, so dark that I can only see a few feet in every direction. The moon is a fingernail sliver, barely lighting up a narrow streak on the water and nothing else.

"Why didn't you follow her?" I say, scanning the beach. Searching the darkness for her. "How do you just lose somebody?"

Bro-dude lifts up his hands, innocent. "Look, man, I don't even know her. She's not my problem."

My knees start to buckle. I hang on to Micah, who passes me off to the girl before he waves to some guys and heads down the beach, cell phones out like flashlights. They shine them into the water.

I run to the ocean's edge. My fear freezes me between the land and the sea. *Don't be in the water.*

Everyone is searching now, up and down the beach, flashlights flicking out like searchlights across the waves. A group of girls Alice went to high school with huddle around me, telling me to calm down, that she's probably fine, that she's probably hooking up in a dune somewhere. The three girls laugh in unison. Alice is one big joke.

"She's not fine!" I yell. "Don't you understand? She's bipolar. We *need* to find her."

The girls stop laughing.

"Bipolar?" one says. "Is that when you hear voices?"

"Or have multiple personalities or something?"

"No, I think it's when you're, like, crazy-happy one second and suicidal the next." They all look at me. "Oh my gosh, do you think she did this on purpose?"

Micah's voice rings out from the darkness.

"Over here!"

I shove my way past the idiot trio and run down the beach, abandoning my flip-flops in the wet sand. The rain falls sideways, hard and stinging as I run through it toward the cluster of lights.

When I reach the group, they're all looking up.

Toward Alice.

She's perched, partway up Deadman's Cliff, on a slick wet rock, wearing nothing but a bra, underwear, and a smile on her face that scares me.

chapter 45

"Lily!" She shouts down to me, waving like we haven't seen each other in ages. "I've had another amazing idea!"

From the bottom of the cliff, I yell up to her, "Come down, okay? Alice? Come down here and tell me."

She shakes her head. "No, no. I have to go up. Up. Up. Up! That's what I'm trying to tell you."

Her eyes are wilder than I've ever seen them. How long have they been like that? Her pupils dart around the rock as she talks, her words coming almost too fast to understand.

"What if I get a running start? What if I leap beyond the rocks? And so, like—BAM!—it hit me." She closes her eyes and presses a finger to her temple. Without her shirt on, the scars on her arms stand out, dark against her skin. "What was my idea? What was I saying?"

"Alice, just come down. It's too wet up there."

Her eyes snap open. "Oh yes, the cliff! So, what if—and this is the genius part—what if when I jump, I don't fall? What if I fly?"

"Alice. No."

"I can do it. I know I can."

A crowd has gathered behind me. Watching her lose it. Seeing her scars.

"Alice," I say like I'm trying not to scare away a baby bird. "This is not a good idea."

"Yes! Yes, it is! You'll see!"

She's climbing again, one hand reaching up to grab a craggy jut-out. Her feet slip on the slick rock, but she scrambles back and hoists herself up to the next level of rocks.

"Stop, Alice. You need to stop."

She laughs, a ringing, echoing trill. It's too high. Too loud. Too uncontrolled.

"Can't stop, Little Sis! I'm going to be brave like you. Like I used to be."

"This isn't brave," I yell up to her. "It's stupid."

She laughs again and keeps climbing.

Micah tells me he's going to run around to the barricaded entrance up top. He takes off in the night. Behind me, people whisper.

". . . bipolar . . ."

". . . Fairview . . ."

". . . crazy . . ."

Cell phone lights punch through the dark. They're filming her. Stockpiling evidence against the sanity of the Larkin sisters. And suddenly, standing here at the bottom of this cliff, all the emotions of the last few days erupt like a powder keg. Why is she doing this? Why now, when things are falling apart, does she have to do *this*?

"Just stop!" Before I can filter my thoughts, I yell up at her, "Why do you have to be like this?"

She frowns down at me. "Be like what?"

"Like this! Why do you have to act so, so . . ."

She stops climbing, her toes balancing on a ledge. She looks over her shoulder down at me. "So crazy?"

"No, that's not—it's just—it's too far. Like when we were kids. Like when you said we should sneak into the school. It's always one step too far, and you just, you just—"

My mind flashes back: I'm six, and I follow Alice into the ocean. She dares me to swim out farther. Go on an adventure.

I'm sixteen, and I follow her into the school. Alice opens the door.

All her impulsive ideas. Her reckless thoughts. Always taking over, and taking me down with her. "You ruin things."

The wild in Alice's eyes turns to anger. "I knew it. I *knew* you were mad at me about the trespassing."

"I'm not mad, Alice. I'm tired of babysitting my big sister."

"Nobody told you to babysit me."

"Oh right. That's all I ever hear. 'Look out for Alice.' 'Don't anger Alice.' 'Help Alice.' Alice, Alice, Alice. Do you know what it's like to find your sister on the bathroom floor with a blade pressed to her skin? Do you know what that *does* to a person?"

Her eyes fill with tears as she stares at me from above. She opens her mouth like she's going to say something, but stops and turns around, lifting her arm high to grab at a rock, her voice half carried away by the wind. "Well, maybe you'll get lucky and I won't fly after all."

Without thinking, I step barefooted onto a rock, hoist myself up, and start climbing. Alice is climbing, too, but I'm faster, and soon I've almost caught up to her, and we're halfway to the top when I grab her ankle. She shakes me off and reaches for the next rock, but I lunge for her one more time.

"Come. Down," I yell, but I miss her—just barely—and as she yanks her leg away, her other foot slips.

And time breaks.

Because it's moving too fast and, somehow, too slow.

And she's falling.

And screaming.

A blur of skin and darkness and tumbling rocks.

And I'm fumbling my way down, and then crawling to her, holding her, and there's blood in her hair, so much blood.

On me.

On everything.

Micah's voice brings me back.

"Someone call 911!" He picks Alice up off the sand, one arm under her knees and one behind her back. Her head lolls backward lifelessly.

And all the monsters in my head shout together:

Please be okay.

Please be okay.

Please be okay.

chapter
46

In the ambulance, EMTs poke needles into her arms, cover her mouth with oxygen. They use words like *nonresponsive* and *laceration*. They look at each other knowingly when they see the scars on her wrists. They have her all figured out.

They ask me questions. So many questions.

How did she fall?

She wanted to jump.

To fly.

History of mental illness?

Bipolar disorder.

She was going to get help.

What medicines is she on?

I'm not sure. Something with a *Z*, or maybe *X*?

But she's not taking it.

Any unusual symptoms?

No. She was doing better.

I was going to fix it.

Any alcohol or drug use?

I don't know. I wasn't watching.

~~I should have been watching.~~

Anything else we should know?

No.

~~I grabbed her.~~

~~I did this.~~

~~Take me away.~~

~~Lock me up.~~

But they don't take me away. They take *her* away.

They wheel her through heavy doors that only open with key cards, and I don't have a key card so I stay on the other side. The waiting side.

When Micah gets there, he dials my dad, and I try to talk through crummy cell reception.

"Honey, honey, what's going on?"

"It's Alice."

"What is it? What's wrong?"

~~I broke her.~~

~~I broke everything.~~

"Lily? Lily, are you there?"

My voice won't work.

Micah takes the phone. Gives the details.

Dad told you not to see Micah anymore.

How many times will you disappoint him?

"They're on their way, but they're all the way downtown," Micah says. He touches his fingertips to a bloody scrape on my arm. "We should get that looked at."

I shake my head. "I'm fine."

315

He sighs and goes to get us something from the vending machine. A woman across from me bounces a crying baby on her knee. Her eyes dart around the room from an ashen face. An older man hunkered down by the vending machine vacantly watches the soap opera on the ancient TV.

We're all waiting

waiting

waiting.

A doctor in blue scrubs exits the special key-card area. He kneels by the woman with the loud baby. She follows the doctor through the portal—she's been chosen.

The rest of us hate her.

"Sorry. It was the best-looking thing in there." Micah hands me a stale granola bar. I take it but don't eat. The thought of food makes my stomach roil. It's already moving in waves, lurching up at the bottom of my throat. Micah puts his arm around me because I can't stop shivering, and I remember that before Alice climbed that cliff, before the Larkin sisters hijacked the evening, we were talking about him, about his dad, his expulsion.

"I'm sorry," I say. "I was supposed to be helping *you* tonight."

"I've said it before, Lily. We're supposed to be helping each other."

He's so calm, and so kind, and so *freaking perfect* that I almost hate him for it. Why does he keep sticking around for this? I pull back and look him in the eyes.

"I get it, you know, if this is too much for you."

If I'm too much.

"Eh." He shrugs. "I've seen worse."

"No, seriously, Micah. I wouldn't blame you. You have your own crap to deal with, and maybe we both have too much baggage, too much chaos, to help each other." I take a deep breath to steel myself. "So I'm giving you an out. Guilt-free."

He pulls me back into him. "You're right. We're probably terrible for each other. But I'm not going anywhere."

And even though I know he probably just doesn't want to be the tool who breaks up with a girl in a hospital, I let him hold me.

"We *will* finish our conversation. I promise," I say.

"And I promise, I'm totally fine if we don't. Not that I don't *love* doing a deep dive into my issues."

He pats his shoulder, and I rest my head on it. We sit like that, his hand on my arm, my head on his shoulder, bobbing up and down with the steady rhythm of his breath, on the waiting side. After forever, a nurse comes in and tells me Alice is stable. I jump up.

"Is she awake? Can I see her?"

"Yes, but first, do you have anything sharp on you?" She puts her hand out like a bowl. "Pens. Bobby pins in your hair. Makeup compact with glass mirrors?"

I shake my head.

"Any iPhone chargers, earphones with cords, lighters, weapons of any kind?"

"No. Why—"

"Standard safety measures after a suicide attempt."

"This wasn't a suicide attempt," I say.

She consults her clipboard. "Says here she has a history."

"Yes, but—"

"And you said she was trying to jump from a cliff?"

"Yes, well, no, it wasn't—"

"Then we treat it as an attempt," she says matter-of-factly.

She leads me through the doors, down a long hallway, and stops outside a room with big glass windows and no curtains. Inside, Alice is lying on the bed, eyes closed, head wrapped in gauze. A security guard stands in the corner of her room, watching her sleep.

"Protocol for suicide watch," the nurse says, nodding toward the guard. "Now, just to warn you, she was very agitated when she woke up, so we've sedated her. Don't be alarmed if she's not quite herself."

As if I know who Alice's *real* self is anymore, anyway.

I inch into the room, trying not to be totally intimidated by the man in the corner with his Taser and expressionless face. Alice has a million wires flowing from her—IVs and electrodes and all sorts of medical paraphernalia. A machine beeps in time with her heartbeat. She opens her eyes when I touch her arm.

"Lily," she whispers. She turns toward me, and I can see the side of her head, bleeding through the gauze.

You did that.

"Alice, I'm here. And I'm sorry, I'm so sorry."

She fades out again, but I stand by her bed, listening to the beep of her heart, inhaling the antiseptic smell of the room. She wakes up twice and doesn't know where she is.

"You're in the hospital. You fell," I tell her. "You're going to be okay."

Is she?

When the nurse says it's time for a catheter change, I touch Alice's arm again to let her know I'm leaving. She wakes, confused, until her eyes focus sharply on me.

"Lily, Lily, you need to listen. Listen to me." She pulls me close, a panic in her eyes like I've never seen. "Promise you won't let me disappear again. Don't let me—"

She mumbles something, but I can't catch it all before she fades.

Then her eyes open suddenly, wide and terrified, looking straight at me.

"Help me," she says, exactly like she did on the bathroom floor all those months ago—small and scared and just . . . less. "Promise."

And even though I feel as helpless as I did that night, I squeeze her hand.

"I promise."

In the waiting room, the nurse tells me to go home.

She puts her hand on my shoulder. "Get some rest and come back in the morning. Nothing's going to change overnight."

"I can't—I'm not leaving."

The nurse pats me.

"Honey, we'll take good care of her. I promise. The best thing you can do for your sister right now is get some sleep."

I nod. She walks back through to the Other Side, and Micah puts his hand on top of mine.

"I'll drive you."

I shake him off. "I'm not leaving."

"But you just—"

"I. Am. Not. Leaving."

Micah sighs and leans forward, his head in his hands. He looks like hell. I can only imagine what I look like.

"Lily. She's right. You need to go home. Your parents are coming, and Margot sounded terrified when I called your house. She needs you."

"Alice needed me!" I say, my voice escalating involuntarily. The nurse behind the desk watches me like I'm a bomb about to explode.

I *knew* something was off. I *knew* the symptoms.

Abnormally wired. Check.

Exaggerated sense of self-confidence. Double check.

Unusual talkativeness. Checkity-check!

"The redecorating and the videos and the talking so fast. I should have done something," I say, pacing back and forth in front of the key-card door. "I should have *made* her get help. Right then."

Micah watches me weave between the hideous green chairs.

"Lily, this isn't your fault."

"Isn't it?" The truth comes bubbling up, unstoppable and ugly. "I was mad at her, Micah. For being *her*, for using up all of Dad's money, for being the black hole that sucks me in, time after time. I might as well have pushed her off that cliff."

The old dude by the TV stares at me. I'm better than any soap opera.

Micah grabs my hand, which is clawing at my side, and he wraps his arms around me. "It's not your fault," he says again. I bury my face in his shoulder. The tears I've been holding back since we got here erupt—heavy, unrestrained sobs that fill the waiting room. I leave a streak of tears and mascara and pathetic on his shoulder. I try to pull away, but he only holds me closer.

"It's not your fault."

"I should have helped her. I could have stopped her. I knew she wasn't taking her medicine. I *knew*."

Micah holds me tighter. "Don't you think I wonder all the time if I could have done something differently to make my dad stay? If we could have loved him more or better—been more or better? That maybe he'd still be here? But I can't think like that. *You* can't think like that. *She* climbed that cliff, Lily. You didn't do this."

Didn't you?

"But it's not just this time. Don't you get it?" I say. "That night, in the bathroom. I knew something was wrong with her before I went out running. I *knew*. But I didn't want to look. I pretended like I didn't see the marks on her skin, didn't notice that she was acting strange. I didn't even answer her text. She needed me, but I wasn't there. Do you know where I was?" I don't wait for an answer. "I was running. I was outside, trying to shave another second off my time. I was running while my sister was trying to die."

Micah brushes the hair that's come loose from my ponytail out of my face.

"You couldn't have known."

"And then, you know what I did after?" I laugh, even though none of this is funny. Except maybe it is. Maybe it's all so freaking hilarious. "I made the bed, Micah! I made it and remade it because the sick part of my brain convinced me that if I could just make that bed, make it perfect, then she would be all right."

Micah holds me again, so tight, I can barely breathe.

"But she's not all right," I whisper into his shoulder.

"It's not your fault," he whispers back.

My shoulders shake against him as he rocks me.

"It's not your fault."

Ridgeline Underground

133 likes

LARKIN SISTERS SNAP AT BONFIRE

95 comments

Girls gone wild, psycho edition. I am 100 percent here for this.

They're not crazy, dumbass. Bipolar does not equal crazy. Crazy is as crazy does

Guys. This isn't a joke. These girls are messed up. They need help.

OMG. I was there. Lily totally pulled her sister down! That's straight up cold!

I hope she's OK! Prayers to you, Alice!

Total attention whores. World would be better without them.

chapter
47

The post on the Underground has a picture—a digital damnation—
of Alice clinging to the cliff, me standing below her, yelling into the
rain, looking abso-freaking-lutely insane.

Ping!

> **Sam:** Holy crap, Lil! Is Alice OK?
> **Sam:** are you?
> **Me:** yeah

no

> **Sam:** look, I know things have been weird, but I'm here if
> you need me
> **Me:** thanks

too late

Micah convinces me to go home when Dad and Staci finally get to the hospital. Dad quickly hugs me before rushing to the Other Side, without a word about the fact that I'm standing next to Micah, who I was specifically told to never see again. Dad doesn't have time to stop to tell me I've let him down, and he doesn't need to. I know.

I've let me down, too.

Let everybody down.

At home, Margot's on her bed, her eyes red and swollen, scanning the pages of *Harry Potter and the Deathly Hallows* frantically. She chews on her fingernails while she reads, like she's trying to bite them right off.

"Margot. Stop," I say, swatting her hand away as I sit next to her. Her finger is red and scabby in the corners of the nail bed. I tell her Alice is going to be fine, even though I have no idea, because what else can I say?

My eyes wander her room, a strange mix of little-girl and preteen: stuffed animals and dolls on her shelves next to a makeup kit.

"You need to sleep," I tell her, tugging the book away. She tugs it back.

"I thought it was working," she says, her finger going back to her mouth. "There's something I'm missing."

I'm too tired to argue with her about the difference between fantasy and reality, so I sigh, give her a hug, and leave her alone with her magic. Back in my own room, I stare at Alice's unmade bed, wishing she were here—whichever form of Alice it happened to be. Manic, red-lipped Alice with her booming laugh, or sullen, short-haired Alice with her eye rolls and cocooning. I don't care which, as long as she's home.

In the dark, I walk the seven steps to Alice's chaotic side of the room, pull back the rumpled comforter, and get in.

Staci and Dad come home well after midnight. I meet them in the front hallway. Staci lights a lavender candle. Supposed to be calming, she says.

"Do you hate me?" I ask.

"Why would he hate you?" Staci blows out the match. "We're just glad you were there. I don't even want to think what could have happened otherwise."

Dad pulls me tight against his chest. It's the first time he's really even acknowledged me since the principal's office.

"She was still a little loopy, but she told us how you stopped her from going higher. You probably saved her. She's lucky to have you. We all are."

~~I didn't save her.~~

~~I can't even save myself.~~

"She's gonna be okay," he adds, standing back to look me in the eye, and I wonder if it's the same lip service I gave Margot. "They're watching her concussion and adjusting her meds. Nothing you need to worry about."

The lavender fills the front hallway, but it's doing little to calm me.

"Don't tell me not to worry, Dad." I say. "I *am* worried. And I know you want everything to be better, but it's not. And she is not okay."

He shakes his head a little too vigorously.

"What happened tonight was bad. But it was an accident. She's getting better. She just needs to find the right dosage."

"Dad! You're not listening." My voice wobbles. I promised to help her. "She's not even taking her meds."

You also promised not to tell.

He looks at me like I'm speaking another language. "She didn't tell me—"

I run up to our room, grab Alice's bottle of unused pills, and run back down. I slam it in front of Dad, who has already retreated behind the French doors of his office.

"Of course she didn't! Because we don't talk about anything we need to be talking about. We're all just pretending Alice is fine. That we *all* are."

He picks up the pills. Then he places them down softly, stands, and turns away from me, to face his rows and rows of books. Tale after tale, characters he knows inside and out, when he can't see the story playing out right in front of him. The unhappy ending we're all headed for if we don't twist the plot, and soon.

"What do you want me to do?" Dad's gesturing wildly with his arms, pacing back and forth in front of his books. I've hit a nerve. "Stuff the pills down her throat? Grind them up and hide them in her Lucky Charms?"

I go around his desk so he has to look at me.

"What if she hurts herself again?"

Dad meets my eyes. We've never talked about that night. Never discussed how he groaned when he saw her on the floor. The raw, throaty sound that filled the bathroom as he scooped her off my lap. Instead, I washed the blood off my hands. He washed the floor.

And we pretended like that was enough.

"Exactly," he says, a quaver in his voice now, too, one hand on his bookshelf. "What if I push her and she does *that* again? I can't— I can't lose her."

I put my hand on his arm.

"Dad, we're losing her anyway."

He shakes his head, his eyelids blinking quick, only barely holding back the tears.

"I don't know what to do." Dad's voice catches in his throat. It guts me. "I mean, I was by her bed in the hospital, and it's like I'm standing there, watching someone I love be in pain, and I'd do anything to stop it. To take it from her. But I can't. And I just feel . . . helpless. You know?"

"I do." The image of me sitting helpless on the bathroom floor with Alice fills my brain. "I know exactly what you mean."

Dad sinks into his chair, his eyes searching the picture of us at the beach like it might have the answers.

"Do you remember this day?"

I nod. "It's the day Alice made me swim out too far."

Dad shakes his head.

"No," he says. "There was a riptide. We couldn't see it from the beach, but one minute you were next to Alice, and the next minute I looked up and you were gone."

"I thought I followed her," I say, trying to remember the details of that day.

"She followed *you*," Dad says. "I swam after you, too, but she got to you first. To this day, I don't know how she managed to get you back through those currents."

I'm six, trying to stay afloat. Reaching for Alice's hand. She tells me we're explorers.

327

I look at Dad, trying to make his words make sense. *I* was the reason we almost drowned. Not her.

"I felt so helpless that day," Dad continues. "But it's nothing compared to how I felt that night in the bathroom. How I feel every single day. What kind of father can't help his own daughter? I'm supposed to have the answers, but I don't." He puts his head in his hands. "Nobody tells you what to do when your child wants to die."

The words fall, so harsh—so true—that they seem to surprise even him. He shakes his head. "So yes, I want to pretend everything is fine because I don't know how to fix this, Lily." His voice is quiet now—resigned and sad and lost. "I don't know how to fix *her.*"

I grasp Alice's pills tight and fight the tears pricking my own eyes at this helpless version of my dad, the man who tucks me into my spot on his chest and tells me everything is going to be okay. That he'll make it okay.

Except this time, he can't.

"She doesn't need to be fixed, Dad. She's not broken," I say. "She's Alice."

In the bathroom, the red-tinged grout screams: *Help me.*

I didn't know how then, and I still don't. And neither does Dad. That truth scares me to my core.

And you told him about the pills.

Alice will hate you more than ever.

She'll disappear again.

Maybe for good this time.

I hear Dad and Staci leave to go back to Alice, and I fill the bath, strip down to my scars, and submerge in the water. Hoping it will clear my head. Cleanse me.

I sink below the surface, holding my breath, the memory of the water, of the tug of the ocean, coming fast and fresh. Alice and I weren't off on one of her wild ideas; we were caught in a riptide. She must have been terrified. But she acted so brave. She saved me.

My lungs burn for air. But I stay below the water. In the silence. The nothing.

The words I yelled to her on the cliff come back, stinging and sharp: *You ruin things.*

I've been so wrong. About everything.

Micah says it's not my fault. I want to believe him.

To let the words absolve me.

But the monsters out-scream everything:

You swam too far.

You let her bleed.

You let her fall.

She's not the one who ruins things.

You are.

chapter
48

My body forces me up out of the water, gasping for breath. My fingers itch. My skin buzzes.

On my stomach, a scab circled by hot, pink skin. It's tender when I pick it off.

One by one, I pick every scab on my stomach.

Psycho.

Crazy.

Hypocrite.

Joke.

Better without you.

I move up my arms, my fingertips searching out little bumps and rough patches. Piece by piece, I dig out the imperfections.

Up my neck—

pick

pick

pick

my chin

pick it all out
my nose
get it all
just one more
my cheek
a little farther
my forehead
you'll grow new skin
perfect skin
pink and new like a baby bird.

I get out of the bath, and the girl in the mirror is covered in spots.

But that girl isn't me.

That's not my face.

My hands.

I'm long gone.

Just a little more.

I continue even though the pain fills me.

Because the pain fills me. I'm here, I'm alive, because I can feel it, really feel it, right there on my skin.

A little more.

A little

more more more more more more more more more more more more more more more more more more more more more more more more more more more more more more more more more more more more more more more more more more more more more more more more more more more more more more more more more more more more more more more more more more more more more more more more more more more more more more more more more more more more more more more more more more more more more more more

more more more more more more more more more more more more more
more more more more more more more more more more more more more
more more more more more more more more more more more more more
more more more more more more more more more more more more more
more more more more more more more more more more more more more
more more more more more more more more

The sound of screaming brings me back.

Margot stands in the doorway, eyes wide, like she's seen a real-life monster. Her cry lingers in the air.

"I—I just wanted to show you . . ." She holds out her Harry Potter book to me, flipped open to a page. "I found something that I think could help. We just need—"

"Get out!" I yell.

Margot doesn't budge.

I grab the book and throw it over her head into the hallway. It lands with its spine smashed, edges splayed out.

"Enough!" I'm still yelling. She shouldn't be here. She shouldn't be seeing me like this. "Enough with the fairy tales, Margot!"

She walks backward as I walk toward her, until she reaches the door.

"What you need is to grow up!"

She hops back as I slam the door.

I turn back to the monster in the mirror.

I pick

and pick

and pick.

I scrape myself away.

*   *   *

After, I toss back a sleeping pill.

    And one of Alice's pills, too.

    They made her numb, she said. Unfeeling.

    I take it without water, feel it's rough edges as it goes down.

    I fall into the easy embrace of unconsciousness.

    I give in to the nothing.

I sleep for days.

    Years.

    Lifetimes.

Dad's always at the hospital.

    Staci puts her cold hand on my forehead. I hide my picked-open face under the comforter.

    "Are you sick?"

    I nod. "I'll feel better after I sleep."

~~Pink and pure and perfect.~~

    Margot stands at my door but doesn't come in.

Sleep is my only escape.

    I double the dose of pills from Dad's drawer and take more of Alice's,

    and I sleep

    and sleep

333

and sleep.
Through school. Through practice.
Through everything.
Tucked in the fetal position,
I wait for rebirth.

Supernova

I am
disappearing—
a supernova
collapsing inward
smothered in black.

I
am gone.

chapter
49

Someone rips open my cocoon and lets the light in.

It's blinding.

"Why aren't you answering your texts?" Micah asks. He dials a number on his phone and roots around for the ringing coming from the other side of my room, swallowed up behind Alice's bed. He tosses me my phone, which has had an alarm going off over and over again for hours.

"Go away," I say, pulling the covers back over me, partly to block the light, partly to block Micah from seeing what I've done to myself. "My dad will make you leave anyway."

"Your dad and Staci are at the hospital. Margot let me in," he says. "She's worried about you."

Scared of you.

"Time to get up." Micah yanks off my covers. "I have a group today, and you're coming."

"What, like therapy? Hard pass. You, of all people, should understand that sometimes you just need to be unconscious."

He tug-of-wars me for the comforter when I try to return to my embryonic state. Micah's voice is calm but firm.

"Yes, but sometimes you need to wake up."

He pulls my shoulders back and flops me over. He can't hide the shock on his face when he sees my skin.

"Shit."

His eyes trail down to my legs sticking out from my long night-shirt. Little, round wounds scream from my body, bright and red and angry.

The memory of what I've done to myself roars to life. Why did I think I could become someone new? That I could scrape off this Lily-ness and reveal someone better, someone who didn't have monsters in her head and an insatiable itch in her fingers?

I hide myself again, half hating him and half humiliated that he's seeing me like this. Face scratched open, wounds still raw.

"Why are you even here? Have you forgotten I got you expelled? What I did to Alice?" I say through the covers. "No one's giving out brownie points for biggest martyr today."

Micah lifts the covers, softly, and studies my face, looking into me like he's done since we first met—back when I was the perfect one. What does he see in me now?

"There's a reason why flight attendants tell you to put on your own oxygen mask first," Micah says.

I roll my eyes, extra dramatic. "I'm not crashing, Micah. I'm tired."

The alarm on my phone goes off again, and when I reach to silence it, a reminder pops up: *state qualifier. 10 a.m.*

The race. I blanked the track meet. Dad needs me to win.

Everybody needs me to win.

336

I need me to win. It's the only thing I haven't irrevocably screwed up. I force myself to sit.

"Good." Micah says, helping me to my feet. "The group's really not half-bad once you—" He stops when I start rifling through my track bag and pull out my shorts. "Wait. What are you doing?"

"Going to my race."

Micah tries to wrestle my bag from me. The room tilts as a wave of dizziness almost knocks me off my feet. I stagger back, and Micah catches me. My head feels like a helium-filled balloon, like it could float away any second. It doesn't help that the house is rocking like it's on the ocean. My pulse pounds in my skull, and vomit burns the back of my throat.

"Lily. You don't look good."

"Rude."

"You know what I mean. You need to sleep, not run." He puts the back of his hand against my forehead. "You're burning up. And sweating."

"I'm fine," I say reflexively. Fine. Fine. Fine. Everything is fine. Besides, how can I be sweating when I'm so cold?

"You're not fine, Lily. Forget group. I'm taking you to a doctor."

I try to jam my leg into my shorts but miss the hole. The room's tilted again.

"You want to help me? Help me get to this track meet. *That's* what I need right now." I wave the shorts at him in frustration. "You're always telling me to speak up. To ask for help. This is me, asking. Help me get to my race."

He groans from the back of his throat, pointing a finger at me. "And then you'll see a doctor? You'll take it easy? Let me feed you chicken soup and Gatorade?"

"Yes, yes. Whatever you say." I hug him tight. I agree to his terms. I'll rest. I'll stop. After I prove that I'm still Lily Larkin, straight As and team records, despite the words on everyone's lips and phones and posts.

I'm still a winner.

Micah shakes his head but helps balance me while I pull on my uniform. I look down at the picked-open spots on my legs. The jersey reveals the damage on my arms, too. I rip both off, and Micah helps me put on a long-sleeve cross-country jersey and leggings instead.

In the bathroom mirror, more disappointment.

No baby bird today, folks.

Just me. Ugly, scabby, and—

disgusting.

The pink skin around one of my wounds has turned red, spreading in a wide circle, hot and tender and clearly infected. I'll deal with that later, I tell myself as I tuck my shirt in tight.

I spend fifteen minutes blobbing on foundation and concealer and bronzer.

"You look great," Micah says when I come out and put on my race-day shoes.

"Your BS is no good here."

Downstairs, Margot is slurping Lucky Charms at the kitchen island. Her usual book and cape are missing. She keeps her eyes trained on her bowl instead of me when I talk to her.

"I'm—"

~~sorry~~

~~ashamed~~

~~humiliated~~

"—going to my track meet. Dad and Staci are at the hospital?"

Margot nods.

"Do you—"

~~hate me?~~

~~judge me?~~

~~wish I was dead?~~

"—want to come with us?"

She shakes her head, still not looking at me.

"You okay?" I ask.

"Fine."

I chug an energy drink on the way. The pill cocktail I've been tak-ing knocked me out good, and it's hard to surface. My brain is a saturated sponge, heavy and soft. The beaches and cliffs flash by so nauseatingly fast that I close my eyes, roll down the window, and suck in fresh air like my life depends on it. Micah reaches over and holds my wrist.

"Your pulse is racing."

"I'm just nervous. Only the top five runners go on to state."

The caffeine hits my bloodstream just in time, punching into my chest and zapping my foggy brain to life. I ignore the fluttery feelings behind my rib cage and hop out of the car in front of the high school across town where we run the state qualifiers every spring. The team is already stretching out, warming up in a small huddle next to a ban-ner for Ridgeline High. Micah heads to the bleachers as Sam beelines for me. She takes in my mottled skin—makeup can only cover so much—and her face falls.

"Lil. I—" Her voice catches.

I want to tell her to cut it out. That I don't need her sympathetic head tilt or her pity or whatever it is oozing from her right now. But my words get caught in my throat, which is tightening as my teammates turn to look at me, their thoughts written across their faces.

Did she do that herself?

She really is crazy.

Crazy and scabby and desperate.

I close my eyes and try to ignore the way my stomach is lurching and my head is spinning. I center myself, envision bolting down the track. Crossing the finish line.

"What is this?" Coach says, looking at my cross-country clothes.

"I couldn't find my regular uniform."

Coach tucks his clipboard under his arm, his eyes closed like he's summoning strength from the god of adults who have to deal with teenagers.

"You missed our last scrimmage, Lily. You've been MIA from practice all week."

"I know, but—"

"Do you think being part of a team means doing whatever you want? Not putting in the time and effort that all your teammates do?" He waits for me to defend myself. Explain my absence. Justify my existence. I got nothing. "You're not running today."

"But—"

"No. Enough excuses. You'll have another shot next year."

The caffeine has reached my heart. It does the cha-cha in my chest so fast, I could jump out of my skin. Next year? Next year is too late.

Panic starts its forward march from my core, radiating out to my fingertips.

You've lost Berkeley.

Now this.
And Alice is worse than ever
and so are you.
Is there anything you haven't screwed up?

Coach yells at everyone to huddle. I'm outside the circle. I walk until I'm off the field, outside the fence, running toward the porta-potties by the parking lot.

I don't make it.

I vomit on the blacktop, sink against the tire of a random car, hugging my knees. An elephant sits on my chest. An invisible hand grips my heart, my lungs.

I can't move.

Stars shoot into my peripheral vision, slow and beautiful, and I slide toward the ground, one thought repeating on loop:

I can't.

I can't.

I can't.

Micah finds me there, muttering. He steps over my vomit and pulls me back up to sitting.

"Hey, hey, Lil, look at me. You can't what?"

The invisible hand squeezes tighter, shutting off my lungs. Paralyzing my heart. Little shooting stars everywhere.

"Win," I whisper, before the world goes black.

chapter
50

In my dreams, I run
and
run
and
run.
My lungs can't keep up.
I'm starving for air.
Stop, legs!
Stop running!
But they don't.
They can't.
Alice is running, too.
I reach out to her.
Our fingers touch
and she's gone.
Vaporized into the night.
I'm alone.

running

and

running

and

running

with no finish line in sight.

I wake in my own bed.

Someone has moved me, wrapped a blanket over me, tucked me in tight.

Did Dad see my scars? Does he know?

Across the room, another shape, wrapped in sheets.

Alice.

She's home.

I crawl out of my cocoon. Drag myself the one million miles between us.

"Alice," I whisper. "Are you awake?"

No answer.

I pull back the sheets.

A waterfall of blood pours out.

Soaking her nightgown.

Splattering onto the carpet.

Flowing into the bathroom, staining the grout.

Staining me.

Her eyes flash open, darker red than the blood.

"Help me."

I try to stop the bleeding.

But it's coming from nowhere.

From everywhere.

"Help me."

Alice reaches out.

I fall back.

"I tried," I scream. "I tried!"

She can't hear me.

Just keeps bleeding

and bleeding

and bleeding

until it fills the room.

Fills all the space.

And washes me away.

chapter 51

I wake again, this time for real, in darkness, on the floor by Alice's bed.

The blood is gone.

But Alice is here.

Her eyes are open, small white lights in the blackness. A fresh gauze wrapped around her head.

"You're home," I say, because it's all I can think.

"I'm home," she whispers.

I reach up to hold her hand, and to my surprise, she lets me.

"I didn't mean to hurt you," I say.

"I know," she says. "I didn't mean to get hurt." She rolls over to stare at the ceiling. "I just kept thinking maybe I could fly as high as I feel. I could fly out of myself and finally be free." A tear streaks from the corner of her eye onto the sheets, making a dark, wet circle.

"I told Dad," I whisper. "About the medicine."

"I know."

"What happens now?"

Alice breathes out, long and slow. "They've pumped me full of all sorts of meds," she says. "So I guess, first, I fade away."

She says this so hopelessly, it crushes me. And all I can think is how she swam out to save me. How she must have been terrified, but she pretended to be fearless—for me. And I've failed her.

"Maybe you won't."

She laughs, a forced chuckle full of hurt. "I will. But maybe that's not so bad. Maybe everyone will be better off without me."

I don't tell her that I feel the exact same way. We've had enough truth—enough pain—for one day. I lay my head against her bed, our hands clasped together as we drift off.

When I open my eyes again, the room spins. I steady myself on Alice's mattress to stand up, trying not to wake her. My head feels light, disconnected, like it could topple off my body if I let it. My side hurts, too, and I lift my shirt to examine the infected wound, which now has angry red streaks that reach, like little fingers, toward my heart. I'm chilled to my core, but my skin is sticky with sweat.

Even though I'm tipsy, a strange energy surges through me.

My mind is alive with a million scattered thoughts.

And Alice's words burst through the rest, loudloudloud.

Better off without me.

The words take my breath way.

And yet, there's something familiar in them. Like the answer has been there, staring me in the face, waiting for me to wake up and listen. Like I've known it all along.

Isn't this what the monsters have been telling me?

You don't belong here.

Isn't that why I slip out of myself? Why the tug of the ocean felt so easy? Why I imagined jumping into the Grand Canyon?

That's when I see the box, tucked under my bed. I slide across the floor, sweep my arm, and pull it out. I run my finger across all the razors and pencil sharpeners and scissors. Maybe Alice had it right on the Night of the Bathroom Floor. If pain is all we're going to feel anyway, why not bring it on?

No!

I shove the blades away from me. I can't do that to Dad. To Margot. To Micah.

They won't miss you.

You're a burden.

They'd be relieved.

I push the box back under the bed and grab my phone instead. I could call someone. Micah. Or Sam. I could tell someone that my brain is finally breaking. They could help me.

If they even believe you,

and they'd probably tell Dad

and stick you in a room with a cop in the corner, too.

I hold my head, try to shake out the monsters. But they won't go. Won't shut up.

Other words swirl through me. Dad. Margot. Micah. Alice.

That's my girl.

Suck out your soul with a kiss.

One for all, right?

The monsters always find me. Why try?

Better off without me.

I grab a pen and a hot-pink Post-it note off Alice's desk and write down the words I can catch.

Fight or flight.
That's what they say.

So what do you do
when your body
is too weak
when your mind
is too crowded
and your lungs
are out of air?

When you're tired
of waging war
on yourself?

When you don't want to live,
and you don't want to die

but your fight has left
drop
by drop
by drop

and the only thing left to do
is fly?

My heart has gone wild, bursting through my chest.
This room is shrinking.
I have to get out.

I put on my sneakers and make my way down the stairs, gripping the handrail all the way so I don't fall.

I step into the night air.

And I do the only thing I can.

Run.

Ridgeline Underground

10 likes

Listen up, Undergrounders. Micah Mendez is looking for Lily Larkin tonight. Please message if you've seen her. URGENT.

0 comments

chapter
52

My heart is pumping too fast.

My whole body is pumping too fast. Like my brain and my blood and my bones are short-circuiting, spilling over with excess electricity. My body is too small to contain it.

My skin is too small to contain me.

I don't know how long or how far I run. The houses around me are unfamiliar. I'm lost in a strange land.

My mind races. The images play like flashes in an old-timey movie reel.

Flash!

Margot screams. Her older sister claws herself to pieces.

Flash!

Dad in the principal's office, so disappointed.

Flash!

Micah in handcuffs.

Flash!

Alice on the bathroom floor.

Tumbling down a cliff.

The monsters sing in unison:

Better off without you.

Better off without you.

Better off without you.

Ridgeline Underground

25 likes

UPDATE: Micah says they've found Lily's phone and a note that indicates she may be in danger. If anyone has any information, please message. Her family is v. worried.

13 comments

Praying

Did you check the loony bin?

She wasn't at school today!

I saw her running earlier.

Where and when?

An hour ago? My neighborhood.

I saw her, too. Maybe 20 minutes or so

Headed toward the ocean

chapter
53

I stand for a long time on the living side of the barrier.

Where people without wings stop.

Below, waves heave themselves into the cliff. Impale themselves on the jagged edges.

And shatter.

They smash and crash and call to me.

Lily—

come.

Join us.

Just let go.

I should feel panicked or scared, but I don't.

I feel calm. A strange peace washes over me.

No more hurt.

No more monsters.

It's the only way.

The wind whips my hair as I put one leg on the bottom rung of the fence and hoist myself over.

Onto the other side.

chapter
54

It's so easy.

It'll be over.

We'll be quiet then.

We promise.

It's the only way.

Another voice breaks through.

"Lily!"

Alice stands behind me, her arms outstretched. Behind her, Dad and Micah.

I take them all in. Dad's face is twisted, his hands clasped together. Micah looks like he's using all his energy to not run toward me.

"Come back," Alice says. The white bandage wrapping her head tortures me.

You did that.

You hurt her.

"Do you hate me?" I ask.

"Of course not. We love you." She inches closer to me. "Come home with us."

I shake my head, trying not to look down, where the white frothy tips crash in the darkness.

"It was your idea," I say. "To fly."

"Not like this, Lily. I didn't mean like this."

"No, you were right. I'll be free."

The voices will stop. They promised me. It will be so easy. And I won't make Dad's face look like that anymore. I won't make Margot cry or you bleed. Don't you see, Alice, don't you see?

It's the only way out.

"It's too much. Too much to carry alone," I say. "Too much to put on the people you love."

She takes a step toward me. I move to the edge of the cliff. The roar of the water crescendos, pulsing in my head.

"Listen to me," Alice yells, straining to be heard over the waves and the wind. "I know what you're thinking. I've been there. You can't see one step ahead of you right now. But this isn't the answer."

"Then what is, Alice? What *is* the answer? Because nobody seems to know."

A massive wave slams into the cliff, spraying us both. Salty water drips into my mouth as Alice's eyes dart back and forth from me to the edge.

"I don't know. But I know you'll never find it if you leave now. So stay, and we'll figure it out together." She moves another step closer to me. "Take my hand."

"You won't even take your medicine!" I yell, tears flowing down my cheeks now. The wind whisks them into nothing. Drowns them in the sea.

"I will." Her hand is still out in the space between us, the pink slashes marring her arm. "I'll find the right meds and you'll get help, and we'll be brave, together."

"I *am* being brave."

"No. No." She shakes her head. "Stay. *That's* brave."

The voices from the ocean are screaming now.

She's lying.

If you stay, they'll all suffer
because of you
disgusting
failure
waste of space.

I feel myself slipping out of my body. As Alice creeps close, I go,

bit

by

bit

by

bit.

Until I'm above me, watching as I teeter on the edge.

I see Alice reaching for me.

Flash!

I'm six again. Alice's hands guide me through the water.

Flash!

They buoy me up.

Flash!

Her hands throw open the sheets as she helps me make friends with monsters.

Part of me wants to reach out to her again. Let her pull me away from the edge.

Because I don't want to go, not really—I just want it to stop. All of it—the monsters, the guilt, the never enough.

It's the only way.

I'm floating away. I feel myself going

going

goi—

"Lily!"

Dad's running toward me, his face contorted. His arms wide, a visceral, guttural cry erupting from his throat.

Flash!

I'm little, choking up water on the beach. Dad makes that same noise from deep within his chest. He rocks me, rocks me, rocks me in the space reserved just for me. *Aren't you proud of us, Daddy? We were on an adventure.* His arms hug me so tight, I can't breathe.

Flash!

His arms carry Alice down the stairs.

Flash!

Mom doesn't come home from the hospital. I don't understand. Moms don't leave. Alice and I hold hands under the covers. Dad folds us in his arms. *I've got you,* he says. *Daddy's got you.*

"Lily!" he screams again.

My dad's cry hangs in the air, louder than all the waves.

Louder than the monsters.

His voice brings me back into my body, and I feel the wind and the tears and the *everything*.

And I want him to tuck me into his arms, chase the monsters away. Tell me everything will be okay.

Even if he doesn't know how.

Because even when he didn't have the answers, he was there.

He stayed.

And I want to stay, too.

My knees begin to buckle. I grab Alice's hand before I fall.

But I don't hit the ground. Strong arms catch me. My head fits perfectly into my spot.

"Dad?"

"I'm here, baby. I'm here."

"Daddy," I whisper.

Cracks splinter through the ice behind my ribs. The words, buried for so long, burst out, sending aching waves ripping through me as I let them fly free.

"I need help."

chapter
55

"Lily."

A light.

"Lily, can you hear me?"

I surface slowly. Little flutter kicks propelling me up, up, up. Dad leans over me. His face fills my vision.

"Dad," I say. "What happened?"

He tells me I'm in the hospital. I'm hooked up to antibiotics. The doctors are helping me now. I'm going to be okay.

My family sits around my bed. Dad. Staci. Alice. Margot.

They tell me they love me.

I tell them I'm sorry.

I didn't mean to hurt anyone.

"Why didn't you te—" Dad starts, but cuts himself off. He shakes his head. "It doesn't matter. What matters is that you're here. And we're here. And we're going to get you help."

I nod. I'm in a hospital gown. Dad has probably seen all my scabs. Probably knows how deep my wounds run.

"I might be beyond help," I whisper.

Dad puts his hand on my shoulder. The weight of it grounds me.

"We'll figure it out," he says. "We're a family. That's what we do."

Alice touches my foot at the bottom of the bed as Margot squishes her way next to me through the maze of tubes pumping into my arm. She wraps her arms around me. Dad keeps one hand on me at all times, like he's reassuring himself I'm real. I'm here.

And I am.

I'm here, breathing in and out.

Listening to the rhythm of the heart monitor beeping through the room.

Even though my brain is mushy and my body aches and I have no idea what will happen next, I'm here.

And so are they.

And their light chases away the darkness.

chapter
56

I spend two weeks in the hospital.

Mending.

Talking.

Making a plan to get better.

An IV in my arm treats the infection from my scab, and the doctors tell me I've pushed my heart to the brink with my combination of pills and energy drinks and stress. My family rotates their visits to make sure I'm never alone. Dad brings a Scrabble board. Staci plays meditation music. When I get up to go to the bathroom, she reaches out to steady me.

"I got it," I say.

She doesn't take no for an answer, just hooks her arm through mine determinedly. Even though I want to fight it, I lean on her. After, she combs my hair while sitting next to me on the bed.

"I'm sorry about all this," I say. "If you need to be somewhere else—"

"I need to be right here." She finishes braiding my hair and smooths back the wispies.

"But you signed up for a husband and got way more than you bargained for."

"It's true," she says, holding the sides of my head lightly so that I'm looking right at her. "Aren't I lucky?"

When Margot comes, I tell her how sorry I am for yelling at her. She cuddles up in my bed, her little fingers running over the scabs on my arms. Her chewed fingernail beds are spotted with scabs, too. Guilt needles me—I told her to grow up, but now I want to tell her to slow down. Stay little and wear capes and believe in magic for as long as possible.

"I really am sorry," I add, "about the other night. And I'm sorry I threw your book."

"I know you are." Margot smiles. "Nobody's perfect."

"Well, for the record, I'm definitely not perfect."

Margot snuggles in closer. "For the record," she says. "I never thought you were."

Alice joins us in bed, and we lie there quietly, puppy-piled like we used to with Mom while she read to us, her words making the dark less scary, making me feel like nothing bad could ever reach us. I didn't understand then, all wrapped up safe in her arms, that it wasn't about the words at all.

When my infection is better, they move me to a room for people whose bodies are fine but whose brains need work. It's bare bones—a bed and a chair and a jam-packed therapy schedule.

My counselor's name is Suzanne. She wears A-line skirts and her hair in a tight bun, and she listens while I talk. She talks, too, about obsessive thoughts and compulsions and why I want to pick my skin. She tells me that what's happening to me is definitely not *all in my head,* at least not anymore. She talks about anxiety and how when it gets stuck in the on position, the whole body goes haywire. She talks about rewiring my brain in baby steps. She helps me set goals, for tomorrow, for next week, for next year—for the Lily of tomorrow. We set appointments as far as the eye can see.

My family talks with Suzanne, too. Sometimes we hold hands, in a circle, like we're saying a prayer. And maybe we are, supplicating a higher power to help us, to heal us, to make us better. We hold on to each other so tight-tight-tight, it almost hurts.

We say the things we've held too long. We say all the words— even the sharp ones that sting coming out. We cry. We laugh.

We *feel.*

And the words I've kept are out, free and flying. And slowly, slowly, I can breathe again.

Sam visits, too. She brings me a card with a lollipop on the front that says, *I suck so hard.*

"You'd be surprised at how few cards there are that say, 'Hey, sorry about your mental breakdown,'" she says.

I laugh, and she laughs, and we feel almost normal. She sits on a chair across from me in the visitors' lounge. She picks at a loose thread in the sofa.

"I should have been there for you," she says.

"I should have told you," I say. "Call it even?"

The anger between us melts away. We make plans for burgers and shakes.

Micah doesn't come. I'm not allowed to have a phone (or razors or shoelaces or hoodies with strings or anything suicide-enabling), so I can't text him. The monsters in my head tell me he hates me. That he finally saw the truth of me and decided he was out. Alice tells me he hates hospitals, not me.

"After his dad, you know. I'm sure that's all it is."

I want to believe her. But when I close my eyes, I see his face, the fear and the pain as I stood on the cliff where his father stood. How can he forgive me?

A nurse brings me pills every twelve hours. Suzanne says they'll help me stabilize, help me stick to the plan. Each time I take the little white, round meds, I feel proud—and defeated, all at once.

"Now we're pill buddies," Alice says during a visit, clinking her water bottle with my plastic cup. She finally told her doctors about how the medicine makes her disappear. They're trying something new, and so far, she's still here.

"Want to hear something sick?" she says. "Sometimes I wish I had, like, I don't know, cancer instead. I mean, who wishes for cancer?"

"That *is* sick," I say. "But I get it. People understand cancer. They show up with casseroles and do bake sale fundraisers and tell you to stay strong." I hold up my little pill cup. "But no one knows what to say to something like *this*."

Alice stares at the pills in her own hand, and then, like she's just remembered something, she pulls out her phone and taps, taps, taps.

"But sometimes," she says, turning the screen toward me, "they say something anyway."

It's the Underground, and a picture of my locker, covered top to bottom with magnetic strips of poetry, pieces of notebook paper, and brightly colored Post-it notes. **GET WELL SOON. HURRY BACK.**

My first thought is fear.

"Do—do they know? About the cliff?" I look around my stark psych room. "About where I am?"

"I'm sure the Ridgeline rumor mill has been churning," Alice says. "But, Lil, look closer."

She zooms in on the smaller messages:

your words saved me

your voice is stronger than you think

guerrilla poets forever

"I didn't think anyone even cared," I say. "That any of it mattered."

I read the messages again, zeroing in on a small note in the corner of my locker.

you are not alone

"Looks like it mattered to someone." Alice raises her water bottle into the air. "Cheers to the original G.P.R.H."

We clink our cups and take our meds, together.

By the time I leave, my scabs are healing.

Not gone. But better.

But the work's not over, Suzanne tells me. "It won't be easy," she says on the day my doctors clear me to return to the world. "But it'll be worth it."

"And you won't be doing it alone," Dad says as he helps me put my personal belongings into a bag. "After all, we may not have our crap together, but together we have a lot of crap."

Margot laughs. "Dad, that's not how it goes."

"Actually." I jump in. "It's kind of perfect."

Dad pumps my hand—once, twice, three times.

Dad and Alice and Staci and Margot escort me out of the hospital. We look ridiculous, my entourage flanking me like a Secret Service detail.

But I don't mind too much.

Because they know all my secrets, all the words I've kept for so long, and they stayed.

Outside the hospital, Margot squeals,

"Micah!"

chapter
57

He's here.

He stands at the end of the sidewalk to the parking lot, chalk in hand. Below us, words adorn each concrete square.

be brave
be smart
beUtiful
be
the
best

do it right
do it now
do it better
just
do
it

stay sweet
stay out of trouble
stay focused
stay
on
track

In the final square, Micah stands, two words at his feet:

just stay

"I'll wait in the car," Dad says. He pats Micah on the back before he goes, and I definitely missed something, because when did *they* get all buddy-buddy? My posse hauls my bags away.

"So," I say hesitantly, piecing together words to articulate the emotions bubbling up in my chest. "You and my dad?"

"Right?" Micah says, eyes wide, and then his voice gets small and tight as he adds, "Turns out nothing brings two people together like almost losing someone they love."

Love. The word bounces in my head. Everything in me wants to touch him, to have him hold me, but he just stands, staring at his chalk-stained hands and then at me for what feels like eternity.

"Don't look at me like that," I say.

"Like what?"

"Like I'm going to shatter. Make fun of me. Be normal."

"Okay, but first I have to tell you something kind of serious." He inhales and closes his eyes, but I can tell he's trying not to laugh. "I saw your butt. Before they realized I wasn't family and kicked me out, they put you in a hospital gown, and I totally saw your butt."

I shove his shoulder slightly. "Well, was it good for you?"

"Oh yeah." He smiles, but it's strained, and his face goes serious again as he looks down at the chalk words below us. "I'm sorry I didn't come sooner. I didn't want to be in the way, and your family was always there and I thought you'd want some time, you know, with your inner circle and all."

I step closer to him, and all I want is for him to grab me and kiss me and remind me that I'm still me and he's still him and we're still *us*.

"You're in that circle, too, you know."

He puts his chalky fingers into his front pockets. "There's something else, too." His hair dips in front of his eyes, and I want so badly to reach out and tuck it behind his ear. "I wasn't sure I *could* be here."

Here it comes.

"I want to, of course. But being on that cliff, seeing you there. Like that. It was . . ." He swallows hard. "It was a lot."

In my chest, my heart thuds.

"And my whole life—my whole damn life—I've pictured what I would have done if I had been there on that cliff with my dad. How I would have stopped him." Micah's crying now, and so am I, partly because I'm a selfish jerk and don't want him to finish this train of thought that clearly ends with him dumping me, and partly because seeing him—strong, self-assured Micah—in tears is about the worst thing I've ever seen.

"But when I was up there, with you, I was helpless. And I hate myself for it," he says. "And after, I just kept thinking that maybe you were right: we're a bad idea. Maybe we're both too broken."

"Of course," I say, wiping my own tears. "I get it. Totally."

He reaches out and touches my fingers with his, lightly. "But—"

My heart clings to that *but.*

"But here's the problem. This life, in general, sucks. And most days, all we can hope for is pockets of air. And with you, I can breathe."

Through his dark curls, he looks at me.

"And I'm not sure I'm ready to give that up. So maybe it's totally selfish or stupid, and even though I'll probably hide in my room sometimes, and you'll probably tell me to shove off sometimes—"

"I would never—"

"You will. There will be days when you're done with it. With me. With therapy. With everything. But if it's all right with you, I want to stay. And keep trying. And failing. And breathing. And *being* with you."

The pain in his eyes sears me.

"And I'm sorry I wasn't here, but I'm here now. And I'm just sorr—"

I weave my fingers between his. His semicolon tattoo touches up against the Band-Aids on my arm from the IVs. I push the hair from his eyes, and that's all it takes for him to pull me close.

"I thought I'd lost you," he says.

"Me, too."

He's holding me so tight, the bum-bum-bum beating inside his chest pulses against me.

"I can feel your heart," I say, my mouth brushing the skin of his neck.

"It's yours."

And he's kissing me, soft and slow, and his black curls tickle my forehead, and I know Dad's probably covering his eyes and Margot's probably squealing, but I don't care. Because all I can think about is the feel of his hands on my back, his mouth on my mouth, and his heartbeat next to mine, reassuring me that we're both here.

We chose to stay.

And the thought makes me so happy, I can't help smiling.

He pulls away, his lips red and splotchy. "Is my kissing amusing you?"

"No, no. I . . . ," I say, searching for the words. "I'm just glad I didn't miss this."

chapter
58

Baby steps.

That's what Suzanne tells me each week when I see her. One step, one day at a time. Some days are good. Some are bad. And some are just days, moving me forward, little by little.

But each day, I feel more like me.

Suzanne was right, though: the work of healing is not easy. She makes me face my biggest fears, doesn't let me erase my mistakes, walks me through what it feels like to fail. Sometimes my anxiety feels higher than ever as we work, but she gives me stress balls to keep my hands off my skin, and skills to bring myself back when I start to slip away. I'm pushing back against the glass, cracking it slightly so I don't run out of air.

The monsters aren't gone.

They visit often, actually.

When the rumors swirl at school about me on the cliff. When the track team goes to state without me and Kali's winning project gets displayed in the lobby. When Damon struts the halls, as cocky as ever, unpunished for his crimes. When the darkness feels heavy and the road back seems far too long.

That's when they come, whispering, yelling, repeating words I don't want to hear.

But Suzanne is helping me choose when to listen.

Which words to keep.

I write those words down. Poems and stories and all the ideas that pop into my head. The new notebook that Dad bought me is almost full only a month after the night on the cliff.

I read my poems to Micah, to my family, to Suzanne. Even though the summer program scholarship is long gone, I keep writing.

"You should share your poetry again," Alice says one night after I've read her and Micah a haiku. Micah's on the floor, filling out an application for a killer summer art program at UCLA. He's not sure about college yet, but it's back on the table. *Baby steps.*

"You could read them on my YouTube Channel. A guest segment!" Alice says, her eyes gleaming the way they do when she gets an idea. She's more like regular Alice every day, full of life and ideas, only the swings aren't as high or as low.

I shake my head. "Not sure I'm ready to share my most personal inner thoughts with a bunch of internet randoms." I take a bite of the pizza Staci ordered. It's actual, real pizza with carb-loaded crusts and cheese from a living, breathing cow. *Like your dad says, you only YOLO once,* she said.

Alice takes a bite and talks with her mouth full.

"So what if they weren't randoms? Like, what if you do it at Tony's? I could get you a slot," she says. She's been doing a shift a few nights a week to save up for school in the fall. She and Dad have decided she's ready to take some baby steps, too. "You could invite people. And everyone can bring something to share."

I chew while I think about how the words have saved me since I got home. How the chalk poetry outside the school got people talking about all their secret wishes and worries. Even though the words are gone at Ridgeline, #mywords #mystory is still going strong online with people posting new poems all the time.

"Would you do it, too?" I ask.

"Sure, why not," Alice says. "I've been working on an amazing new stand-up set for my channel."

"I'm in, too," Micah says.

The electricity I felt as a guerrilla poet of Ridgeline High surges through me again.

"So, we're doing this?"

"Sounds like it," Alice says. "Now we just need people to come."

A Night in the 100-Acre-Wood

Join us at Tony's café.

Bring your art, your poetry, your songs, your whatever.

As long as it's real.

#mywords #mystory

I am

I am
pills
in the cupboard
scars
on my body
monsters
in my mind.

But I am
more
than my
diagnosis.

I am
setbacks and
switchbacks and
wrong turns.

I
am
terrified.

But
I am
here.

I am
I am
I am

I am
not fixed
because
I am
not broken.

I am
a work in progress—
a lily
in embryo.

And when my petals finally unfurl,
I'll blossom,
wild
beautiful
and free.

chapter
59

The café is packed.

Sam has brought the whole track team, and Micah recruited every last one of the Artists. The room buzzes with conversations and laughter and life.

Dad, Staci, and Margot are sitting front and center. Sam's tuning up her violin to play a piece she wrote, and Alice is pacing in the back, freaking out about doing her set in front of Dad for the first time.

Gifford is here, too. She introduces me to the lady by her side.

"Lily, dear, this is a friend of mine from the English Department at UC Berkeley," she says, her eyes wide, sending me a message. *This lady's important. Listen up!* I shake the woman's hand.

"This is exactly the kind of thing we're always pushing in the department," she says, holding up our poetry-night flyer. She hands me her business card. "I'd love to talk more. Stop by my office if you're ever on campus."

"Yes, yes, of course," I say.

Gifford winks at me as they take their seats.

Before the man in the afghan kicks off the evening, Micah signals me over to him. He's wearing the bright orange vest from his roadside trash pickup hours that he's still finishing since his expulsion.

"I've always liked a man in uniform," I say, pulling him closer by both sides of his vest.

"Court-mandated community service does it for you, huh?"

He leans down and kisses me softly.

"You nervous?" he asks, nodding toward the poem in my hand.

"Petrified," I say. "But it's gonna be okay."

He steps back, aghast. "Lily Larkin, don't tell me you've lost the will to worry?"

"I'm afraid no amount of therapy will change that."

"Which is exactly why"—Micah smiles and produces a book from behind his back—"I wanted to officially welcome you to the Hundred Acre Wood."

I take the thin, golden-spined version of Winnie-the-Pooh, with its bright drawings.

"I thought you didn't believe in the power of the wood anymore."

"I was wrong."

"I'm sorry. Could you speak directly into the mic, for the official record?"

He leans forward to the fake microphone I've put in front of his face. "I, Micah Mendez, was wrong." He laughs. "Was that good for you?"

"Better than I ever imagined."

"But seriously, I don't need to change the whole world. Maybe a few friends who get it—who get me—is enough. And who knows? Maybe, someday, the world will catch up." He surveys the room of people who have showed up to share their stories, their pain. "Tonight sure feels like a step in the right direction."

He kisses me again, and whispers, "I know you, Lily Larkin. Don't you ever forget it."

I take a deep breath. This moment feels so pure, so sure, but the future is anything but certain.

What if Micah gets sick of you?

What if you don't get into Berkeley?

Or therapy doesn't work?

And Alice relapses?

I stop the monsters in their tracks—*baby steps, Lily*—and I kiss him back.

When it's time to start, I look out at my friends and family from the stage. The sight of them, the people who stayed no matter what, fills the spaces in my chest where I used to hide all the things I couldn't say. With the light shining in my face, I open to my own page, my own words, and begin to read my latest poem.

"I am . . ."

My voice hangs in the air after I've finished the final word. I lean into the microphone one more time.

"Tonight is terrifying for me, as I'm sure it is for many of you. So thank you. For being here. For listening. For speaking up."

The crowd claps as I hand the mic to Alice. "Knock 'em dead."

She takes the stage, wearing a T-shirt that shows off the scars on her arms. But with the light on her face, it's hard to notice anything but her smile.

Dad wraps his arm around me in the front row as Alice starts her set.

"Proud of you, kiddo." My head settles into my spot. His chest shakes as he laughs while Alice comes alive on the stage. On my left, Micah holds my hand, and he's laughing and I'm laughing and the sound of it fills me.

I don't know what tomorrow will hold, but I'm here, existing in the in-between.

Screaming into the void.

And for now, that's enough.

And so am I.

author's note

As a teenager, I had a near-constant barrage of thoughts telling me I was not good enough, not smart enough, just not enough. It wasn't until I became an adult that I finally learned the word for the monsters in my head—*anxiety.*

Anxiety is a tricky beast. It can show up in a million different ways, and unfortunately, it's become a catchall word for normal worries. But the anxiety I felt, the kind Lily feels, goes beyond everyday fears. She has an anxiety *disorder,* a debilitating and often undiagnosed condition that has a high correlation with self-harm and suicide.

So many people silently battle the anxiety monsters that tell them they'll never be enough, that convince them to cut or pick or take the pills to make the thoughts stop. When I tell readers that I'm writing about this kind of anxiety, they often tell me about their own struggles with mental health, or those of friends, some who have tragically been lost along the way. I vividly remember one girl in the front row of a middle school in Washington, DC, who raised her hand and asked in a tiny voice, "What's the answer? How do you fix it?"

But she was really asking, How do I fix *me? The Words We Keep* is my attempt at an answer: You don't fix you, because *you* are not broken. You are already whole, even if you need help. And you are not alone.

I wrote this book for the anxious teenager I used to be (and, let's be honest, the anxious adult I still am), who needed to know that her diagnosis didn't define her, that there is no shame in getting help. I also wrote for that timid girl in the front row. And, reader, I wrote it for you, because whatever you struggle with, you are already enough—just the way you are.

I've lived a full and successful life hand in hand with my anxiety, but I had to stop hiding from it, stop running from it. If the words *you* keep are too heavy to carry alone, speak up. Get help. You deserve it.

National Suicide Prevention Lifeline
988
988lifeline.org

Substance Abuse and Mental Health Services Helpline
1-800-662-HELP (4357)
samhsa.gov/find-help/national-helpline

The notOK App
notokapp.com

acknowledgments

When my editor asked me to write something "from the heart," I had no idea the deep dive I was about to do into my own anxiety. Even though it was challenging, I'm so grateful I took this journey alongside Lily to finally face the perfectionism and fear that has always been part of me.

This story would not have taken shape without the people and experts who spoke with me about their experience with an array of mental health issues. Thank you to therapists Leah Jaramillo and Lynne Sill at the Anxiety & OCD Treatment Center in Bountiful, Utah, and Misty Covington at West Ridge Academy, for helping me understand my characters, and also more about myself! Kim Simkins, thank you for opening your heart to me, and Tom Hewitson, thank you for showing me how art can heal. To others who shared their struggles with me anonymously, thank you for being vulnerable— and brave.

Thank you to Wendy Loggia for seeing the potential and beauty in Lily's story. I'm forever grateful for the faith you had that I would find the right words. Brianne Johnson, you could see the story that needed to be told way before I could. And to Rebecca Sherman, let's bring more words into the world together!

To my critique partners—the WIFYR gang and my Knuckles group—where would I be without you? I thrive on our brainstorming sessions, your loving encouragement, and your harsh feedback when needed. And a special thank-you to my beta readers—RuthAnne, Samantha, Cary, and Sarah.

I could not have written this book (or really done anything in the abyss of 2020) without the support of so many friends and family. I am truly blessed to have my own Hundred Acre Wood of people who love and accept me for just who I am.

Dad, thank you for all the dad-joke material and for all the "I love you" hand squeezes throughout my life. You were always there, no matter what.

Mom, thank you for raising me surrounded by books and go-round stories and family histories (even when I didn't want to hear them!). You encouraged me to tell my own stories one day, and I knew you were in my corner, cheering me on.

And I can't forget my second parents, whom I claim as my own. Don and Kathie Stewart, thank you for embracing me so fully with all my quirks.

To my sisters, Jenny and Katie, I thought of you both so often while writing these sister scenes. We didn't have these exact struggles in our home, but we did have puppy piles in bed, secrets swapped in the dark, and the amazing luck to have our best friends in our own family. Thank you for having my back, rooting for me, and sharing a lifetime together!

It certainly takes a village to raise a family and write a book, especially at the same time. My incredible friends make it possible. To my Backyardigans—Meredith, Kim, Kacey, Heather, Jill, Meghan,

April, and Bree—you are my go-to people, and there isn't a problem we can't solve during a walk or a late-night get-together.

Of course, thank you to the members of my own little family, each of whom inspired bits of this story:

Ellie, you are the toughest girl I know. I'm constantly in awe of your willpower, your determination, and your amazing brain. Avery, your creativity inspires me daily, and I know you're going to wow the world someday. Cayden, you are my model of living out loud and loving every minute of it. Keep dancing, baby!

Kyle, you are the one who makes it all possible, the one who has valued my dreams and made sure I had the time and support to make them come true. You truly are phenomenal.

And finally, a shout-out to the anxious teenage girl I used to be: You're going to be okay, and you are more than enough. Don't you ever forget it.

Turn the page for a preview
of Erin's stunning debut!

"This story made me laugh and cry. . . . So much hope and strength!
Get it on your TBR today!"
—Erin A. Craig, *New York Times* bestselling author of *House of Salt and Sorrows*

SCARS

LIKE
WINGS

ERIN STEWART

"This story made me laugh and cry. . . .
So much hope and strength!"
—ERIN A. CRAIG, *New York Times* bestselling author
of *House of Salt and Sorrows*

"Endearing and profound."
—BOOKLIST

1

One year after the fire, my doctor removes my mask and tells me
to get a life.

He doesn't use those exact words, of course, because he's paid
to flash around lots of medical-degree terms like *reintegration* and
isolation, but basically, the Committee on Ava's Life had a big
meeting and decided I have wallowed long enough.

My postburn pity party is over.

Dr. Sharp examines my skin grafts to make sure I haven't inadvertently grown batwings in my armpits since our last monthly
pat-down. Scars can be screwy little suckers, and since my body
is 60 percent screwed up, it takes Dr. Sharp a full twenty minutes
to check me over. The tissue paper covering the vinyl exam table
crinkles beneath me as my aunt Cora watches attentively from
the sidelines, scribbling notes in her gargantuan "Ava's Recovery"
binder while her eyes follow Dr. Sharp.

He removes the bandana from my head and then my clear
plastic mask, his fingers grazing my scars.

"Everything's healing beautifully," he says, without even a hint of irony. The coldness of his fingers registers above my eyes but fades as he moves to the thicker grafts around my mouth.

"Well," I say, "you can put lipstick on a pig, but it's still a p—"

"Ava!" gasps Cora, who is not only my aunt but also the self-appointed CEO of the aforementioned committee on my life.

Dr. Sharp shakes his head and laughs, revealing two deep dimples on either side of his smile, which only makes him even more like one of those McHottie doctors on TV who bang each other in the on-call room between saving lives. I blame his smoldering eyes and strong jawline for the butterfly swarm in my stomach every time he touches my grafts. It also doesn't help that I'm keenly aware he has seen me naked approximately nineteen times. Sure, it's on an operating-room table, but naked is naked, even covered with gauze and nineteen surgeries' worth of scars.

But we never address that awkward elephant in the room, just like I never mention the fact that he once literally took a chunk of my butt and stretched it across my face to make a new forehead.

Dr. Sharp hands me a small, salon-style mirror so I can admire his handiwork.

"No thanks," I say, giving it back.

"Still having trouble looking?"

"Unless I grew a new face overnight, I already know what I'm going to see."

Dr. Sharp nods while typing a note into my chart, and I sense a forthcoming committee meeting about my resistance to reflective surfaces. It's not like I haven't seen my face. I know how I look. I choose not to keep looking.

With a dimply smile, Dr. Sharp holds up my plastic mask.

"I think you'll be happy to hear that you can get rid of this little guy."

Cora squeals and awkwardly side-hugs me, careful not to apply too much pressure to disrupt the all-important healing process.

"You couldn't have given us a better gift today, Dr. Sharp. It's been a year, this week actually, since—" Cora pauses, and I can almost see her brain trying to come up with the right words.

"The fire," I jump in. "One year since the fire."

Dr. Sharp hands me the mask, which has been my constant companion every day, twenty-three hours a day for that year. Its one job: keep my face flat as it heals so my scars don't bulge out in fleshy blobs. The doctors and nurses reassure me constantly that the mask has made my scars heal so much better, although I'm unconvinced it can get much worse than the patchwork of discolored grafts I call my face.

"You'll still need to wear the body-compression garments until we're sure the scars won't interfere with your movements," Dr. Sharp says. "But I do have one more piece of good news for you."

Cora gives him the slightest nod, which tells me that whatever comes next is a direct result of an Ava's Life meeting. My invitation must have gone straight to spam.

"Now that you don't have to wear the mask, I am authorizing—and strongly recommending—that you return to school," he says.

I flip the mask around in my hand without looking up.

"Yeah, that's a hard pass," I say. "But thanks."

Jumping off the sidelines, Cora lays her massive binder by the sink and half sits on the patient chair with me, lightly tapping my thigh.

"Ava, I know you're bored with those online classes, and you're always saying how you wish things could go back to normal."

Normal.

Right. Old normal. Ava Before the Fire normal. Normal normal.

"That's Never. Going. To. Happen," I say. "I'm not going to waltz back into my old school and have everything be the same."

"You could go to the school by our house, like we've talked about. Or pick any school you want," Cora says, undeterred. "You know, a fresh start? Make new friends and begin a life here."

"I'd rather die," I mumble.

I've been doing fine at home taking classes online in my pajamas. Where no one can see me. Where no one can point and stare and whisper as I walk by like I'm deaf as well as deformed.

"I know you don't mean that," Cora says. "You're lucky to be alive."

"Right. I'm a human rabbit's foot."

Why am I the lucky one because I survived? Mom, Dad, and my cousin Sara are probably dancing through a celestial meadow somewhere or happily reincarnated as monkeys in India while I face an endless loop of surgeries and doctors and stares from strangers.

But I can't compete with tombstones. Death trumps suffering every time.

"If it were Sara, I'd want her to live a full life," she says. "And I know your mother would want you to be happy."

Her attempt to use dead people to win this argument irks me.

"I'm not Sara. And you're not my mother."

Cora turns away from me, and so does Dr. Sharp, pretending to concentrate especially hard on the computer screen rather than acknowledge the tension that fills the exam room like smoke. I hate that Dr. Sharp is here for this embarrassing toddler tantrum, but he's partly to blame for blindsiding me with this development.

Cora sniffles quietly, and I wish I could take back my jab. She didn't ask to be my makeshift mother any more than I asked to be her understudy offspring. We're both trying to navigate this sick twist of "luck" the universe threw our way.

Dr. Sharp clears his throat. "Ava, the fact is, we're concerned about your level of isolation. Reintegration is a major part of your healing process, and we all think it's time to start," he says. I refrain from asking him who this mysterious "all" includes, since my concerning hermit status is news to me. "What if you go to school for a trial period, and then we reassess our reintegration strategy? Say two weeks?"

Cora looks at me hopefully, tears still wetting her eyes, as the guilt of the lucky creeps into my chest. The guilt of the one who lived.

This week marks one year for her, too. One year without her daughter. One year taking care of me, the girl who survived instead.

I can't give her Sara, but I can give her two weeks.

"Fine," I say. "Ten school days. If it's not a complete train wreck, then we'll talk about more."

Aunt Cora hugs me so tight that I act like it hurts more than it does so she'll stop.

"It's only two weeks," I remind her. "And it *is* going to be a complete train wreck."

"It's a start," she says.

I re-cover my scarred scalp with my red bandana as Cora and Dr. Sharp exchange a triumphant look. I toggle the transparent mask between what's left of my hands, fighting the urge to put it back on.